THE BONE FIELD

THE
BONE
FIELD

Leonard Krishtalka

gatekeeper press

Columbus, Ohio

The Bone Field

Published by Gatekeeper Press
2167 Stringtown Rd, Suite 109
Columbus, OH 43123-2989
www.GatekeeperPress.com

ISBN: 9781642370171
eISBN: 9781642370164

LCCN: 2018935478

Printed in the United States of America

For
The Carnegie Museum of Natural History
and the Carnegie bonehunters

CONTENTS

"... and some run up hill and down dale, knapping the chucky stones to pieces with hammers, like so many road-makers run daft. They say it is to see how the world was made!"

—Sir Walter Scott,
St. Ronan's Well, 1823

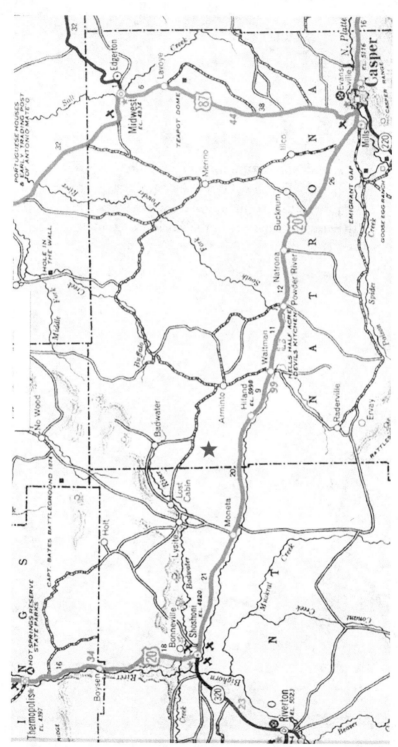

Badwater area, eastern Wind River Basin, Wyoming
★ Buck Spring Quarry

PROLOGUE

FINAL NOTICE

From: ARMY OF CHRIST
To: PETER MARCHAND
Date: March 17, 2001

    Blasphemer of the Lord's word
    Defiler of Genesis
    Debaser of Creation
    Whoremonger

WE WILL EXECUTE THE LORD'S JUSTICE

CHAPTER 1

WHEN THE PHONE rang, Harry Przewalski was stapled to the wall. He'd been putting up a large street map of Pittsburgh to cover the crack that spidered across the wall behind his desk. He'd aimed the staple gun, squeezed the trigger, and missed badly. The staple shot into his thumb, through the map and into the sheetrock. Cursing, he yanked his hand from the wall and grabbed the phone.

"Przewalski".

"Detective Parswitski, please?" A good voice. Professional. Not good with names.

"It's Przewalski. You got him." He cradled the receiver on his shoulder, worked the staple out of his thumb and sucked on the two points of blood welling up through the skin.

"Yes . . . of course. This is the Carnegie Museum of Natural History. I'm calling for Director Mayer. She said you would remember her. She would like you to meet with her today at the museum, if at all possible. She apologizes for the short notice. It's an urgent matter. She said to tell you that Peter Marchand has disappeared, that you would understand. Is eleven o'clock convenient?"

That gave him thirty minutes. Harry glanced over at his blank appointment book. "That works."

"Excellent. Thank you. Please come to the main office on the first—"

"Thanks. I know where it is."

He hung up, still sucking his wound. Mayer knew him. He knew her. He also knew Marchand, their star paleontologist. He'd worked with him, digging up the past, excavating the intrigues left by a vanished world imperfectly preserved.

None of it mattered after Nicole, his exile into nightmare. He escaped to a war, came back with a gun and got a license to detect. The dirt he excavated now was recent, loose, uncompacted. If there was a corpse buried, it was fresh, not fossil.

Harry opened the can of Drum tobacco on his desk, pulled out a gummed Zig-Zag paper, rolled a thin cigarette, and lit it. The ashtray already held six mashed butts. His mouth felt like a smokestack. His only rule was to lay off the smokes when a client was in the office. He needed to quit cold or get more clients. Cigarettes rotted the body like death, from the inside first. Even he could smell it.

Outside it was raining as hard as it had yesterday, and probably as hard as it would tomorrow. This was Pittsburgh in early August. Oppressive, thick heat alternated with bouts of rain, the moisture above the river valleys holding the city a humid hostage. Occasionally, a brisk west wind along the Ohio River would blow the sky clear. Not today. He owned a raincoat but had no idea where it was. He turned up the collar of his jacket and lowered his head, as if ducking through the rain would make him any less wet. By the time he reached his car two blocks away, he was drenched.

CHAPTER 2

THE CARNEGIE INSTITUTE squats on three blocks along Forbes Avenue. Its exterior walls boast 165,000 square feet of sandstone blocks, the interior 6000 tons of Italian marble. It was built by Andrew Carnegie, industrialist and robber baron, in the heyday of the gay nineties. The Institute was his pact with Pittsburgh—culture in exchange for steel, smoke and an eighty-hour work week. Culture to Carnegie meant his noble quartet: art, science, music and literature. From the outset in 1896, the Institute housed an art museum, a natural history museum, an opulent music hall, and an enormous public library, inscribed "Free To The People."

Wednesday's midmorning traffic was still heavy. Harry cursed as he maneuvered his yellow Corolla rustbucket around the potholes on Boulevard of the Allies, then hit every red light on Forbes. In the gray rain, the Institute loomed dark and foreboding, as if its sandstone skin had contracted black lung disease. For eighty years, the ash and smoke from the coke furnaces of Carnegie Steel and U. S. Steel had hung the air sunless, tarring the city and the people. Executives kept spare white shirts at the office to change into at noon. Lungs were not changeable, Harry thought. Andrew Carnegie liked the motto,

"It is the mind that makes the body rich." But it was the bodies of steel workers that had made him rich.

Harry cruised the visitor's parking lot behind the Institute, an open, multi-tiered affair terraced into a steep hillside above a ravine. It was full except for an open slot by the Museum of Art marked "DIRECTOR." He wouldn't be needing it. According to the *Pittsburgh Post-Gazette*, the director was in Europe, recruiting the last pieces of art for the Carnegie International, a contemporary art extravaganza begun by Andrew in 1896 and held every four years. The art museum had expanded in the 1970s into a new building, a dull granite and glass bunker welded onto the elegant Victorian exterior of the Museum of Natural History. An acerbic architecture critic called it a sterile mating of science and art.

Harry hunched through the rain into a short vaulted tunnel, the Institute's employee entrance. He took the worn marble stairs two at a time to the director's office on the first floor. His hair was plastered to his head, his jacket and trousers soaked against his body. The attractive redhead behind the desk inspected him over the top of her glasses, slowly, carefully, almost playfully. She was tight—tight-lipped, tightly coiffed and dressed in a tight suit. Although she was seated, Harry guessed she was tall, with the long, loping legs, tight stockings and a tight body. Even her desk was tight—no paper, no pins, no pens, no coffee mug. Her name tag read "Liza."

"Mr. . . . uh . . . Priz . . . Prizwalski?"

Harry smiled. "It's 'Zhe-val-ski.' Like the Mongolian wild horse."

Liza flashed a small set of tight teeth. "Yes. I can see the resemblance." She got up and came around the desk. "I'll show you in." He'd guessed right. She was tall, long-legged and loped. Also quick-witted.

Samantha Mayer stood up from her desk at the far end of

the carpeted office and walked over to greet him. Gray hair, streaked white, maternal except for the steel-blue eyes. The beauty of her youth still beckoned from between the lines on her face.

"Harry." She grasped his shoulders and studied him, almost maternally. "Damn, it's good to see you. Thanks for coming on such short notice. What's it been: seven, eight years? Here, sit." She led him to a set of leather sofa chairs. "I . . . I wish you could've come back after . . . after Nicole . . . that horror. And the war."

He forced a smile. His past was in a fifty-gallon drum stuffed with body parts. The museum had become hollow terrain. "Tell me about Marchand, Sam."

"He's gone missing out there," she said, leaning forward, a strained urgency in her voice. "We need to find him. We need *you* to find him. You . . . you know our ways better than anyone."

Harry shifted uneasily. "I'll listen."

"Good. Did you see the paper this morning?"

"Yeah, checked the obits and bankruptcies. To see if I was dead or just broke."

Mayer laughed and handed him a *Post-Gazette*. "Front page, below the fold."

POPULAR SCIENTIST MISSING

by Meredith Shue

CASPER, Wyoming, Wednesday, August 3 — The disappearance ten days ago of renowned Carnegie Museum paleontologist Peter Marchand from his fossil-hunting expedition's campsite in the badlands of central Wyoming west of Casper remains unexplained. According to Fremont County Sheriff Burt Crumley, Marchand has not been seen or heard from since July 21.

Carnegie Museum curator Diana Palantier, a colleague of Marchand's and one of the scientists on the expedition, told police, "It had been a long day at the dig site. We all had dinner and went to bed. Nothing unusual happened, except we haven't seen Peter since that night."

Palantier, who has taken over direction of the dinosaur excavation in Marchand's absence, said that Marchand is accustomed to going off by himself. "We're not worried," she added. "He's an independent spirit."

Marchand, who is also an adjunct professor at the University of Pittsburgh, is known for his studies of dinosaur evolution, especially his radical theories about changes in the Earth's climate during the Age of Dinosaurs.

"So, we're getting worried now," Harry said, skimming the rest of the article. "It's been two weeks."

Mayer sighed. "Right. The reporter in camp, this Meredith Shue, she wants to know why he isn't around, where he's gone off to. She interviewed him in June here in Pittsburgh. Did a piece on the expedition in the *Post-Gazette* before they left for Wyoming. Diana calls in from the field. She isn't concerned."

"What about the sheriff out there in Shoshoni?"

"Diana's talked to him. He's checked around. No sign of Peter. Nothing suspicious either. He's just up and vanished. Then this hit the paper today. It's embarrassing. We need to find him. Like I said, you know us. And you know him."

Yeah, he knew them. Marchand and the other Carnegie curators were the resident research scientists in charge of the sixteen million animals, plants, fossils, minerals, and anthropological objects in the museum. Most were a parochial lot, cloistered behind their collections, specimen-focused and issue-deprived, obsessed more with order than ideas. Even their titles—curator of this and that—evoked hermetic keepers of dead objects.

Mayer was one of the exceptions. Before becoming director, she'd run the museum's mammal collection, the 133,000 stuffed bats, rodents, marsupials and shrews arrayed in cabinets in endless rows, like the plague's army at dusk. Glass vials held their skulls and skeletons, picked white clean in the bug colony. Minus eighty-degree freezers held their muscles, kidneys, hearts and livers for DNA sequencing. The animals hailed from all continents, tagged, numbered, and catalogued, documenting the life we were losing from the planet.

Mayer looked out the window at the buses splashing through the potholes on Forbes Avenue. "There's one more thing, Harry. Probably meaningless. This past spring, Marchand mentioned that he got a threatening note. In the mail."

"What did it say?"

"Don't know. He made light of it. Thought it was a stupid prank."

"Who was it from?"

"Apparently, some Christian fundamentalist. Or someone pretending to be one. Peter doesn't suffer them well. He baits them. 'Bible-suckers' he calls them. He debated one here last winter, the head of some group from San Diego called Genesis Responds. Made him look like an imbecile."

Harry shrugged. "Why not let Marchand come back when he's ready, Sam? You know him. He's probably gone off with a woman."

She grimaced. "Could be. But he's already with one in camp, a graduate student. And, of course, Diana is there as well. You haven't met her. She and Peter were together until last year. She's the only one who's lasted for more than a few months.

Frankly, I can't imagine what the hell he's doing. We want you to find out."

Harry bought time. He walked over to a large painting of *Diplodocus carnegii* on the far wall. It was a dinosaur triptych, the tiny head and sinuous neck on the left panel, the extended whip-like tail on the right panel, and the gargantuan limbs and torso in the center. A reptilian bridge—four pillars supporting a ninety-foot span. It eventually became a bridge to extinction.

Returning to the Wind River Basin, he thought, would mean sleeping with a jettisoned lover. He remembered the badlands, prospecting the endless mudstone undulations for bony remnants of an ancient tarsier or hedgehog or opossum that had scampered through a steaming jungle fifty-seven million years ago, after the dinosaurs had become extinct. Days could pass between finds. Then, abruptly, a bit of petrified jaw or skull or skeleton would break the pattern of light hitting the scree on the cracked mudstone slope—a strange being from the past eroded to the surface. He'd squat beside it, roll a cigarette, smoke, and savor the singularity of the moment. Then he'd reach down and pluck it out of deep time.

He turned to look at Mayer. "All right, Sam, I'll look into it."

She broke into a broad smile. "Thank you, Harry. Now, I'll admit to being presumptuous. I had Liza book you on a flight to Casper tomorrow morning. She'll have a check for you before you leave. For expenses." Mayer stood up and led him out of the office. Liza winked at him as he walked by.

"Preston Stewart would like to see you," Mayer continued. "Do you know Preston? No, of course you couldn't. He became president of Carnegie Institute after you left the museum. Gird yourself," she said, frowning. "He'll give you the speech on discretion."

Harry knew Stewart. A few years ago, his wife Pitty, short for Patricia, had picked Harry's name out of the phone book for a tail job. She had suspected her husband of straying. The case was done in a week. Stewart liked a gay bar off Penn Circle called Planet Uranus, which was a few light years in the wrong direction from the Institute. It was known for a lot of rough sex and imaginative use of animals. If word got out, Stewart's excursions would bring a swift, polite boot out of Carnegie Institute, Ligonier's exclusive Rolling Rock Club, and Pittsburgh's social elite. That's what had worried Pitty. Philandering was tolerable, but only with the right class of people.

Harry followed Mayer past the marble pillars in the museum's grand foyer to the president's office. It had been three years since the rendezvous at Planet Uranus. Stewart hadn't changed. Natural selection among CEOs favored sixtyish males on whom the prep school look had aged well. They looked alike, as if they'd been cloned from the same bit of puritan DNA—a feminine face gone craggy, short gray hair, immaculate grooming, good teeth, thin lips, detached until death. It also meant less work for the undertaker in readying the face for the coffin.

Stewart rose slowly from his chair and stretched out his hand. "Been doing this sort of work for a while, have you?" he asked, raising his eyebrows.

"Long enough," Harry quipped.

"Harry was a graduate student here," Mayer interceded. "He then went on to other things."

"Well then," Stewart said, "you understand how concerned we are about discretion, about keeping the public confidence. We are not an institution that simply loses its scientists. Or can suffer negative press. I deeply regret having a reporter there. I can't imagine why she was given permission to observe the dig in the first place." He shot an accusatory look at Mayer.

"Preston," she reminded him, pointedly, "*we* asked the *Post-*

Gazette to send a reporter with the expedition. You thought it would be good publicity for the museum."

"The reporter won't be a problem," Harry said.

"Good." Stewart allowed himself the slightest of smiles. "Have Sam take care of your needs. I'll be looking for a report from you by the end of the week. I imagine we can wrap this up quickly if it's properly handled."

He turned back to his roll top desk and picked up a folder thick with papers. They were dismissed.

In the museum office, Liza stood up behind her desk and handed him the check. "Go get 'em Prizwalski." He asked her to stick out her left hand. She grinned, then wriggled her fingers at him. No ring.

"How about dinner tonight? And a bonus—a short course on Przewalski's horse. And a pronunciation guide."

"Hmmm." She furrowed her brow. "Let's see. You're tall enough. Sam thinks you have character enough to hire you. That's more than most. It's worth a shot, Mr. Zhe-val-ski."

CHAPTER 3

HARRY LEFT THROUGH a basement corridor at the back of the museum crammed overhead with pipes, electrical conduits and new internet fiber. Two narrow-gauge rails, half-buried in the concrete floor, ran down the corridor and disappeared under a pair of massive steel doors marked "Big Bone Room." Behind them, he knew, were racks of dinosaur skeletons: *Diplodocus, Camarasaurus, Allosaurus* and *Stegosaurus,* their monstrous limbs, backbones, ribs, shoulder blades, and pelvic girdles coated with black pitch. They'd been chiseled out of the fossil-rich badlands in Utah and Wyoming by Carnegie's bonehunters a hundred years earlier and shipped back to the museum in railroad cars. Some of the skeletons were still in their original wooden packing crates, entombed in Jurassic rock, waiting for the pace of science at the museum to catch up with history. The crates were made from the last of the American chestnut—the extinct housing the extinct. The building hadn't changed, Harry thought. It looked the same, smelled the same, a static continent that refused to drift.

Outside, he waved at the security guards in the glass booth. No interest. He thought he could walk out with a small dinosaur. Or Warhol's twelve-panel Elvis in the art museum. Security was a nightmare. The Institute had fourteen entrances and a maze of basement passageways, most of them unguarded. Most of the security guards were in their seventies, snoozed in the galleries, and couldn't protect their own pockets. Visitors to Dinosaur Hall regularly snapped off the last tail bone of *Apatosaurus* and *Stegosaurus* for souvenirs. The first thief got the real one. All the others got plaster replicas.

He drove back to his office on West Carson, a converted storeroom on the top floor of a dead steel mill on Pittsburgh's South Side, across the Monongahela. He rolled a Drum and blew the smoke into the empty space. The office reminded him of the badlands, spare, stark, almost desolate. The furniture had been abandoned when the mill shut down: a scratched wooden desk, a metal file cabinet, gray and dented, a cheap steel garbage can and an old red armchair. It was a faded leather piece from the sixties, a handsome dowager opposite his desk, waiting for whoever took the trouble to find him. A small end table sported an ashtray, a few cycling magazines and a *National Geographic* atlas. Two Eugene Smith photos of Pittsburgh blackened the side wall—*Smoky City, Dance of Flaming Coke.* The mill's foundry had provided the smoke.

A barge hooted, chugging downriver to the Ohio loaded with coal. Harry stubbed out the cigarette, pulled a can of air freshener from the desk and sprayed. Two windows looked out onto the rusting rail yards along the south bank of the Monongahela. He couldn't see much through them. They'd grown cataracts, a grimy memento of the foundry being coated in its own soot. The PPG building across the river in downtown Pittsburgh rippled upward through the dirty panes, a steepled skyscraper stenciled out of steel and fluid sheets of glass, disjointed by pollution's parallax. Seurat could have painted it, Harry thought, an impressionist cathedral rising to the heavens in a metallic blur, as murky as the religion it professed.

On the wall behind the armchair hung two framed pro-team

cycling jerseys, La Vie Claire and Team Z. His father had gotten Greg Lemond to sign them. Lemond had turned wistful, his father recounted. His fingers had lingered on the cloth, as if the memory of beating Hinault and Fignon in the Tour de France was stored in the cells between the threads. Both teams were extinct.

His father had raced in the peloton across Europe, a Polish domestique to Eddy Merckx in Belgium and Fausto Coppi in Italy. In the end, it petrified his life, Harry thought. Naming his son Edward Harry after Merckx. Naming his retro bike shop in East Liberty *Velo Europa*, his Bianchi road frame hanging behind the counter, his memories permanently anodized on the steel tubes, silver-brazed, lugged, celeste green.

CHAPTER 4

NICOLE HAD KISSED him that December morning, skipped down the stairs of his walkup, crossed the street to her brown VW Rabbit, and driven north to a farmhouse near Saxonburg. They'd been lovers for six years, she a social worker, he a paleontologist, plotting their lives into the future.

Her patient, Viola, was an elderly woman beset with frequent depression and anxiety. She hadn't answered Nicole's phone calls for a few days. Neither had her grown son, Donald, who still lived with her at the farmhouse. Viola had fallen a few months back, but she'd steadfastly refused to move to a care facility. She insisted she had Donald to care for her. Nicole had seen him once or twice during visits, a dark-haired shadowy figure flitting between doorways, then creaking the floorboards in an upstairs room. Viola would sit in her living room in a faded upholstered armchair, worn bare in parts, much like her mind, the prions in her brain at times strung out, at times in melancholia.

That morning Donald came out of the shadows, outwardly calm, inwardly seething at the world, at his mother. As Nicole rapped on the door and went into the farmhouse, he grabbed her by the hair and throat and dragged her to the barn. If she screamed, no one heard. He locked her in an iron cage, gave her water, watched her drink, shocked her with the cattle prod, and saw the red welts make topography on her skin. Then he stripped and raped her. When she lay there compliant, it enraged him; her body still, silent, not pleasuring his violence. He used the cattle prod to enter her. When he saw her hips leap off the ground and heard the long horrific scream, he killed her. Then he sawed her into parts, into lengths and widths that would fit into a fifty-gallon rusted metal drum. Police found the drum outside the barn under a roof gutter. There were two others beside it, also rusted, also filled with the dismembered bodies of mutilated women. One of them was Viola.

After Nicole, the madness was too unhinged to fix. A counselor advised him to bury himself under strata of normality interleaved with forgiveness. Perhaps seek pastoral guidance. No thanks, he'd told her. He was a rationalist. He had no truck for religion—his talent for delusion wasn't powerful enough. He'd never been one to find comfort in scriptural deliverance. Unless, of course, it was the proverbial eye for an eye. He told her that the only weapon he had was reason, but it was never designed to anesthetize evil, or scrub memory from the lobes of the brain, or forgive inhumanity.

The counselor asked him what he felt. Most of the time he felt nothing, he told her. Numb. Empty. Losing Nicole had marooned him on some alien piece of terrane, adrift, at sea without bearings. When he did feel, it was rage, almost uncontrollable. It frightened him. Frightened he'd become as mad as the psychopath who had killed her. Frightened of these savage fault lines in him he'd never mapped. He had no solid earth with which to seal them. He had no vocabulary with which to describe them. He had nothing to halt the daily subsidence of sanity. He was in a vacuum, he told the counselor, an abhorrence living in violation of Nature.

The Carnegie waited for Harry to come back to the stacks of dissertation notes on his desk, to the jaws and teeth, fossilized blue and amber, sitting beside the Zeiss scope, waiting to reveal biological rhythms in evolutionary time. But he never did. He chose the sanctioned deposition of fury. He volunteered for a desert war, to hunt a different quarry in a different set of badlands, where death came up red, not blue or amber. By the end, he hadn't had to kill. He knew he'd lucked out. He also knew it would not have purged the rage.

CHAPTER 5

ON THURSDAY, IT took Harry longer to climb the two flights of stairs to his bedroom than to pack for Wyoming. He grabbed his bedroll and duffle bag and tossed in a week's worth of field clothes, a ball cap and an old pair of field boots. On the way to the airport, he thought of Liza and smiled. They'd had dinner Wednesday evening at a French restaurant on the South Side he couldn't afford. But it stocked Fischer LaBelle beer from Alsace.

He'd told her about Nikolai Przewalski, the Russian colonel whose 1881 expedition encountered the short, stocky horse on the Mongolian steppes. Harry didn't know whether or not he was related—the wars in Europe had destroyed too many records. It was either kinship or coincidence that his father's name was also Nicholas. He told her about his mother, in a nursing home, her mind having drifted across that ocean of cognition to dementia.

Liza told him her last name was Kole. Used to be Kolakofsky. Her grandparents changed it to be less ethnic in the melting pot. She joked with Harry that maybe it was time to quit being a Mongolian horse.

After dinner, they'd had Scotch at his place. He'd kissed her. Then she'd risen from the couch, nonchalantly slipped off her clothes, faced him, arms folded across her breasts, and whispered huskily, "Until you quit smoking those tobacco sticks, this is what you're missing;" then she put her clothes back on, pecked him on the cheek and left.

Harry flew into Casper from Denver on a Frontier two-engine prop. It tracked Interstate 25 north until Fort Collins, then skimmed low along the eastern flanks of the Rockies, across the sweep of blood-red Triassic hogbacks and Jurassic bluffs. To the east, the vast short-grass prairie fanned out toward Kansas in a shimmering yellow and brown heat. To the west, the mountains sliced out of the earth without warning, stark, jagged, snow-capped and invitingly cool. Deep evergreen forests were shaved here and there into the irregular strips of logging operations. Straight ahead the sky was an obstacle course of ominous thunderheads billowing to 22,000 feet. The plane pogoed rather than flew, pitching and yawing through a minefield of late afternoon thermals.

The turbulence stopped when they cleared the long rim of Casper Mountain, descended over the belching Amoco refinery and banked west into the wind to land. Parched scrub desert ran to the haze at the horizon, scarred here and there by a dry wash and an alkali flat. The buffalo grass had become thin and burnt brown since the June rains. It didn't look much like home on the range. To the west, over Casper Arch, the land broke up into badland canyons of striated yellow and red rock.

The plane came straight in, the engines unnaturally loud in the desolate landscape. The 104° heat hit like a choke hold in the seconds it took him to climb down out of the plane and cross the tarmac to the terminal.

Mayer had said Diana Palantier would have him picked up at the airport. It was small enough that Harry could stand just inside the gate and scan the entire terminal for his ride. There weren't any candidates. Business types in outsize cowboy hats and pointy boots at the Hertz counter. A Shoshone woman with a lot of luggage. A janitor mopping the clean floor. A couple of teenagers working the candy counter.

At the far end of the terminal stood an enormous bronze statue of a cowboy astride a bucking bronco, left arm flailing and legs spread-eagled toward the roaring crowd. The horse was frozen in a vicious kick, about to toss the bronco rider into the imaginary dust. It was a Frederic Remington made big and banal for the nineties. Harry half expected a rodeo buzzer to sound every eight seconds.

It was three-forty. He had a map to the campsite. He'd wait a half-hour, then get a rental. He dug into his duffle for the Drum and Zig-Zag papers. The Marlboro Man was the icon for Wyoming. It hadn't yet banned smoking in bars and airports.

After ten minutes, he rummaged through the duffle for the book Megan had given him. Then he remembered. It was on the plane. He'd stuck it in the seat pocket during the turbulence, preferring the geologic chaos of the Wyoming terrain for his last bumpy moments on earth. Maybe the next passenger would appreciate it.

They were different biological species, he and Megan, their temperaments reproductively isolated. She wanted to live in a *New Yorker* novella amid characters immersed in narcissistic introspection, too infatuated with malaise to get on with life. Their relationship was a dustbowl, the lovemaking proper, prefab, without sweat. Keeping separate places had kept the affair from crumbling. They could feign commitment and forgo passion. They'd looked for things in each other that neither possessed, then resented not finding them.

They'd decided on an intermission a few months ago, both free to entertain intimacy elsewhere. Liza was a beginning. Wyoming was a convenient sequel.

CHAPTER 6

"**Y**OU THE DETECTIVE looking for Marchand? Diana asked me to get ya."

Harry looked up. It was one of the kids from the candy counter, a tall, strapping boy with red hair and a suspicious bulge in one cheek.

"And you are?" Harry asked.

"Darryl . . . Darryl McCarthy." The boy shifted uncomfortably from boot to boot and took off his baseball cap. A working face, two-tone: forehead milk white; burnt bronze below the eyebrows. He'd spent long hours in the baler.

"You're my ride?"

"Yeah, I was just talking to Tanya." He motioned over to the girl behind the candy counter. The white forehead blushed.

He led Harry out of the terminal into the blast furnace that was central Wyoming in August. The parking lot looked like a truck dealership. Most of the pickups were Chevys and Fords, with Dodge running a bad third. Darryl pointed at a beat-up blue and white Ford half-ton. It was a chiropractor's delight—no arm rests, no seat belts, no shocks, no window cranks. Springs erupted through the upholstery. The floor was littered with crushed pop cans, rags, Copenhagen chew tins, and an oil spout. Something was dripping out of the underside of the heater. The dashboard, a thicket of exposed wires, had one gauge, the speedometer, but the needle didn't move.

"It's my dad's truck."

"Who's your dad?"

"Uh, he's the foreman for Karlsen Ranch, over where the bonehunters are staying. Up by Badwater."

The truck bucked onto the main road. "The clutch is shot," Darryl explained. "Been like that since I started driving this outfit."

Everything in Wyoming bucked, Harry thought. Pickup trucks. Turboprops. Airport art. The license plates bore a miniature of the terminal's bucking bronco. Bucking was the state emblem.

"When was that?" Harry asked, making conversation.

"When I was nine. I'm fifteen now." Darryl smiled at him, proudly, his face already baked beyond his teenage years. To emphasize his manhood, he spewed a stream of brown saliva out the window, spattering the sides with sticky juice.

"Chew that stuff long enough and Tanya will prefer to kiss a pail of worms."

"Naw," Darryl said, sheepishly. "My dad chews too."

They headed west on US 20-26, a two-lane highway bordered by barbed wire and sagebrush. He had left Pittsburgh in a heat so heavy it was smothering the city. Here he could taste the dust. The hot, dry wind through the open windows shriveled his lungs. They passed Natrona on the left side of the road, population 10: a house trailer attached to a small clapboard building and two abandoned gas pumps in the sandy front lot. A faded Sinclair Oil sign with a green cartoon *Brontosaurus* hung on the side of the building.

Harry wondered whether the kid knew anything about Marchand. "Where do you think Marchand took off to,

Darryl? You didn't happen to see him drive past your place that night?"

"Who, me?" Darryl was genuinely surprised. "Naw, I haven't seen the bonehunters much. We been busy hayin', my Dad'n me. This is the first time in town in a month. Except for church. And that's only at Powder River." Darryl pointed down the road.

"Where do you go for fun in Casper?"

"Well, there's ... uunh ... there's the Tokyo Massage," Darryl said, trying hard for nonchalance. "It's near the airport. The Holiday Inn has dances every Saturday. That's about it. Oh yeah, there's Bronco Bullies over on West Yellowstone. It's a bar with wet T-shirt contests. Also lots of fights."

"You go there often?"

"Naw," Darryl grinned, embarrassed. "I'm underage. Can't take the truck on the highway at night until I'm sixteen and get a license. Don't need a license for the ranch roads."

"You think Marchand went to one of these places that night?"

Darryl thought for awhile. "Dad says Peter don't need that. Anyway, he didn't take his outfit. It's too far to walk. About eighty miles from up above Badwater to Casper on the roads."

"You mean he left his truck in camp when he took off?"

"Yeah, didn't they tell you?"

Harry avoided the question. "So he probably hitched a ride."

"Could've. There ain't much traffic on the Badwater Creek road, 'specially at night. Course, he could'a hopped the wire and hiked over country to the highway. Here's Powder River."

They passed a café decked out with antelope horns, a scatter of log homes and trailers, another extinct gas station and a small church. Population 20. On the other side of the highway, in the middle of a pasture, stood a large hangar of recent vintage, a long gray loaf of riveted sheet metal. Out front, a crude, hand-lettered sign announced:

ANNUAL Sheepherders Fair
July 16–17, 2001
Food. Music. Sheepherding contest

"Was that fun?" Harry looked over at Darryl.

"Yeah, but I messed up on the hooking." Seeing Harry's blank stare, Darryl continued. "Y'know, y'run after the sheep with the hooked stick to get 'em down and tie 'em up."

Harry nodded. The Calgary Stampede must also have had humble beginnings. "Did the bonehunters go?"

"Yeah, they even entered the mutton stew cook-off, but lost to those Basque herders from the other side of Shoshoni."

"Marchand too?"

"Yeah, he was there with his girlfriend. Lynn. They had a big fight. She got mad enough to kick a hog barefoot. He was pretty drunk. Dad says maybe he's fooling around on her, maybe a married lady, that one of these days Peter'll get his nuts shot off." A dad's double-barreled warning to his son.

They crossed over a rise and were suddenly in jumbled terrain. Sheets of tan and purple rock hurtled out of the ground and stopped in midair. To the south, the first of the badland canyons dissected the land toward the Rattlesnake Hills. A brash billboard announced "Hell's Half Acre." A café and tourist store teetered at the edge of an escarpment overlooking the stark red and tan ravines.

At Waltman, population 6, the truck turned north onto a gravel road and grew a long, thick tail of dust. Harry checked the bed of the pickup to confirm that his duffle and bed roll were being buried in Wyoming dirt. Eight miles north they rumbled across a Union Pacific rail line and veered through a ramshackle collection of house trailers and makeshift cabins. A rusted sign on a pole creaked in the wind: Bighorn Hotel, Arminto, WY. Below it lay a heap of charred bricks and debris.

"When did it burn down?" Harry asked somberly.

"Couple years ago," Darryl said. "Lightning strike during a gully-washer. Went up like kindling, my dad says."

It had been their watering hole on the way back to camp after a blistering day in the badlands. Harry remembered the massive sweep of the mahogany bar, the slight cant of the pool table to the northwest, the pronghorn on the wall with the crooked antler, the acre of dance floor and the chromed jukebox that played memories from a 1960s prom. The guest rooms on the second floor were small, silent tableaux from the 1880s—a brass bed, a simple dresser, and an enameled washbasin.

A half-mile out of Arminto, they turned west, paralleling the southern flank of the Bighorn Mountains. Darryl bumped across a cattle guard and roared past the junction with the Badwater Creek road that climbed northwest into a scatter of cedar trees. Harry let himself lose his mind to the dry, spare terrain. The hotel, reduced to rubble, had jarred him. He felt emotionally trepanned: archaeologists thought that ancient tribes bored holes in their skulls to treat migraines, epilepsy and mental illness. Perhaps it was to extinguish memory.

Suddenly, they swerved south off the road onto a dirt track that rutted across the sagebrush prairie. Darryl handled the pickup like a veteran, shifting to slow down and speed up, riding the ridges above the ruts to avoid high-centering the truck. He circled a large butte and careened down a rocky slope onto a flat mudstone escarpment that overlooked an expanse of badlands.

They pulled up alongside three trucks parked at the edge of the cliff: a battered green 1973 Chevy pickup, a rented blue Blazer, and a white Jeep with "CMNH" and a long-necked dinosaur stenciled on the door.

"Here ya go. They're over there." He pointed to a gray hillside across a ravine.

CHAPTER 7

HARRY CLIMBED OUT into a stiff wind. The sky was laden with storm clouds, thick black and blowing in from the horizon. He grabbed his duffle bag and bedroll from the back of the pickup and threw them into the Jeep. Darryl bucked the truck into reverse, spun the rear wheels and roared away, kicking up a dust bowl. The wind sand papered Harry's face.

He squinted across the ravine at the quarry, a surgical wound gouged out of the terrain. People dotted the side of the hill, camouflaged against the gray and tan rocks, staring at the new arrival. He wondered whether they hoped he was Marchand come back. It was four-fifteen, probably close to quitting time. One of them, a woman wearing a large hat, waved him over.

Harry remembered when Marchand had first brought him here years earlier for a quick reconnaissance. He checked for the jagged gash on the butte across the gully. It was still there, a geologic fault where the earth had trembled and smacked the red layers up against the gray ones.

At the edge of the escarpment, Harry started down a mudstone ridge covered with a scree of small, ironstone pebbles. He regretted not digging out his field boots. The footing was treacherous, like walking on ball bearings. The Carnegie crew had worn a narrow trail along the spine of the rocky ledge, down to the dry gully, and up the opposite slope to the quarry.

Halfway down, he spotted a flash of orange bone against the gray, cracked mudstone. It was part of a turtle shell, dismembered and buried eighty million years ago when Wyoming was a steamy Amazonia choking on palm trees and ferns. Downpours fell two or three times a day. The canopy, understory and forest floor teemed with insects, crocodiles, turtles, snakes, dinosaurs, and small furry mammals that could have doubled for opossums, weasels and shrews. Large rivers roared eastward and inundated the forest floodplain, burying the carcasses of the ancient animals in an instant muddy grave. Now the place was a bone field.

Harry crossed the sandstone ledges at the edge of the gully, where rattlesnakes like to lose heat in the shadows. Above him, in the quarry, two men in shorts crouched over a massive bone perched atop a thin, excavated pedestal of rock. It looked like a sauropod femur, about five feet long, black, shiny, glistening in the sun, waiting to be encased in a jacket of burlap and plaster. The large-hatted woman seemed to be directing the operation. Below them, on the hillside, the raw, dull mudstone was spattered with splotches of brilliant white plaster, as if Jackson Pollock had been out here flicking his paintbrush.

Harry noticed a second woman at the far end of the quarry. She was sporting a chartreuse bikini top, skimpy white cut-offs, a bare blond head, and a long blond braid down her back. She spied him, lifted a green canteen and drank as if performing, letting her sleek neck rise and fall with each swallow. Harry wondered if that was Lynn, Marchand's current interest. She said something to the two men, gesturing at Harry with her water bottle. They turned to watch him scramble up the slope to the quarry.

Big Hat greeted him. "You must be the detective Sam called about. I'm Diana Palantier." Her voice was a surprise, raspy and tough. It didn't match the tiny hand she stuck out at him. She was dwarfed by her hat, a garden-variety straw job with a wide, flattened brim.

"I had Darryl bring you here instead of camp. I hope you don't mind."

"That's fine," Harry said. He could barely make out the face talking to him from the shadow of the broad-brimmed hat. It looked like it went well with the voice. "I'm Harry Przewalski."

She started to laugh, almost a gentle cough. "Really? I thought Sam was putting me on. There's a horse—"

"Yeah, I know," he interrupted. "Przewalski's horse. No relation."

Diana twisted her mouth. "Very funny. Let me introduce you." She pointed to a tall man sitting cross-legged in a corner of the excavation, with small, round dark glasses and a bandana around his head.

"This is Morris Burke, our collection manager for paleontology at the museum." He nodded and went back to cutting a burlap sack into long strips, soaking them in a bucket of water, then immersing them in a bucket of plaster of Paris.

"And this is Edwin Simeon, a professor from Cornell." Harry turned to find a portly man stumbling toward them over the rocks. He was red-faced despite his pith helmet, clearly suffering from the heat.

"Very glad you're here, detective. Very glad. I'm starting to worry about our friend Peter."

Harry shook Simeon's hand. It was sweaty and soft, almost baby-soft. Simeon had spent his career in the field observing, not digging.

"We have three graduate students with us," Diana continued. "Lynn Calvert, Gunther Bruckmann and David Jacobs."

Calvert studied him for a long moment, then turned away for another swig from the canteen. Harry didn't normally gawk at women, but Calvert radiated sensual nonchalance: green eyes, pouty mouth, long legs flowing out of the shorts, small breasts pushing high against the tight bikini top, a young stomach, languid shoulders. Her face radiated a resentful mournfulness. Perhaps because Marchand had taken off. But it seemed something deeper. Abruptly, she grabbed a black T-shirt and slipped it on.

Harry turned to find Diana watching him with a tired, bemused smile. She was used to men gawking at Calvert, no doubt beginning with Marchand. Bruckmann and Jacobs nodded at him. They were an odd team: Jacobs, short and pudgy, like a doughboy, with thinning blond hair; Bruckmann, also blond, not much taller, but barrel-chested and robust. More incongruous was Jacobs' gray T-shirt. Across the front, big red letters instructed: "Trust In . . . " Across the back, it said who: " . . . JESUS." Harry wondered how Jacobs managed to square scripture with science.

"This everyone?" he asked.

"Yeah, the whole crew. Minus Peter, of course," she added, drily. "And there's a reporter from the *Post-Gazette* here. Meredith Shue. She's wandering around here, somewhere."

Jacobs and Bruckmann finished wrapping the dinosaur limb in damp toilet paper and began applying the plaster-soaked burlap strips in methodical, overlapping folds to the contours of the bone.

"Listen," Diana interrupted, somewhat impatient, "we're just about done for the day. But we have to get the rest of the plaster on before it hardens. You'll be out of the way over there." She pointed over to the edge of the quarry. "We'll talk later. I'm sure you have questions. Why don't you sit down on those rocks and think about what you want to ask. You can start with Edwin over there. Or Meredith." She turned back to the plastering operation.

Big hat and bossy, Harry thought. He picked his way toward Simeon between the rubble heaps and an exposed, gridded jumble of dinosaur skeletons.

A young woman, breathing hard, came around the end of the butte, scrambling awkwardly over the rocks. She looked as if she'd hiked out of a Banana Republic catalog, attired in khaki hat, khaki shirt, khaki shorts, khaki socks, khaki boots. She was also typecast as a newspaper reporter: inquisitive eyes, boxer's chin, mop of brown hair protruding from below the hat. The badlands were clearly a new beat for her, evidenced by her scabbed knees, a shallow scrape on one leg and blistered lips. Her pale, freckled skin had begun to resemble a slab of pepper steak.

"You're the detective?" she panted, beaming at him.

Someone was happy to see him. "Harry Przewalski. Miss Shue, right? *Post-Gazette*?"

"Right. I'll trade you Meredith for Harry. You saw my piece?"

Harry nodded. "Back in Pittsburgh. It stirred the multitude."

"It was meant to. Let me guess––it got Carnegie to put you on an airplane."

Harry nodded again. "You were circumspect."

"Meaning?"

"You didn't speculate on Marchand's whereabouts."

Meredith gazed out at the badlands, then, almost sympathetically, motioned at Calvert. "Well, there's gossip. I'll publish it when it's fact."

"What's the gossip?"

"Marchand's shacked up with one of the locals. Apparently it's happened before."

"Anything else?" Harry prompted.

"Well," Shue continued, "he might have just hung it up after all these years. His career, I mean. Just taken off."

"Why would he do that?"

"Not sure. Just a feeling from interviewing him. Desperate for a new life. Free from academia . . . scientific pressures."

"What kind of pressures?"

"What I hear all profs complain about. I work the academic beat—Carnegie Mellon, Pitt, Carnegie Institute. I sensed he was fed up with the system. Endless streams of students. Endless proposals for research grants. Ruthless professional politics, rivals itching to bring you down. He called academia 'the place of the long knives.'" She looked pointedly at Simeon, who was straining to overhear the conversation. He glared back at her.

A brown ant had begun to forage in the sunscreen on her sunburnt leg. Shue brushed it off. Yesterday, in his office, Preston Stewart had dismissed Shue as an amateur not capable of digging up serious copy. He ought to start worrying, Harry thought. She had the nose for detecting the story beneath the topsoil and the savvy to excavate it.

"When did you interview Marchand?"

She grabbed a notebook from her back pocket and quickly leafed through it. "In Pittsburgh. A week before they came out here. Then twice here. He seemed oddly distracted, disillusioned with the project, almost impatient for the field season to be over. He seemed to be . . . what did Graham Greene call it . . . a burnt-out case. So he just walked out of camp one night . . . and hasn't come back."

"How do you know he walked out?"

She raised her eyebrows. "Simple. All the trucks were in camp the morning he turned up missing." She waved at the escarpment. "Including his old green Chevy over there."

Calvert began gathering the hammers, chisels, pails, brushes and burlap strips into a neat pile. Quarry work was done for the day. The dinosaur thigh bone lay swathed in white, an alien artifact on a gray planet. Burke, Jacobs and Bruckmann spread oilskin tarpaulins over the exposed bones, weighed them down with rocks, and shoved the 100-pound sack of plaster under another tarpaulin. Every time Lynn bent over, her skimpy cut-offs rode up, flashing the white of her thighs. Harry noticed Jacobs stare and look away, flushed yet disgusted, seemingly at war with himself.

Diana motioned to Harry. "Time to go, Har—" A lightning flash a few hills over electrocuted the air. The thunderclap was instantaneous and explosive. Harry almost dived for cover. It wasn't Iraq. It wasn't a bomb.

"Okay, let's move it!" Diana barked. She led them single file down the well-worn path into the gully and up the other side to the trucks. The wind hit full force as they emerged out of the ravine. The saltbushes and sparse prairie grass doubled over, straining to stay rooted. Thunderclouds rolled across the sky like black tumbleweeds.

"Let's motor before the storm hits," Diana shouted above the wind, somehow managing to keep the brimmed hat on her head. "Harry, ride with me in the Chevy."

Simeon and Meredith jumped into the Blazer. Harry suddenly regretted not renting his own truck in Casper. He would tomorrow. Jacobs, Calvert, and Bruckmann piled into the Carnegie Jeep with Burke at the wheel. As the caravan lurched along the two-wheel track out of the badlands, the first heavy drops of rain thumped against the roof and windshield, pummeling the dust back into the ground.

Diana took off her hat and turned to him. "Do you smoke?" It almost sounded like a challenge. The face that went with the raspy voice was kinetic. It moved in three directions when she spoke—mouth zigzagging northwest, an eyebrow arching up, a sharp chin hooking left.

"When I can't help it," Harry finally answered. "Which is most times. I'm trying to give it up. Someone told me I tasted like an ashtray."

"Well, this is the smoking truck," Diana replied. "Yeah, I'm also trying to quit . . . and failing. I might taste like an ashtray, but these days no one would know it." It could have come out sentimental, but didn't. She paused, then rasped, "Fuck this noise." She tossed him a pack of Pall Malls, unfiltered. "Grab me a cigarette. Light it for me. Get one for yourself."

Harry lit a couple of cigarettes and handed one to her. The first drag felt like a shared, consummated sin. Harry weighed telling her about Marchand, that he'd been his student, that he'd done paleontological time in these badlands, that he knew they'd just tramped over ancient dirt laid down in the Cretaceous. But it was hard to talk over the roar of the engine. The truck had lost its muffler. The windows were frozen open. He slid toward Diana to avoid the spray of rain and mud kicked up by the front tire. She gave him a quick look, her kinetic face now set on rough, her eyes pinning him to the back of the seat.

They bumped off the dirt track onto the wide, county gravel road. To the west, Harry knew it led to Lost Cabin; to the east, the junction with the Badwater Creek road and, beyond that, Arminto. Diana shifted into four-wheel-high and accelerated to highway speed. The slashing rain was beginning to turn the clay into a slick, treacherous muck. A spine of utility poles ran along the side of the road, sending lone wires to the distant hills at unpredictable intervals. Harry couldn't see any ranch houses.

"It costs a rancher about a hundred dollars a foot to bring electricity to a house from the main trunk," Diana shouted over the engine and wind, reading his mind. "It's a thousand dollars a foot to dig a well. And then you hope the water is good. Much of it isn't anymore with all of the oil and gas drilling around here. Trading water for money. The well at Darryl's place is foul. But, hey, they've made a bundle from providing access roads to the drill rigs. And they spend it on having water hauled in weekly from Casper."

"How long have you been coming out here?" Harry shouted back.

"About seven years. Three at the quarry. Peter's been working in Wyoming and Montana much longer. Now he has this dinosaur bone bed. It'll take years to excavate. Peter doesn't like a big field crew. More than six or seven in camp is a crowd."

At the junction with the Badwater Creek road, Diana turned north and climbed into the sparse cedar hills, dipped west down into the Badwater valley, and followed the winding creek past hay meadows and across a series of cattle guards. At a massive set of power lines, Diana downshifted and pitched north onto a two-wheel dirt track toward the flank of the Bighorns. A quarter mile up, a barbed wire gate was strung tight across the road. Must be cattle in the upper pastures, Harry thought. He remembered the drill and cursed silently. The passenger in the lead truck opens the gate for the others.

Diana turned to him. "D'you know how—"

Before she could finish, he stepped out into the mud and driving rain, and tromped over to the gate. Almost by rote, he pried the wire loop over the top of the wooden gate post, yanked the post out of the bottom wire loop, dragged the gate to the side of the road, and stood in the rain waiting for the three trucks to pass. Diana eyed him suspiciously as the Chevy went by, baffled that Harry had somehow acquired this arcane talent of opening barbed wire gates.

He stretched the gate back across the track and forced the wire loops onto the post. By the time he got back into the truck, his clothes were plastered to his skin and his boots were carrying his weight in mud. Diana studied him again, that mercurial face now somewhat clement. She jammed the truck into gear and bounced it up the rocky track. Harry turned and looked back at the barbed wire fence line. Marchand must have worked that gate in the dark the night he walked out of camp.

CHAPTER 8

CAMP WAS AT 9000 feet, a rocky, green meadow abutting the foothills of the southern Bighorn Mountains. To the north, the meadow led to the high summer pastures for the cattle and sheep. To the south and east, it overlooked the scrub-grass desert, flat and expansive except for the sudden breaks of gray and red badlands. The storm had missed camp, deflected by surrounding ridges. At 9000 feet, the meadow remained cool through the midday heat. At night it would freeze.

Diana parked the Chevy beside two tall trees that sheltered the ruins of an extinct homestead: a stone foundation, rotting timbers, a sagging barbed wire fence. Upslope, a clapboard outhouse listed to the west. It would house the predictable latrine food chain: flies, brown recluses, lizards, and the occasional rattlesnake.

A large, white canvas mess tent rose between the fence and outhouse, anchored by stakes and guide ropes. Personal tents dotted the meadow, brilliant blue domes rising incongruously from the straw-burnt scrub grass. At the edge of the meadow, a small stream burbled up from a natural spring. Harry noticed they'd dammed it with a pole and tarpaulin into a shallow bathing pool. An overgrown rose bush by the pool sagged under a tangle of towels and wash cloths.

The original homesteader must have explored long and hard before putting his life down on this sylvan piece of Wind River Basin. Marchand, Harry thought, was now the homesteader here, the biogeographic successor, if only as a vicarious summer immigrant.

"In the morning, if the haze is low, you can see the Wind River Mountains to the west." Diana had come up quietly behind him, the big hat again hiding her face. "Also the trucks on the Casper-Shoshoni highway about twenty miles south."

She pointed to the meadow. "You'll tent over there. David and Morris will give you a hand. Get your gear arranged before dinner. Grab a bath if you want." She pointed at the rose bush. "Listen, the water's damn cold. And the guys say you'll feel it where it counts. Old-timers out here call it cowboy birth control. I guess it beats abstinence."

Before he could answer, Burke and Jacobs came around the side of the mess tent lugging a bundle of blue nylon and canvas, a bag of stakes and a sheaf of aluminum poles. Harry moved a few rocks and spread the tent out on the flattest spot left in the meadow, if flat meant an eight-degree slope. He'd sleep uphill. They were still using Springbars, Harry noticed, the only ten-by-ten tents that could withstand violent thunderstorms and sixty-mile-an-hour winds. They were an engineering marvel, suspended from a skeleton of poles kept taut by the trademark springbar across the top. Ten-penny pegs at the corners and sides kept the tent from becoming a blue dirigible over the Bighorns. The zippered, triangular windows were set low, perfect in the middle of the night for a kneeling whiz out of the tent instead of a cold trek to the outhouse.

"Ever been to Wyoming?" Burke asked.

Harry nodded, pounding in the corner stakes. Burke and Jacobs threaded the poles through the loops and hoisted up the sides. Harry tied back the door flaps, tossed his gear into the tent, unrolled his sleeping bag, unzipped the windows, and watched the western horizon catch fire through the mosquito netting.

Jacobs lingered outside, nervously shuffling his feet. Finally he stuck his head in. "Got an air mattress or a foam pad? You'll feel every pebble if you don't."

"No," Harry said.

"We have a couple of spare pads. Or you can take Peter's. He won't need it tonight. He might not have any more nights here. I'll go get it." But he remained half in the tent, half out, not making a move to go, crossing his feet and rocking back and forth as if he needed to piss badly.

Harry took the bait. "Why? Do you know where he is?"

Jacobs said nothing. His eyes darted around the tent, his body rocking, his hands deep in his pockets visibly agitating his groin. Harry was sure that Jacobs was fighting a full bladder.

Finally he blurted out, "I bet Karlsen shot him. He's a good Christian. But he wouldn't turn the other cheek if he found his wife and Peter fornicating." Jacobs pointed toward the haze smothering the scrub prairie. "I bet he's buried out there on the Karlsen Ranch. It'll take more than you to find him. It's tens of thousands of acres."

Jacobs turned and dashed off toward the outhouse. Harry thought about a shallow grave on the plains. Deep enough to cover a carcass. But, unlike Marchand's dinosaurs, not deep enough to petrify it. If he was buried out there, it wouldn't be for posterity.

He unpacked a towel, picked his way between the bushes

to the stream, stripped, and gingerly immersed himself in the pool. He made himself smile when the water seized his crotch. As he reached for the washcloth, he swore he saw Bruckmann behind the rose bush staring at him through the dusk.

CHAPTER 9

T HE SCENE OUTSIDE the mess tent was as congenial as a Serbo-Croatian picnic. No one spoke. They might as well have taken vows of silence. Harry remembered how field crews became toxic after a few weeks. There was no escaping one another's irritations, like a marriage gone bad: waking together, eating together, quarrying together, shopping together, bathing together, and waiting in line to use the same crapper. Words became venom. Pique became poison.

Lynn stood in a cloud of smoke, madly forking pieces of chicken, baked potatoes and ears of corn on a Weber grill. She had cleaned up—a white, V-neck T-shirt, jean cutoffs, and wet blond hair streaming down her back. Humming a Linda Ronstadt tune, "You're No Good." No doubt fingering Marchand.

Bruckmann hadn't changed from the sweat-stained shorts and shirt he'd worn in the quarry. He seemed to be plotting, squatting by the fence, alone, staring south into the distance, furiously choking down a cigarette. Simeon, in fresh khakis and a vest, was more professorial—and more portly. He nursed a beer and looked worried, as if he were the object of Bruckmann's plot.

Jacobs sat in a lawn chair, writing field notes in an orange, hard-covered log book. He kept rocking, likely fighting another trip to the outhouse. Burke, sprawled in a canvas chair, was tallying specimen numbers against a gridded schematic of the quarry in his field book. Shue was working on the next Pulitzer piece for the *Post-Gazette*. She had ditched the all-khaki outfit for jeans and a taupe sweater. Her hair was slicked back. It made her look tougher. Harry didn't doubt she was.

In the mess tent, Diana was uncorking a red wine for dinner. Her makeover was astonishing: fresh jeans, a white shirt, sandals, earrings, and black hair parted on the side. For the second time in one day, Harry found himself gawking at a woman in Wyoming. She turned from the table, and methodically arranged her face into a smile.

"All set? Tent? Bath?"

Harry tried humor. "Yeah. I'm sterile."

She didn't laugh. "Congratulations. We're eating."

Science marched on, Harry thought, but field life didn't. The mess tent was a throwback. Tarpaulins on the ground to keep the dust down. A table set for dinner. Makeshift benches on either side. Tables against the side walls of the tent strewn with hammers, chisels, cans of glue and acetone, plaster, old newspapers and a pile of topographic maps. There was one concession to the modern—a small propane refrigerator. That explained the chicken, fresh salad, and milk on the table. Beer and soda pop were on ice in the coolers. The wine was likely a Marchand tradition.

They sat in what seemed to be ritual order: Bruckmann, Shue and Calvert on one side of the table, Burke and Jacobs on the other, Palantier and Simeon at the ends. It reminded him of a black-and-white photograph taken a hundred years earlier at Sheep Creek, Wyoming, north of Medicine Bow. A large, canvas wall tent. The door flaps are tied back. Inside, eight Carnegie bonehunters sit on wooden crates around a table; sullen, stiff, hunched over, silently spooning beef, beans and bread from enameled bowls. They're exhausted from the pick-and-shovel work in Quarry D, removing the thick overburden of rock above the exposed bones of a dinosaur skeleton. It is eighty-four feet long and new to science. It will be named *Diplodocus carnegii* and become the centerpiece of Andrew Carnegie's new museum in Pittsburgh, nicknamed "the house that Dippy built." For Harry, the skeleton at Sheep Creek was the measure of the profession. It was discovered on Independence Day, July 4, 1899. The Carnegie bonehunters didn't take the day off.

Harry squeezed in beside Burke. Jacobs was murmuring a prayer under his breath. Harry grabbed some salad and a roasted potato, and poured himself some wine.

Diana nodded at him. "The floor is yours, detective."

"Wait!" Lynn interrupted, flashing a warm, welcoming smile. "Speaking for myself, it's good to have you here, Mr.—"

"Harry works."

"Okay, Harry. You've probably been told stories." She indicted each one at the table with a short, intense stare. "I don't care. Peter and I are . . . together. And I want you to find him. The damn sheriff out here won't. Doesn't matter where Peter's gone . . . or with whom." She looked out the wide door of the mess tent toward the distant ridge of badlands to the east turning crimson in the setting light. "If that's the case, so be it."

Jacobs tittered. Lynn ignored him.

"Okay," Harry acknowledged. "That's good. You want him found. I assume all of you want him found. And the Carnegie Institute wants him found. Quickly. Quietly. I need each of you to tell me what you know. Start with the day he disappeared. What went on in the field. Then here in camp that night."

Diana sighed. "We've been through all this with the sheriff in Shoshoni. What's his name . . . Crumley?"

"I'm not Crumley," Harry said patiently. "Run through it for my benefit. When did you last see Marchand?"

"All right," Diana declared, exasperated. "Thursday, July 21. Nothing unusual happened. We got back from the quarry, ate, finished our field notes, went over the next day's schedule, read a bit, and went to bed. The next morning, he wasn't at breakfast. Or in his tent. He walked out of camp sometime during the night."

"Who was the last one to see him that night?"

"Lynn was last," Meredith volunteered, shooting her a probing glance. "She usually waited up for Peter."

"Bet no one waits up for you," Lynn shot back, her eyes frozen green. She nodded at Simeon. "Dr. Simeon was still wandering around with his flashlight when I went to my tent. So was David."

"The young lady is quite right," Simeon intoned. "I retrieved my shirt from the bathing area on the way to the tent. Mr. Jacobs was returning from a visit to our homesteader's pissoir. No one else was about. Except Peter, of course. He was drinking here in the mess tent. He had just put a new propane cylinder in the lantern. But you won't get anywhere this way, detective."

Harry ignored him. After years of too much alcohol, Simeon's nose and cheeks looked like a relief map of a delta draining the purple-veined headlands.

"So you left Marchand alone. What time was this?"

"Just after ten," Simeon said.

"That's pretty exact. How can you be so sure?"

"Mr. Jacobs tunes in the baseball scores on that radio every night." Simeon pointed to a battered Panasonic boom box with a bent aerial.

"How long did Peter stay up? Anyone hear him go to his tent?"

No one spoke. They all looked at Lynn.

Diana finally answered, calmly. "Peter typically does not go to bed right away. He likes to get in his truck, drive out to the badlands, sit and drink. Usually till well after midnight. He returns at one or two in the morning. Sometimes at three. He's been doing it for years out here, every night, weather allowing, of course." After a moment, she added, softly, "Often he has a companion."

Harry looked at her face, now averted, muscles tightened, an Erector set of bones moving quickly under the skin to annul the past.

"And did he drive off that night?"

Again, they looked at Lynn.

"Yes," Lynn said. "He left about eleven-thirty. The motor woke me up. But by the time I got out of my tent, he was already down the track to the gate. Lately, he wanted time at night in the badlands by himself. I figured I'd see him when he returned, so I went back to bed."

"Anyone else hear or see the truck leave?" Harry scanned the table.

Shue chimed in. "The first week or so the truck would wake me up. Not anymore. I didn't hear him leave camp or return."

For the first time, Bruckmann spoke; but first, he raised his hand as if he were in school. "I heard Peter leave in the truck. Happens every night, so I didn't go out to see it. Anyway, what Peter and Lynn do is their business."

"All things are God's business," Jacobs murmured into his napkin, wiping the barbecue sauce from his mouth.

Only Lynn heeded the sermonette. "Shut up! You pathetic little twerp," she hissed. "You can't stop looking at my chest, can you? Not that you can do anything about it. You know what Peter says? 'Not with your balls wrapped in Genesis.' "

Jacobs smiled, then lowered his head, but not before eyeing

the cleavage at the V in her T-shirt. Harry noticed that no one seemed perturbed, as if this were a nightly exchange.

"Which truck did he take?"

Burke answered. "The green Chevy. It's his." He got up and lit a propane lantern. Outside, dusk had gone to dark. The wind had picked up, each gust billowing the sides of the tent and testing its anchors.

"When did Marchand come back?"

"It was late, later than usual," Lynn replied. "About three-thirty in the morning. I woke up and checked my watch when I heard the truck drive into camp. Peter got out, slammed the door, then opened and slammed it again. I guess he must have forgotten something. Then he went to his tent. I stayed in mine and went back to sleep. I figured he still wanted to be alone." She tried to sound nonchalant, but her face registered the pain of rejection like a fresh wound.

"Anyone else hear the truck? Or see Peter return?" Harry asked, surveying the faces. Simeon was beginning to look pickled in alcohol. Burke was fighting sleep. Meredith had pulled out her notebook and was scribbling. Diana was staring into the memory of an extinct romance. Jacobs kept eyeing the platter of half-cooked chicken as if he were battling temptation.

"I did," Bruckmann admitted. "I heard Peter return and get into his tent. But nothing after that. I went back to sleep."

"What about later? Anyone hear him leave camp?"

Negatives all around.

"Who was up first that morning?"

"I was," Jacobs stated, "but I usually am. I wash up at the stream, open the mess tent, start the coffee, and check to see if the deer mice have gotten into any of the food."

"What time was this?"

"Between six-thirty and seven."

"And Peter was already gone?"

"I presume so. He didn't show for breakfast. But if you're asking if I checked his tent, the answer is no. Never know who you might find in there." He looked at Lynn, who ignored him. She turned to Harry.

"I checked his tent first thing. He was gone. The bed was a mess, but it always is. Pete's not a neat guy."

"Okay," Harry said, "let's see if I've got this straight. That Thursday night, July 21, Marchand is here in the mess tent alone from about ten till eleven-thirty. Then he leaves camp in the Chevy pickup, comes back about three-thirty in the morning, goes to his tent, and then leaves again sometime in the next three hours. But this time he walks out. His Chevy is still here in the morning. And no one hears a car or truck come to pick him up. Right?"

Everyone was silent until Simeon slurred, "Thash right, detective. Told you you weren't going to get anywhere." His nose had become redder, the delta now swollen with more wine.

"I think we've all had enough for now," Diana declared, getting up.

Harry grabbed a flashlight and ducked out into the cold blackness of the night. Hard-cut stars glinted across the underbelly of the sky. He walked up to the outhouse, turned on his flashlight and swung the wooden door open. It was the homesteader's original two-holer. Clean. No graffiti. Functional.

"HURRY UP!"

Harry spun around. Jacobs had suddenly come up behind him.

"Hurry up," Jacobs repeated, rocking back and forth in discomfort.

"Go ahead. I can wait."

Jacobs dashed in and slammed the door without checking the wooden floorboards. Harry wondered when they'd last found a rattler lying in wait.

CHAPTER 10

"A S I KEEP saying, but no one seems to be listening," Simeon fulminated as Harry returned to the mess tent, "it is outrageous that every day, in this age of science and technology, we are forced to renegotiate the Enlightenment!"

"Edwin!" Diana barked. "You're right! No one is listening! We've heard this before."

Simeon plowed on, too lubricated to care. "Daily we are beset with the three stooges of reason. Creationism. Multiculturalism. Deconstructionism. Creationists say God tells them the facts. Multiculturalists invent the facts. And deconstructionists say there are no facts. They belong in a nursing home for vestigial ideas."

Jacobs, his face tense, got up at the mention of God and left. Lynn kept working at peeling the Olympia label off the beer bottle. She looked adrift in a distant choppy life. Meredith studied a map of Wyoming as if she were divining where Marchand had skedaddled. Diana was trying to read. Harry couldn't make out the book. Bruckmann stood outside puffing on a cigarette.

"OK, EDWIN!" Diana shouted. "You're plastered. Go to bed!"

Simeon looked around, burped, slowly stood up and weaved out of the tent. The others followed. Diana looked at Harry with relief.

"Christ, I need a beer and a goddamn cigarette! Harry, you want one?"

She grabbed a Pall Mall from a pack on the table, lit it, and threw the pack to Harry. His Drum was still in the Chevy truck. Harry smelled the tobacco and gave in. Damn, he thought, the first drag is like the first long kiss. He heard the high-pitched chorus of Springbar zippers being opened and closed. It sounded like the mating call of a mutant species of frog.

"It's after ten o'clock. No Jacobs? No baseball scores tonight?"

"I guess not. You've probably detected that David is religious . . . fundamentalist."

Harry couldn't tell if the cynicism was real or inadvertent. "Yeah, I saw the T-shirt, heard the prayer. Tell me about him. Has he been a student long?"

"This is his second year with us. We never noticed this Bible stuff last year. So either he found religion lately or kept it well camouflaged. He's also put on a fair bit of weight. He seems distressed about it. We think he's taking medication for some condition. Maybe there's a connection. For all that, he's a pretty good student. He's studying dinosaur reproduction, eggshell ultrastructure. I'm sorry; ultrastructure is the makeup— "

"I know what ultrastructure is," Harry asserted quietly. "Strange, a fundamentalist studying paleontology. You'd think he'd have a hard time reconciling the contradictions."

Diana looked at him oddly. "What do you mean?"

"An old universe. An old Earth. Continental drift. Evolution. Fossils. Extinction. All those animals and plants that aren't around anymore. Clearly creation wasn't perfect. Or meant for the long haul. Paley said God was the divine watchmaker. If so, God made a Timex, not a Rolex."

Diana sat back, her face registering astonishment, then confusion. "Harry, for a detective—"

"Yeah, I'm pretty well educated," he finished the sentence for her. "We gumshoes like to be typecast."

She looked at him, pained. "I'm sorry, Harry, I didn't mean . . . never mind. Except," she held up her palms in defense, "don't take this the wrong way, but I'll say it again. For a detective, you know a hell of a lot about the history of science and evolutionary biology. C'mon! William Paley from the 1700s?"

Harry passed on the opportunity to explain. He lit another Pall Mall. "Tell me more about David."

"Okay," she nodded, still puzzled. "Yeah, he's probably conflicted about paleontology and religion. Also, the strain has been terrible on him and the rest of the crew since Peter disappeared. They feel abandoned. Peter's the reason they're here. He energizes them. His exuberance is infectious. Now they're orphaned, just going through the motions. Peter was the intellectual glue in camp. He turned dinners into rousing debates. Politics, religion, paleontology, the latest stupid dinosaur theory. In the quarry, Peter played jazz on the boom box—Pittsburgh's own Roy Eldridge. Now the dig is as solemn as a goddamn funeral parlor."

"What did you talk about the night he walked out?"

Diana thought for a moment, reached into the backpack behind her, brought out a notebook, and leafed through it. "I keep a log. Here it is—July 21. I hadn't seen Peter get so angry in a long time. He was fuming over an article in that week's *Nature* . . . sorry, *Nature* is a British scientific journ—"

Harry cut in. "I know what *Nature* is, thanks."

Again she eyed him quizzically, but decided not to quiz. "The article was about the worldwide illegal commercial traffic in fossils. A lot of it comes from here and goes to Asia. Collectors and department stores. There was a stink a few years ago about a *T. rex* skeleton nicknamed Sue. It made all the papers. The FBI seized it from commercial collectors in South Dakota. It was about to be shipped to a Japanese buyer for six figures. Illegally collected from an Indian reservation."

She reached over to the cooler, cracked her third beer, took a long guzzle and lit a cigarette. "Hell, go to any fancy rock shop in Jackson Hole, Beverly Hills, Santa Fe, New York. Any tourist spot. They're selling fossil rhinos from Nebraska, fossil fish from the Green River shale in Wyoming, fossil sharks and pterosaurs from the Kansas chalk, fossil insects in amber from the Dominican Republic, and of course, zillions of fifty-cent trilobites and shark teeth. Illegal, most of them. Harry, if these were Indian objects—pots, arrowheads, jewelry—the authorities would pounce on the commercial collectors. Archaeology is protected by the Antiquities Act. But fossils aren't. So we're seeing the plunder of paleontological science."

The two mantles in the propane lantern began flickering. The steady hiss of the fuel turned irregular.

"It's sack time," Diana conceded. "Any of this been helpful, detective . . . sorry, Harry?"

He nodded. "It's a start. I'll be talking to Jacobs and the others alone."

"Start with Lynn. As you know now, she and Peter are a steady ticket."

"Like you and he were, once," Harry probed.

Her face jerked into surprise, then resentment. "Christ, we sure are up on the gossip."

"Detectives traffic in gossip. It's our lingua franca—cheap and mean. The smelly fog around a bit of truth. Gossip at Carnegie traffics in the latest Marchand fling. But I'm not here to find out your history between the sheets with him or anyone else. I'm here to find where he went off to. Gossip says he went off with someone."

Diana gave a short laugh. "He'll turn up when he's ready. Do you know what he looks like?"

"Yeah. I've met him."

"Really? When?"

Harry took a cigarette from her pack, fingered it, and decided he might as well chain smoke and open the past.

"It's been a few years. Before your time. I was a doctoral student. At Pitt. I worked with Marchand at the museum. Spent three field seasons out here. I drank at the Bighorn Hotel in Arminto before it burned down. I know the dirty history of the Okie mansion in Lost Cabin. And I know there's a roller on the Lost Cabin–Arminto Road where you can get liftoff in a Chevy Suburban at sixty-five miles an hour."

She stared at him, shocked, her mobile face making the connection. "I'll be damned. I wondered. What're the fucking odds? Someone named Przewalski majors in paleontology, becomes a detective, and is hired by a museum to find his former professor. Never mind. What happened?"

"A little tragedy," Harry said. He remembered the morgue, being asked to identify body parts. "But we're not here to talk about me. Where would Marchand go each night?"

"Oh hell," she waved her hand toward the hills outside the mess tent. "There's a butte out there. It overlooks the badlands. Near the quarries. Spectacular by moonlight. For Peter it was a nightly reverie, a getaway from the field crew, the grind of camp, the quarry work."

"Also a getaway for romance," Harry reminded her.

"Oh yeah? If you mean me, often we would just talk. Peter's not so young anymore. He was eleven years older than me when we hooked up. Still is."

She took a long swig from the beer bottle. "Anyway, this

summer he was going out there without Lynn as often as with her. Maybe he's getting tired of her. Not surprising. Sex alone doesn't bind. Peter needs the companionship of ideas, intellectual jousting. Lynn's not stupid. Just isn't wired that way. But she genuinely cares about him. She's worried. And hurt. Now *she's* the one he's left for another woman. I feel for her. When they first took up, I tried to warn her about Peter's track record. For all his scientific accolades, Peter still needs to keep conquering women to sustain self-esteem. Rather tragic."

Pop psychology from a spurned lover, Harry thought. "The morning he turned up missing, July 22, you worked as usual?"

"Yeah. It was a Friday—we work till noon and go to Casper for the night. We didn't hang around waiting for Peter. He knows the drill. His truck was here."

"Where did you think he'd gone off to?" Harry pressed.

"Who knows? We thought he might want some time alone. Maybe up the meadow in the pastures with the Basque sheepherders." She motioned to the Bighorns in the north outside the tent. "I know he's around somewhere. Peter's just not someone you worry about."

"So you left for Casper that afternoon without him."

"Yeah. If you want to know the truth, I didn't care. I was pissed off. Who does he think he is, just taking off? We have a three-year, half-million dollar research grant from the National Science Foundation. It's funding this field expedition. He's the fucking leader. If he thought I would stop the excavation until he returned—that he's essential—he's wrong. I can't make him come back from wherever he's wandered off to. Or whomever he's holed up with. I can't worry about his emotional state. I've got a deadline. August 12. Get as many of those goddamn dinosaur skeletons out of the ground as we can. Close up camp. Head home. That's the schedule. That's job one for me."

The indignation sounded too righteous. She wasn't worried,

but Harry wondered if she too felt orphaned. "What did you do in Casper?"

"Hell, same as we do every week. Same as you guys did in Casper back when. Stay at the smelly Day's Inn for the night, get a long shower, maybe a movie. Saturday, do laundry, get groceries, stock up on beer. It's a break. There's a good Middle Eastern restaurant in Casper now. You like that food?"

"No," he said too quickly. He had a flashback to the slaughterer slicing the sheep's throat in the alley behind the kebab place in Tehran. Another dismemberment. He felt his throat gag. "You got back to camp Saturday afternoon?"

She nodded.

"Still no sign of Marchand?"

"None. I drove over to Karlsen's to see if he had stopped in there."

"Why Karlsen's?"

"This is George Karlsen's land, part of the ranch. He also owns the section the quarry is on. Peter sometimes visits him at the house in Lost Cabin. Anyway, Karlsen didn't even know Peter had gone missing. Does that save you a trip?"

"No. Then what?"

"I came back here, to camp. Sunday morning, when he still hadn't turned up, I drove back to town myself to look for him. I sent everyone else out to the quarry."

"Why? You insisted Peter could take care of himself."

Diana hesitated. "I was afraid he might be on a drunk. Maybe got beat up and rolled. Peter carries about a thousand in cash in his wallet. He hates traveler's checks. The rest of the field funds are in a bank account in Casper."

"Where'd you look for him?"

"Bars. Motels. I used a picture of him that Lynn carries around. Nobody had seen Peter. I called Sam at the museum. And Crumley, the sheriff in Shoshoni. He came out, nosed around camp, asked the same questions you did, checked the bars and motels in Shoshoni, and had the sheriffs in the towns around here do the same. Nothing. Crumley isn't concerned. He knows Peter's reputation. I think he suspects Peter is shacked up in some motel with some woman around here. Probably using a different name to escape a husband's or father's shotgun. Hell, maybe Peter got a lift with a trucker to God knows where. Anyway, ten days later, still no Peter. Then Sam called you. And here you are."

The propane lantern had gone out. The tent was dark except for a surgical beam of moonlight that knifed through the hole for the stovepipe in the sloping canvas roof. A tent zipper buzzed in the distance. A minute later the door on the outhouse creaked. Then it creaked again, then the zipper, then quiet.

"Midnight bladder break for someone," Diana noted, motioning with her head. "Probably Jacobs. Or Simeon. He drank enough to fill two bladders. Fucking windbag is too old school to piss out of the tent."

Harry let it go. "Tell me about you and Marchand."

He sensed her stiffen. She grabbed a cigarette, stuck her hands into her pockets, and got up for a stroll around the tent, as if she suddenly needed physical distance.

"It was over with Peter a year ago," she stated with forced dispassion. "The break was as friendly as those things can be. We've worked together since without any problem. If you want to know the truth, it's been more of a soap opera for everyone else than it's been for us."

"How long were you together?"

"Five years."

"So you were a graduate student."

"No, a post-doc. A naïve one. I thought it was a true meeting of mind and body, or some such adolescent crap." She sounded more mystified than bitter that such a thing had happened to her.

She finished her stroll and, without warning, sat down beside him in the dark, brushing his hip and shoulder. The sudden contact was electric, surging through him like a voltage arc. He waited for the delirium to clear, for his nerves to quit jangling in heat.

"Peter doesn't like women over thirty-five," she declared, jerking him back to reality. "Maybe we remind him of his own mortality. That's the standard theory, isn't it?"

"I don't know. Most social theory is just current prejudice hunting for a correlation. Typical shelf life is a week or so. Same for paleontology."

"That's a pretty cynical indictment."

"You're right. Anyway, did Peter already have somebody younger in mind?"

"In mind!" Diana exclaimed. "He already had somebody younger in bed! *Our bed*! I've never been so pissed in my life!"

"What then?"

"Nothing. Hey, Mr. Detective, when something's over, it's over. Including this." She got up. Their conversation was done.

Outside, the temperature had dropped half a century from the afternoon's 100-degree heat in the badlands. Harry shivered. The night had brought the long arc of the universe, iced and impenetrable under a risen moon. The black vault of space loomed over the earth like a dark, descending fright. Five thousand years earlier that sky had awed a band of nomadic pastoralists in the Near East into inventing the word "firmament."

CHAPTER 11

I T HAD BEEN seventeen years since Harry had last slept on the ground. It had gotten harder. The wind kept fluting arpeggios through the holes in the tent poles. Field mice turned the walls of the tent into ski slopes, climbing up one side and schussing down the other. Diana had buzzed him badly, burrowing into his hindbrain like a wanton mole. He couldn't sleep. Being back in the Wind River Basin had unraveled the neat loops of history. He'd deliberately abandoned the art of digging up the past for some bits of petrified truth. Nicole's murder had triggered it. The war had settled it.

He needed space and a smoke. His Drum was in the Chevy. Maybe Diana had left the pack of Pall Malls in the mess tent. He put on his jeans, jean jacket and sandals and stepped out into the cold moonlit wind. He noticed a sudden glow in the shadows by the old stone foundation. It was Bruckmann, puffing hard, his cigarette pulsing red with the rhythm of a police light. Harry hadn't seen anyone smoke so intensely. Bruckmann himself seemed to be burning, the cigarette a chimney for his own internal combustion.

"What did Diana tell you?" Bruckmann coughed.

"Everything. Nothing."

Bruckmann's laugh was harsh. "They fought constantly. She and Marchand."

"What about?"

"Everything. Nothing." He bent over, nipped off a bit of sage, and singed it with the end of the cigarette. "I've seen her get mad enough to push him off a cliff. Don't let the small size fool you. She's tough enough to do it. Mean enough, too."

"Is that what happened?"

Bruckmann laughed again. "I guess you better find a body before you start to look for a killer."

"You're sharp. That's the first thing they teach us in detective school." Harry didn't bother hiding the sarcasm. "So where's the body?"

Bruckmann shrugged. "There's a million places to hide a body out here. You'd die trying to find it."

"Where would you start? If you were me."

Bruckmann snorted in amusement, smoke spurting out of his nostrils. "I wouldn't be you, detective."

"No," Harry agreed, "you wouldn't."

Bruckmann resumed his smoking. Harry walked back to his tent, his urge for a cigarette stubbed out.

CHAPTER 12

HARRY WOKE INSIDE a wet furnace. The early morning sun burned yellow and hot through the east wall of his tent. With the windows zipped up, the Springbar was a canvas hothouse. His bed roll was drenched in sweat. He looked at his watch: 7:30, Friday, August 5. Noise filtered back from the trucks. They were getting ready to leave. Sleeping uphill on half-buried rocks had made his body feel pummeled, as if an acupuncturist had stuck fat needles in the wrong spots.

At the mess tent, breakfast was done. Simeon was brushing his teeth, alternately spitting into the prairie grass and gargling water from a paper cup. Bruckmann and Burke were loading ice chests and water coolers into the Carnegie Jeep for the overnight trip to Casper after the quarry work. Diana, obviously impatient, brushed past Harry, got into Marchand's green Chevy, tossed him his packet of Drum tobacco and gunned the motor.

"Sorry. Can't wait." She glared at him from under her 200-gallon hat. He'd failed the morning wake-up test. "You can catch a ride with Meredith. She's in the crapper."

Harry gave her a pained smile. He poured a mug of leftover coffee from the pot on the Coleman stove, dragged a canvas chair to the clearing, sat down toward the west, lit up a Drum and let his mind run out to the faint snow-capped ridge of the Wind River Range. He watched the Carnegie caravan disappear in the dust down the dirt track. The roar of the two engines lingered in the morning stillness. In the distance, miniature tractor-trailers floated in the haze along US 20-24 between Casper and Shoshoni. Marchand could have hiked to the highway that night for his ride to a new lover or a new life.

"Good morning, detective." Meredith Shue came up behind him. "Quite the vista. You thinking Peter is still in the territory?"

Harry yawned and gulped some coffee. She was back in her safari outfit. Her hair was an accessory, advertising a windblown wildness.

"It's too early for thinking. Right now I'm still guessing— and not educated ones at that."

"So, you haven't made much progress." It was almost a rebuke.

"Progress? Sure I've made progress," Harry quipped. "The bunch of them are as relaxed as a land mine. Something's eating Jacobs if he doesn't eat it first. He needs to trade in his bladder for a larger model. Bruckmann must be a beta tester for R. J. Reynolds. Simeon is headed for a pickled liver. Diana has inherited a field crew she doesn't want. And Calvert is living the warning that doubt is the brother-devil of despair. Someone I can't remember said that in English 101."

"Yeah, she's pissed that Peter's probably with someone else. From what I hear, she's not the first. You know that Diana preceded her."

Harry nodded. "Yesterday at the quarry you intimated that Peter was a burnt-out case. That he'd likely fled his life and career. Anything specific make him run?"

Meredith pulled an orange from her pocket and peeled it, spraying juice in her lap. "His students, for one. Jacobs irritated him. His religious carrying-on. Peter didn't hide his annoyance at having him in camp."

"How?"

"Any number of ways. Usually in the evening, after he'd had too much to drink. He made wisecracks. About the Bible. About primitive superstitions. He'd goad David—how could he believe in a virgin birth but not evolution? Or the Flood and not the genetic code? The night Peter disappeared he got drunk. He mocked David. Said he was worshipping the myths of a bunch of shepherds who fucked their sheep at night. I'm quoting. It got old."

"How did Jacobs take it?"

"Pretty well. Jacobs may look like a wimp, but he's not. He doesn't shy away from moralistic needling, usually about sex, and usually directed at Lynn. He's part of the Grove City crowd north of Pittsburgh. Aggressive. Religiously militant. I wrote a piece about them last year."

Harry remembered them protesting outside the museum against the evolution exhibits. They had thick skins impregnated with martyrdom's trifecta—piety, dogma and divine conceit. They were sure God was theirs.

Harry eyed Shue's half-eaten orange and was suddenly famished. Since leaving Pittsburgh, all he'd had was a dry, USAir turkey sandwich, a few pretzels on Frontier's bucking bronco, a bit of salad, and a half-roasted potato. He went to the mess tent and returned with a box of corn flakes.

"Any other problems?" he asked Meredith.

"I'm not sure. Bored with Lynn, maybe, ready to move on. Maybe torn about Diana. Something happened between him and Bruckmann before he took off. I think Diana knows but isn't saying. Anyway, Peter practically stopped speaking to him. Made it all business. Otherwise, they've avoided each other—as much as you can out here." She motioned to the mess tent. "Most evenings, Gunther left right after dinner. Same with Burke."

"Know why?"

"No, but here's a guess. It seems Burke is gay."

Harry shrugged. "So? Surely Marchand doesn't care. That closet is pretty much open. Certainly in academia."

"Except that he began avoiding Morris. Like he did his students—Jacobs, Bruckmann, and Lynn."

Shue popped the rest of the orange into her mouth. "Actually, Simeon might have troubled Peter the most. There's this nasty undercurrent between them."

"Professional jealousy?" Harry suggested.

"Maybe, but I think it goes deeper. Peter was one of Simeon's first doctoral students at Princeton. But he quit abruptly, transferred to Michigan for his degree, then went to the Carnegie. A year later, Simeon left Princeton for Cornell. Also abruptly. Maybe a tenure issue, but I think it was something more personal. At Cornell, he became a distinguished professor of geology and paleontology. Out here, Simeon second-guesses Peter's every action in the quarry. And disagrees with his theories."

"What theories?"

"That dinosaurs were hot-blooded. Peter says that their bony joints and growth rings are all wrong. He called *Jurassic Park* bullshit propaganda. Simeon was one of the consultants."

"That all?" Harry asked.

"No. Peter has a crazy idea—at least Simeon thinks so. It's about the Earth being so warm during the Mesozoic, you know, the Age of Reptiles." Harry let her think he couldn't recite the geologic eras and periods. "Peter maintains the whole planet was tilted differently during that time than it is today with respect to the sun. Simeon says he's nuts."

"Hey," Harry countered, "that's standard issue for academia.

It's an intellectual shooting gallery, a highbrow cartoon. Profs regularly ambush one another's theories. The violence is verbal. There are no casualties, no body count, just bruised egos."

"Yes, I know," Shue acknowledged, and hesitated. "But ... Simeon keeps hinting at something more sinister ... that this business about the tilt of the Earth is not original."

"Whoa!" Harry sat up. "Plagiarism? Is that what he's talking about?"

Shue shrugged. "I don't know. Maybe. Simeon's never used that word."

A haze began to condense out of the bright morning sky, obliterating the Wind River Mountains and shrinking the horizon. They tossed their overnight bags into Shue's rented Blazer and bumped down the rocky track to the barbed wire fence. Harry did the gate routine and wondered how long it would have taken Marchand to hike out that night. About fifteen minutes down to the gate; a half-hour for the three-quarters of a mile to the Badwater Creek road. Someone could have been waiting for him at either spot.

"Where did you learn to do that—the gate thing?" Shue asked.

Harry hesitated, then relented. History, like memory, eventually forced its way to the surface. "Out here. Years ago."

"Really? Doing what?"

"Bonehunting with Marchand. Field work for a paleontology degree."

Meredith wrenched her body around and gaped at Harry. The sudden jerk of her hips brought her foot down hard on the accelerator. The truck hurtled down the track, shot across the Badwater Creek road and slammed into the far ditch alongside the hay meadow. Harry wasn't belted in. His head went sideways, whacked the door frame and headed toward the windshield. He threw his arms onto the dashboard in time to keep from ramming his skull through the safety glass. But he couldn't stop his head from hitting the glove compartment and bouncing back. The throb was instantaneous. So was the knob on his forehead.

Slowly, he reached across, turned the engine off, opened his door and slid out into two inches of mud in the ditch. Yesterday's storm had turned the hard clay into an amorphous ooze. He bent under the truck to see whether the skid plate was hung up. It wasn't, but the right front wheel was buried to the axle. He climbed around to the driver's side. Shue hadn't moved. Her hands were welded to the steering wheel, her face ashen.

"C'mon out, Meredith," Harry said, gently, unbuckling her seat belt. "Walk around a bit. Get your bearings." She leaned on him, clambered out of the cab, then climbed up the bank to the gravel road. Harry kicked the mud off his boots, got into the Blazer, started the engine, shoved the stick into 4-low, and began rocking the truck until the front tire became dislodged from its muddy sump. He jammed the gear into reverse, stomped on the gas, felt the tires bite and plowed the truck backwards up the side of the ditch onto the road.

"I'll drive." Harry gave Meredith a forced, reassuring grin as she climbed in. A bit of red had crept back into her pallor.

He drove slowly, windows down, losing his senses to the fresh sage growing alongside the hay meadows. The road tracked Badwater Creek, which originated quietly in the southern Bighorns and picked up Dry Fork, Clear Creek, and other small washes as it meandered west. Irrigation siphoned the creek to a trickle at Lost Cabin. It was a dry wash at Bonneville, twenty-five miles on, and a salt flat where it emptied into Boysen Reservoir, north of Shoshoni.

Geographic names were briefs of history, Harry thought. The water in Badwater Creek wasn't bad, just temperamental. After a hard, fast rain in the mountains, the creek would roar out of the foothills, storm over the banks, uproot the cottonwoods and drown the outlying scrub land and hay meadows. Shoshone Indians christened the creek in the early 1800s after one of its sudden tempers engulfed the floodplain and swept away their encampment. The Badwater flood of 1923 dislodged a train and washed out twenty miles of track near Bonneville.

Shue turned to look at Harry. Her face was now more chagrined than shocked.

"Harry—" She started to reach for the swelling on his forehead, thought better of it, and grasped his arm instead. "How's your head? You okay?"

"Yeah, fine." He gingerly touched the lump. "I've had worse headaches. Ever sit through a long organ concert?"

She managed a laugh. "That was a bombshell . . . you and Marchand. When . . . when was that?"

"Might as well have been in the Pleistocene," Harry said. "An apt date for an extinct life. Before you became a reporter for the *Post-Gazette*."

"No one told me! And I'm kicking myself for not turning it up. Fucking blew that one."

It was the first time he'd heard Meredith swear. "It's not important."

"Maybe so. We're alike, Harry . . . journalists . . . paleontologists . . . detectives. We dig up what history tries to bury. What happened?"

"A history I've managed to bury. Check the *Post-Gazette*. Back issues. The story's there."

It had been front page news for weeks—Nicole raped, tortured, murdered and dismembered. Then there was the trial. The *Post-Gazette* had mentioned Harry as her friend.

Shue didn't press it. She took out her notebook and scribbled something.

Harry gunned the motor as they climbed out of the Badwater valley through Cedar Gap. The hundred feet of altitude produced ecological magic. Brilliant green patches of stunted cedars rose incongruously out of the dry, rocky scrub.

At the junction with the Lost Cabin–Arminto road, Harry turned west toward the badlands. If Marchand had hitched or arranged a ride that night, Harry wondered whether he'd turned east and headed for Arminto and Casper, or west to Lost Cabin, and Shoshoni. By the time they reached the dirt track to the quarries, Harry wasn't any closer to an answer. But he'd counted fourteen antelope along the side of road.

CHAPTER 13

THE ROCKY GRAY bluff that overlooked the badlands was high enough to catch the wind. Dust had begun to gather to the west and blow across the sage flats. Gusts bent the grease bushes and chased a few pebbles over the edge of the cliff. Across the ravine, the buttes rose in stacked, eroded swaths of gray. Higher up, bands of hard mudstone, dyed a deep, bleak red, looked as if the earth had cut itself and bled.

This was the naked edge of the Earth, Harry thought; canyons, stark and rubble-strewn, seemingly clawed from the ground by a gigantic steam shovel. Weathering was ceaseless, the land trying to stay in equilibrium with the elements—and failing. It was like the geology of a love affair, Harry felt, the silent abrasion of its intimate contours to a flat, monochromatic terrain. He'd seen too many in this business.

"So you know this place, detective," Meredith remarked.

Harry climbed out of the truck, leaned against the door and rolled a cigarette in the wind. This raw, desolate terrain overwhelmed him. He wanted to grasp the whole of it at once, all of its immense, savage, chaotic quiet. He knew he couldn't. The badlands were primeval and had always been so. It was the only aesthetic geology was good at, a beauty so terrible it hurt the heart.

"Yeah, I know this place." Across the gully, the quarry was a superficial nick in the hillside, a blemish in the bluish-gray skin of the badlands. "It's useless to ranchers. No water. No grass. But it's good for bonehunters. And geologic irony."

"What do you mean?"

"There was a carcass that got buried in the late Cretaceous mud of Montana. A mammal, about the size of a shrew. It's jaw was found and named *Purgatorius* by a paleontologist with a medieval sense of humor. It might be the first primate, as far as we know. The irony is that it's the first evolutionary inkling of an eventual descendant, us—*Homo sapiens*—who return sixty-six million years later to prospect the badlands for the remains of our forebears."

No one greeted them at the quarry. Lynn, in bare feet, was brushing dirt from a set of ribs. She'd traded in the bikini for a white T-shirt and painter's pants. Burke and Bruckmann, stripped to their shorts, were swinging picks at the rock layer overlying the skeletons. Behind them, Jacobs pounded chisels into the cracks to wedge the splintered blocks free. Each ping of the chisel rang out through the badlands as if tolling a fall from geologic grace. Slowly, methodically, they worked along a ten-foot front, exposing the underlying bone bed that ran into the hillside. Diana stood watch, guarding that they didn't cut too deeply and disturb the bone layer.

She gasped when she saw his face. "What the hell happened?" She reached out to touch the knob on his forehead, then quickly pulled back.

"Meredith. First encounter with four-wheel drive. And touchy brakes."

Shue blushed and didn't elaborate.

Diana glanced at Meredith and shook her head. "I guess they don't teach that in journalism school." She pointed to the gully below the quarry. "Here's the twenty-five cent tour. We were prospecting down there. There was a lot of bony scrap at the base of the hill. Turned out to be dribbling down from a femur eroding up here. The pelvis and the vertebral column went into the hill. When we took off some overburden, presto—more skeletons. Now—"

"Any guess on how many individuals?" Harry interrupted.

She glared at him. "I was getting to that. Around forty. Both juveniles and adults. Some represented by only a few elements. Four species, maybe five. You want to know which ones?"

Harry doubted he could remember his dinosaur taxonomy. He played along. "Sure."

"Okay. There's the hypsilophodont, *Thescelosaurus*; the duck-billed *Anatosaurus*; the dome-headed *Pachycephalosaurus*; and a sauropod that looks like *Nemegtosaurus*, which is a first for North America. If it is, it migrated across the Bering Land Bridge in the late Cretaceous from Mongolia."

Meredith checked her notebook, holding the pages down in the wind. "What about the egg nests? Peter pointed them out to me."

"Right." Diana motioned toward the center of the quarry. "Over there, by Lynn. About fourteen nests. Or at least clumps of eggs. Who knows which nest goes with which dinosaur. Or how we're going to match juveniles to adults to eggs to species. Two small skeletons over there are preserved over nests. Maybe they were brooding females. Or males. Maybe not. Could just be haphazard . . . you know . . . one of them died and fell on an abandoned nest. But this might have been a communal nesting ground for different species. Cooperation to protect the eggs and hatchlings against predators."

"But," Meredith ventured, "Peter told me living reptiles don't do that. Or birds."

"Did he now?" Diana remarked acidly. "Well, he's right. It's a pretty radical hypothesis. It would be a first for dinosaurs or any other egg-layer."

"The bone bed seems pretty extensive," Harry said. "You're going to be out here a few more years."

"Right. The skeletons continue into the hill. We started quarrying three years ago. We'll need about five more field seasons to get everything out. The overburden is a pain. It's about two feet thick at the quarry face and gets thicker into the hillside. Next year we're going to dynamite off the top of the hill to get down to the bones before everything erodes to shit. If there's evidence for dinosaur brooding or species cooperation, it'll be here."

Diana took her hat off and mopped her brow. "Anyway, we have bodies piled on bodies. Most of the bones are so thick and intermingled that we have to plaster them out in blocks. Seems like it was a catastrophic event. Sudden death by volcano. The Cretaceous version of Pompeii."

Harry walked around the quarry gridlines and knelt down. The dinosaur skeletons were welded into a macabre death scene. Their long necks had wrenched back over their bodies as the muscles dried and stiffened. Their last moments of life had been spent in braying panic, a frenzied stampede toward the river through the volcanic ash and poison gas. Finally, they collapsed in a heaving mass on the floodplain. Killer and undertaker that piece of nature was, Harry thought. Eighty million years later, the floodplain was a bone orchard. Paleontology was the study of death on Earth.

"Where are the blocks you've plastered out?" Harry looked around for the telltale pile of bones encased in burlap and white plaster.

"Over there." Diana motioned to the gully below the end of the butte. At the base of the slope, along the raised bank of a broad sand wash, ten or so white plaster jackets lay gleaming in the sun like enormous bleached sarcophagi, misshapen, mirroring the outline of the bones and the fault lines in the quarry rock. Harry recognized the sauropod limb bone they had plastered out yesterday afternoon. It was marked "3-34" in large black numerals.

"Each jacket," Diana continued, "gets numbered and entered in the field catalog—the grid coordinates, the bones inside, the skeletons we think they belong to. Single bones are simple—"

"So, number 3-34 down there," Harry interrupted, "is—"

"Bone 34 from skeleton number 3. It's the large sauropod." Diana pointed to a large, wood raft-like structure attached to a long rope at the far side of the quarry. "We lash the jackets to that sled and lower them down the slope."

The sled had worn a smooth run from the edge of the quarry down the side of the hill to the pile of plaster jackets. Harry remembered seeing a similar wood sled in an old, silent, black-and-white film at the museum. In 1909, Carnegie's bonehunters discovered a spectacular cache of dinosaurs halfway up a steep rock exposure in northeastern Utah, near Vernal. The film captured them inching the plaster-jacketed bones of *Apatosaurus* and *Camarasaurus* on the sled down the cliff face. The whole cliff in Utah is now jacketed in glass and concrete as Dinosaur National Monument.

Harry pointed to tire tracks that snaked up the sand wash and led out of the badlands. "Is that how you'll haul the blocks out of here?"

"Yeah. McCarthy will bring in a flatbed truck and a front-end loader. Otherwise, we stay out of that creek bed. Too chancy. Sudden gully washers. It's the main drainage for these badlands. So we come in from the escarpment each day. Sometimes one of Karlsen's calves wanders into the wash. We tell McCarthy and he drives down here to fetch it."

Harry circled over to Simeon, who was straddling a set of

massive vertebrae at the far end of the quarry. He looked like a bloated manatee still dressed for the Arctic—a navy gray gabardine shirt, khaki pants, wool socks and high-top Red Wing boots. Old school, Diana had said. At least he'd traded in the pith helmet for an authentic-looking Aussie bush hat, likely made in China.

Harry rolled a cigarette and watched Simeon carefully brush away the dirt, then coat the bones with a penetrating preservative.

"Getting anywhere, Przewalski?" Simeon growled.

"It's early. Like excavating this bone bed. I'm quarrying the edges of the case."

"Nicely put. One edge you might consider is that the esteemed Dr. Marchand skedaddled because the scientific heat was getting too hot for his kitchen, if you'll forgive the mixed metaphor."

"What do you mean?"

"His scientific empire was beginning to crumble under the weight of counter evidence. So he ran. It's the power of empiricism, the truth will out, and other such homilies. Very simply, the scientific community was discovering that his retrograde theories were not supportable." Under his breath, he added, "nor original."

Harry cupped his hand around a match and lit his cigarette. "Plagiarism, professor? Is that what you're intimating?"

"Careful, Przewalski!" Simeon hissed, anxiously checking to see if anyone was within earshot. "That's heresy to an academic. Like questioning the celibacy of the Pope." He stopped brushing and squinted at Harry.

"Peter, I imagine, was afraid to face his peers in the adjudicated arena of refereed journals or professional meetings. So he fled, his theories tucked safely between his legs. That's where most academics carry their theories, Przewalski, between their legs. Their erotica is fed by mental acrobatics, not sexual ones. Underneath the philandering, most academics actually suffer from asexual angst, so they overcompensate. Marchand could be the archetype of the syndrome. I learned better long ago."

"No doubt," Harry noted dryly. Simeon looked more asexual than a *Paramecium*. "Where do you think our archetype ran off to? More philandering?"

"A reasonable hypothesis, but unlikely. Jacobs over there keeps blubbering about Marchand and the Karlsen woman having a dalliance. But I can't see her husband putting up with that for very long. After all, this is Wyoming. Males here are afflicted with a psychological neoteny—they retain their juvenile cowboy machismo well into adulthood. Maybe it's because they have to overcome the ignominy of being paid $300 a month to out-think a cow. In any case, ego and rifles are a lethal mixture here, because both are hair-trigger." Simeon took a swig of water from his canteen and licked his lips.

The badlands were losing their shadows to high noon. Harry watched a lizard fishtail across the loose rubble and disappear into a crevice in the weathered rocky slope.

"Magnificent, aren't they?" Simeon mused, staring out at the jagged cliffs and desolate chasms. "Przewalski, few realize that the badlands are the ultimate dialectic between good and evil. Ever since humans first encountered them, the badlands have evoked primordial Creation. French explorers shunned them as *mauvais terres*—literally, 'bad lands'—because they lacked water, shade and signs of life. Victorian England thought they were the chaotic remnants of the devil's evil, a sinful Earth heaved up by the cleansing Flood. Then, America reversed divine aesthetics. The austere sweep of the badlands—a Grand Canyon—manifested the Creator's power and majesty."

Simeon lifted his bush hat to wipe his pate, took another

guzzle of water from his canteen and splashed some on his face. He waited patiently for Harry to finish rolling another Drum before continuing.

"But geology ultimately deciphered Creation. The badlands are a simple, endless war of attrition between earth and sun and wind and water. The Greeks tried to tame this war with a taxonomy of the gods, one for each element: Aeolus for wind, Helios for sun, Poseidon for water, Gaia for earth. Science wasn't as romantic or poetic. It countered with something much more prosaic—the lexicon of erosional geology."

Simeon got up and brushed off his pants. At the other end of the quarry, Lynn had started putting away the rock hammers and chisels. Bruckmann and Burke spread tarpaulins over the exposed bones and weighed them down with sandstone boulders. Harry went around the butte to relieve himself, only to startle Jacobs, who quickly pulled up his zipper, adjusted his shorts, and began clambering across the ridges to the trucks. By the time Harry got to Meredith's Blazer, the others had raised a dust trail to the main road.

CHAPTER 14

RIDAY AFTERNOON, HARRY rented a red two-door Bronco at the Casper airport. The scenery into town hadn't evolved much since he'd been here with Marchand: Tokyo Massage, Amoco refinery, the *Casper Star-Tribune* building, oil-field drill rigs, used truck lots, an army-navy store, a taxidermy shop, an American Chop-Suey restaurant. The oil and gas boom in the late 1970s and 1980s had brought a few glass and prefab cement buildings to downtown Casper, a generic mall to its eastern outskirts, and acres of cloned housing south of the Platte River.

The Bronco was a blast furnace. It had baked all morning on the Avis lot. The air conditioner gave up after half a mile. Harry rolled the windows down. By the time he parked downtown, dust and sweat had hardened into a layer of cement on his upper lip. The revolving sign over the Wyoming National Bank building flashed 2:32 and 107 degrees. The streets were empty. A few shoppers gasped quickly between the air-conditioned stores, asthmatics in search of respirators.

Harry had two pictures of Peter Marchand—a snapshot from Lynn and a PR photo from the Carnegie Museum. The taxidermy shop was closed. In the window, bleached white skulls gaped at the street; bears, wolves, beavers, badgers, more frightening in death than in life.

Harry went into Tub 'O Suds, a small laundromat next door. The matron, a woman in old jeans, was filling the dispenser with boxes of soap. Her skin had acquired the color and texture of detergent. Lamarckian inheritance, Harry thought. He showed her the picture. She barely glanced at it.

"I ain't never seen him," she said flatly. There was no discussing it with her.

A young woman with long, straight hair watched him while she piled clothes into a machine. A little boy clung to one of her legs, sucking a lollipop, sticky green juice running down his chin. A baby slept in a stroller. She turned her back and raised her shoulder, warding him off like an apparition.

Harry checked the seedy, neon monotony of bars on Main Street. No one had seen Marchand. He drove a few blocks east, past a JCPenney, two banks, a movie theater and a western-wear shop. He parked in front of Red's Bar. It had a fake saloon front with swinging doors and smelled as if the floor had been varnished with stale beer. His eyes adjusted to a dim, dust-scattered light. At the bar, he ordered a red beer without the beer. The bartender looked like a hard drinker. His nose was large enough to store a small dog.

Harry slid the snapshots of Marchand across the bar. "Know this guy?"

The bartender picked up the pictures, flipped them over, studied the underside, and flipped them again, as if this was his first encounter with photography. "Could be, not sure."

"When was the last time you might have seen him?"

"Dunno. Last week sometime."

"What was he doing?"

"Shit. Struttin' around, same as usual. Hey, Dwayne," the bartender yelled. "Weren't you here last week when this feller come in with the snakeskin boots?"

A tub of a man pushed his chair back from a table in the corner. He carried a ledger over to the bar, wheezing like a tractor as he made his way across the room.

"Dwayne Slocum. Accountant."

The bartender showed him the pictures. "Wasn't this guy in here last week? Had them new boots? You couldn't miss them boots."

"I do believe he was," Slocum said, holding one of the pictures toward the light and squinting at it. "He came in with Earl Blodgett's son."

"Who is Earl Blodgett?" Harry asked.

"He's a rancher over near Kaycee. Good man, but that son of his never will amount to much," Slocum volunteered. "Dropped out of school and lost a bunch of his dad's money in some real estate deal. Boy's afraid of hard work."

Harry bought him a beer and whiskey. "What about the guy in the pictures? Know anything about him?"

Slocum downed half the beer and sucked his lower lip. "Who's askin'?"

"Private detective." Harry slipped him a card. "A relative of his died. Left him some money. Just trying to find him."

"It might be him," Slocum finally offered. "Hard to say. He was wearin' a hat."

Two men sauntered over from the end of the bar, one short and skinny in overalls, the other tall and skinny in a blue-checked western shirt with imitation pearl snaps, two pockets, and a big grease stain.

"Detective here is lookin' for this guy," Slocum stated.

Tall and skinny wiped his hands on his jeans and picked up the photos. He had oil splotches on his work boots. Auto mechanic, Harry guessed.

"Not sure. Mebbe. Might be him that came into the shop first part of the week. Never took his hat off. Had an old Camaro. Needed a new transmission. Didn't ask what'll it cost, just told me to fix it, and paid cash."

"Any idea where he is?" Harry asked.

"Gone to Cody, I guess."

"Cody?"

"Yeah, that's where he said he was headed."

"Did he have anyone with him?"

"Yeah, some blond gal with him, nice lookin'...and stacked." He winked.

"Did you get his name? On the work ticket."

"Uh, uh."

"Was the Camaro his car or hers?"

"Dunno. I fixed it. He paid cash."

"Wyoming tag?"

"Yup. Had some matches in the front seat from Jack's Antelope Lodge, if that's any help. Kind'a thought he'd been stayin' there with the blond." He sounded envious.

Harry threw a twenty on the bar for the drinks.

At the Antelope Lodge, Jack said that the guys at the bar were blinder than a dead steer. You'd need a lot of whiskey behind the eyes to make the guy with the snakeskin boots and the blond into Marchand. He'd registered as Slim Peterson, stayed in Room 14 for a week, drove a Camaro, paid in cash, and was headed to the rodeos in Cody. Jack thought he was a bronco rider on the circuit. He didn't know the blond.

CHAPTER 15

I F MARCHAND WAS on a binge with a woman, it was somewhere else. At ten-thirty, Harry quit peddling Marchand's picture at motels and watering holes. He was tired of the country and western music, songs mewling on about lost loves, women and pickup trucks. Like Marchand's life. They'd left a dry axle turning in his head.

He found Diana and Simeon at the steakhouse next to the Day's Inn. She was in shadow, drinking and smoking. He could see the alcohol wasn't working. Knots pulsed her forehead. Simeon was downing Coors, barricaded behind a fort of empty bottles. Either his book, *The Dinosaur Hunt*, was infuriating him or his face had become pickled into a permanent scowl. Harry ordered a burger and the only single-malt Scotch they had, Ebradour. It was new to Harry. Maybe to all of Scotland.

"Shit down, Shoveliski." Simeon was half sauced. "Shurprise, shurprise. Diana here tells me you once studied with Peter. Dissertation on fossil primates from the basin. Should have stayed the course. Still could, you know . . . finish your degree . . . never too late." He tried to wink, but his eyelid was too weighted with Coors and merely flapped shut.

Harry was in no mood for drunken nostalgia. "Too late for me. Some cynic said that history is made up of events that probably didn't happen or don't matter. Both hold for paleontology. That's what makes it so attractive."

Simeon tried to lift his hand in protest. "Not sho . . . so, detective." He downed the last Coors and added the bottle to the fort. "No matter. Found our wandering Peter yet?"

"No."

"Found anything at all?" It was an accusation, but Simeon didn't wait for the defense. He wobbled out of his chair, crammed a handful of peanuts into his mouth, sucked the salt off his fingers, and left.

Harry's first sip of Scotch burned his throat. He rolled a Drum and let his head begin to jettison the blind alleys of the day.

"Your past here," Diana said, a tenderness in her voice he hadn't heard before. "It eats at you . . . what you gave up." She put her hand on his arm, then quickly withdrew it.

Harry shook his head. "Remember Cartmill's dictum-- becoming a scientist to get truth is like becoming an archbishop to get girls. Marchand became an archbishop. I hope he hasn't lost his frock."

"He came through town, then?" She tried hard to show she was not afraid of the answer.

"Not likely. Let it go." The tour of bars had made him testy.

"Harry! If you're trying to protect my feelings because he was here with a woman, don't! I have no feelings left to protect. So tell me."

Diana slid her chair out of the shadows over to his and leaned close. Red lips. Licorice-black hair, parted on the side like a man's. He watched her mouth move. If he had information, she could seduce it out of him.

"There's nothing to tell. You know about Roberta Karlsen. According to the kid you had pick me up at the airport, she and Marchand didn't try to hide their romance. The heavy dancing session at the Sheepherders Fair. Did she run off with him to do more dancing in private?"

Diana laughed. "Not a chance. George Karlsen is a big rancher in this state. He moves in pretty high circles in the Republican Party. Rumors started last year that he was readying a run for the governor's office. Rumor also had it that he was caught with a bunch of girls at a Republican Party shindig in Jackson Hole. In any case, he's gone a lot to political functions. I'm sure Roberta is aware of the rumors. The Sheepherders Fair was a chance to get even in public. But it was innocent enough."

"Marchand could have visited her. The evenings he left camp without Lynn."

"Roberta's not that stupid. It's almost impossible to carry on affairs out here without being noticed. The Karlsen ranch has too many employees for Peter just to drive up in the evening, stroll into the house, and pretend that Mrs. Karlsen has developed a sudden interest in dinosaur paleontology. Hell, you can't drive to the liquor store in town without everyone learning whether you bought Heaven Hill or Jim Beam. The Karlsens have the old Okie mansion in Lost Cabin. Roberta sometimes stays there, but the traffic is too visible. And forget a rendezvous in any motel around here. She's too well known."

"They could have met in the badlands."

"And what?" Diana scoffed. "Humped in the front of a pickup? Made out in the bed of a Chevy littered with pop cans and rocks? I don't think that would be Roberta's style."

"Maybe. Lust conquers style," Harry quipped, unsparingly. "She wouldn't be the first."

Diana glowered at Harry, angry at the implication. "Roberta wouldn't throw her life away—the ranch, the power, the prospect of being the first lady of Wyoming—over a fling with Peter. He's not worth it. Maybe five or ten years ago, but not now. I know it. She knows it."

"Yeah, well, lust also undresses reason. Decisions made below the waist. It's why Marchand traded you in for a different model. He's a fool." Harry slumped back. The words had spurted out, unwittingly, before he could staunch them. "Sorry, that was more verdict than desire."

Diana blushed, turned away, then turned back, her face recovered.

Harry tossed back more Scotch. "Bruckmann says you and Marchand argued all the time."

Diana lit a Pall Mall and waved her hand, agitated. "Sure, we argued. His nightly drinking bouts. His midnight sojourns. His personal life. He was getting distracted. We started leaving camp later and later every morning. If he went off by himself in the evening, Lynn would sulk and be pretty useless at the quarry. She'd get into a jealous snit if a woman at the supermarket in Casper looked at him sideways. Their spats about Roberta ruined the camaraderie, such as it was. He kept riding David about his creationism. He overreacted to anything Edwin raised about the excavation. He was starting to make lousy decisions. So, of course we argued."

Harry chewed his burger and downed the Scotch. "Bruckmann intimated that your arguments involved more than work."

"Yeah, he would, the sneaky bastard. Anyway, Bruckmann's on a short string hims—" She caught herself, stubbed out her cigarette and signaled to the bar for another bourbon.

Stalling, Harry thought. "What's the string?"

"Nothing. It's professional. Nothing to do with Peter's leaving. Nothing to interest you."

"Try me."

"Sorry, Harry, it's private."

He shook his head. "Not good enough. Once Marchand went missing, he lost all privacy. Privacy is okay. Except when it's a cover for lousy behavior. Religion got this early on. With sin, confession trumped privacy."

"Damn you, Harry," she spewed, "I don't need a fucking lecture about sin."

"No, you don't. But you need to know that some people I'm hired to find turn up dead." Harry let that take root. "Tell me about Bruckmann."

Diana gaped at him. "You're . . . you're . . . you're not serious," she stammered. "Oh my god . . . I never thought—" She gulped some bourbon, her hand white-knuckled around the glass. She wiped her mouth on her sleeve, then seemed surprised at the sudden brownish streak down her arm.

"Tell me about Bruckmann," Harry repeated.

"Fine! About two weeks after we got here, Peter told me that he suspected Bruckmann of selling Carnegie fossils to dealers. Maybe in Europe, maybe to the Middle Eastern market in Yemen. The foss—"

"What led him to suspect Bruckmann?" Harry interrupted.

"Damn it, shut up!" she snapped, glaring at him. "I don't need prodding. You rattled me and I don't like it. It doesn't happen often."

She lit a cigarette, inhaled deeply, and blew out a fury of smoke.

"Peter thinks Bruckmann might be selling canine teeth from saber-toothed cats, or chunks of mammoth and mastodon tusks—ivory. Probably collected around the turn of the century. We're not sure. You know this shit is prized in Asia and the Middle East. Dagger handles. Grinding up the ivory for aphrodisiacs. Ignorant bastards think it'll make their little peckers stand up longer."

She downed the rest of her bourbon and slid the glass across the table. "We're talking tens of thousands of dollars on the black market. We found out by chance this spring. We were doing an inventory of the fossil collection in the Big Bone Room for a grant proposal. About fifty items turned up missing out of two hundred and fifty thousand. Otherwise we wouldn't have known. Hell, some of those cabinets haven't been opened in years."

She paused. "Christ, I'm dry; I need some water. Want some?" Harry nodded. She got up, strode purposefully to the bar, and came back with a pitcher of ice water and two glasses.

"At first, we thought the specimens might have been misplaced. Or on long-term loan. Peter and I decided to keep it quiet till we checked. We didn't even tell Burke. Collection managers fret over their collections like brood hens. He would have started turning the place upside down. Word would have gotten out."

Diana lit two Pall Malls and gave one to Harry.

"We checked the loan records, the old accession records, and all the basement storage rooms. Zilch. Then Peter happened to stop in at a grad student party at Bruckmann's apartment. He noticed an envelope on a bureau from a well-known French broker who sells to Japanese and Middle Eastern dealers. That doesn't make Bruckmann guilty. I get letters all the time asking to buy or sell fossils. But the letters come to me at the museum, not my house. Peter has excellent connections with paleontologists in France, at the Muséum National d'Histoire Naturelle in Paris. Before we left for the field, he wrote one of them in confidence to check into it."

She chewed on a piece of ice. "That's the Bruckmann story. I know what you're going to ask—did Peter get an answer from the Paris museum? I don't know. If he did, he didn't say. I didn't see any letters from France. Peter usually picks up our mail at Waltman, the closest post office. Anyway, it was the first time he shared his suspicions about Bruckmann. He said he wouldn't confront him until he had indisputable evidence.

Gunther is his favorite student—aside from Lynn, of course. And he didn't want to believe the worst. But he was worried enough to talk to me about it. He didn't bring it up again before he walked out."

"What about Bruckmann's lifestyle in Pittsburgh? Any changes in the past year or so? New car? Other extravagances?"

Diana shook her head. "No. He wears the same clothes, drives the same car—an old VW Beetle."

"Where does Peter keep his mail? In his tent?"

"Yes. Lynn went through it the morning he was gone. She says she didn't find anything."

"Any chance Lynn found the letter incriminating Bruckmann and is covering for him?"

Diana exploded in laughter. "Lynn and Gunther? They hate each other! They're in deep competition for Peter's affection. You're tired, detective. You're losing your edge."

Harry smiled at her, suddenly tempted to lean closer and breathe the scent of her hair. "Yeah, probably so." He pushed his chair back and stood up.

"Just put it on my room," she told the bartender, pointing at Harry's glass and half-eaten food.

"I can buy my own Scotch," he said without thinking.

"I'm not buying your Scotch," she snapped. "The museum is covering your expenses. This will save you the trouble of keeping a receipt."

"I don't bill drinks," he snapped back.

They walked from the chill of the bar into the thick heat of the night. Diana bit her lip in frustration. Harry fought the urge to hold her. He was close to violating the rules of the game. She could beguile him. She had last night and again tonight.

In the motel, the hallway reeked as if the air conditioner were spewing mold. An ice machine groaned on the second floor. They stopped in front of her room.

"I didn't mean to rattle you," Harry said, trying to recoup the evening. "Don't worry about Marchand. He'll show."

She put the key in the lock, turned and faced him like a prize fighter, legs apart, fists clenched.

"Of course you meant to rattle me. I want him back, but not in the way you think. If he's dead, he probably deserved it. But I don't think he is. We were lovers once. That's over. Now we're colleagues. It's cliché, but I might be the only friend he's got. That's the thing. I should know where he is."

She was close enough for him to smell the bourbon. He imagined tasting it on her red lips. The day had caught up to him, drowning his sense in the alcohol, in the ghosts of his time in this place.

When her door closed, so did another near the end of the hall. Harry caught the flash of blond hair and bronze skin. Calvert needed lessons in eavesdropping.

CHAPTER 16

SHERIFF BURT CRUMLEY looked like a burnt boot. Years of sun had dried and cracked the skin on his face. He sounded hoarse, like a burro with a bad cold. He was also unconcerned about Marchand.

"Hell, Przewalski, I cain't be bothered with a missing bonehunter. It ain't a police matter. I went up there when the lady called . . . what's her name . . . Miss Palantier. Looked around, talked to her and the bunch of 'em, didn't find anything suspicious worth sniffin' after. I checked out Shoshoni. Nothin'. I checked with the sheriffs in Casper, Riverton, Buffalo, Cody and Thermop for this tall, gray-haired dude who could have a woman in tow. Nothin' then and nothin' since. Man's an adult. He's allowed to take off. There ain't no crime in that. Hell, I might take off too if I had his way with women. Man could talk a cow out of her calf."

Harry had woken early Saturday morning in Casper, thinking the sheriff in Shoshoni was worth a shot. He'd grabbed a quick breakfast at the steakhouse, which had evolved into a pancake eatery overnight, and left a note for Diana at the motel. He drove west past the Casper airport and into the prairie along the southern uplift of the Bighorns. The foothills rose and fell in the long shadows of the morning light, the languid breathing of a reclining nude.

In the swales, the last of the summer's hay waved against the sky. Most of the meadows were already cut to the stubble. In the fields along the highway, the hay stood baled into huge loaves, rectangular blocks and cylindrical rolls. Harry wondered how the different geometries were adaptive, but gave up. The loaves of hay were the most aesthetic, rising from the plains to feed the multitude. By the time he reached Shoshoni, Harry had done the math. Along US 20-26, bales and rolls were running dead even. Loaves were a distant third. So much for hay aesthetics.

Crumley shifted his weight behind the desk and rubbed his face. He had been sheriff of Thermopolis for twenty-one years, then retired into this job in Shoshoni, fifty miles south along the Bighorn River.

"Just doing the leg work, Sheriff," Harry said patiently. "For the Carnegie Museum in Pittsburgh. They're worried."

"I know why you're here and I know where the museum is at," Crumley broke in. "The bonehunters been comin' out here for years. I see their Jeep with the dinosaur comin' through town to Riverton or back from the breaks. They stop at Yellowstone Drug for shakes. Mr. Marchand's usually got some young woman in tow. When he drives, it's over the limit. I let it go, because they're not likely to be liquored up on the way to the breaks or comin' back. Now he's gone and leaked out of the landscape. You're here to find out where he went and why before he embarrasses your eastern museum. Well, the odds ain't with you. He's been gone since July 22. Today is August 6. Your trail is two weeks and one day cold, and I've already been over it. Like I said, Mr. Marchand's an adult. Leave him be wherever he wants his peace and quiet. He doesn't want to be found."

"Maybe, maybe not," Harry persisted. "Marchand wasn't

spotted in Casper, Riverton or Thermopolis, but you're still not suspicious about his disappearance?"

"Listen, Przewalski," Crumley leaned over. "If I was suspicious about every fool tourist who decides he's had enough of these parts and vamooses, I'd be a damn poor sheriff. It don't mean nothin' that Mr. Marchand wasn't spotted. They probably drove right through town, gas tank full, no reason to stop."

"They? Do you know that he met someone that night?"

"No, I don't and it don't matter much. Unless he's an antelope, odds are he didn't jump over fences in the dark and hike twenty miles to the highway. Likely someone picked him up on the dirt road and took him out of these parts. Hell, there are people hitchin' rides on 20-26 every day. Most get picked up after awhile. It's like marriage. Someone always comes along. Just a matter of waitin' long enough."

Harry smiled. "Speaking of marriage, was his ride out of here Mrs. Karlsen?"

Crumley leaned forward and gave Harry a beady look. "Przewalski, you best be careful before you make these damn fool allegations. Roberta Karlsen is a respected citizen in this community. George Karlsen might be governor of this great state one of these years. Maybe even this year. People have been shot for saying less."

"But she too is missing." It was a cheap gambit, Harry thought.

Crumley sat back, put his feet up on the bare desk and folded his arms.

"Now how would you go about knowin' that?"

"People talk. Wait long enough, information comes along. I called the ranch this morning. Asked to see Mrs. Karlsen. She's on vacation, they told me. Look, Sheriff, you know these people. If she ran off with Marchand, I can go back to Pittsburgh, tell them not to worry, their star scientist is safely bedding the wife of the next governor of Wyoming, then collect my fee and pay the rent."

Crumley eyed him like the borehole of a 30-30.

"Afraid you haven't earned the rent yet. Roberta is on vacation with relatives in Salt Lake. George sent her there after the ruckus at the Sheepherders Fair. Not that anything's going on between her and Marchand. If there was, we'd know it. Lots of folks out here sleep around. Same as anywhere else. But not Roberta. She's in Salt Lake and Marchand ain't. I checked. You have my word on it."

Harry got up, walked over to a Mr. Coffee that was half full, grabbed a spare cup and helped himself. A picture on the wall behind the desk showed a younger Crumley in uniform, shaking hands with Lyndon Johnson. Harry couldn't make out the background or the date, but if it was Vietnam it must have been early on. A side wall featured a picture of the current governor of Wyoming. In the corner, an American flag hung above a tropical plant. The pot was inscribed: Costa Rica. The rest of the office was government issue: fake walnut paneling and a green metal desk and file cabinet, dented enough to date from the sixties. Crumley's wooden inbox was empty. His outbox had a form with his signature on it.

"Any other women in the area he might have left with?" Harry knew it was a throwaway.

"Nope," Crumley stated, also getting up and helping himself to coffee. His cup said "Wyoming Is for Lovers" and pictured a big red heart with two sheep in the act. "For all we know, he walked to the dirt road or the highway, got a lift to town, and took the first Greyhound bus west or east. Can't prove it though. I checked with the drivers and the station. No one saw him that night or the next morning. Also checked the airports. He didn't fly out of Casper or Riverton. So I filed a missing person's report. Can't do much more than that. Like I said, there's no evidence of any crime."

"Did you find anything in his tent? Notebook? Map?"

Crumley threw up his arms in exasperation. "Think I'd be sitting here on my backside jawing with you right now if he had left a goddamn map with a circle around the place he was headin' for? Or a long essay on the state of his head? His tent was pretty ragtag, but nothin' was missin'. At least according to Miss Calvert. I guess she spent enough time in there to know."

"What about his overnight bag or backpack?"

"Still there. Same with his clothes. Like he wanted to leave his whole life behind. Except for his wallet. He took that and a good chunk of change, accordin' to Miss Palantier. You stayin' out at the camp? Check on it yourself tonight. Surprised you haven't already." Crumley got up to swat a big horse fly that had landed on the governor of Wyoming.

"Did you learn anything talking to Diana and the others?"

"Enough to know that they're a sad bunch without Marchand around. And pretty wound up. That Jacobs looks like a fattening hog. His mother must have raised him on pork and proverbs. He's a Bible-thrower. He doesn't like Mr. Marchand's playing around. Or Miss Calvert's. He mumbled something about whoring and Mrs. Karlsen, which is probably where you got it from. That German guy, Bruckmann, he's still mad that the Krauts lost the war. They're all the same, that bunch. Squeeze 'em hard enough and out comes a little Adolf. Didn't get much out of him. Miss Calvert's just sore that Marchand left without her. She'll have fifty more Marchands before her pretty life is done. Didn't get much out of her either. That Cornell professor, Simeon, keeps flappin' his lips like a saloon door. He doesn't let you forget he gets paid lots of money at some eastern university to say big words about animals that aren't around anymore. I bet when he's with a woman he's as limp as neck-wrung rooster. He asked me if I was going to hire a Shoshone to track Mr. Marchand's footprints across the sage flats. He was either puttin' me on or he's dumber than a sack of horse shit. Told him that, too. The other guy, Burke, is pretty quiet. Not much to say, and didn't say much. Miss Palantier is pretty edgy now that she's runnin' the show."

Harry was impressed. Crumley was a quick study. He had gotten their names and temperaments down in one meeting. No notes.

Crumley took another swig of coffee. "We went over the whole business. He went out alone in his outfit around eleven-thirty that night, came back around three-thirty, then must have buggered out on foot before six-thirty that morning. My guess is he met someone, probably on the Badwater Creek road just below camp. Maybe he hired someone at a bar to meet him and drive him out so we couldn't trace his truck. He has lots of cash. Enough to hire someone to pick him up—hell, enough to be in Mexico. Now you know as much as I do."

"What about Marchand himself? You know him."

Crumley sat back and looked up at the governor of Wyoming, who now had insect guts on his earlobe. He rubbed his eyes and refocused.

"Not much to say. Man comes here every summer, does his work, and goes back home. Couple of years ago he lit out for a few days, then showed up. Happened again last year. Could've been a woman. He doesn't let the professor thing spray all over the place like that windmill from Cornell."

"But he didn't tell you if she was a local or not," Harry prompted.

"Or whether she had brown hair, blond hair, or antlers," Crumley quipped. "We didn't talk women. We had a few beers over politics. He's a bit of a liberal. He thinks the ranchers out here are on cowboy welfare because of the cheap grazing rights. Shit, to the government everything is welfare—universities are welfare for the professors, research grants are welfare for bonehunters, cheap grazing is welfare for the ranchers, defense is welfare for the weapons industry, milk prices are welfare for the dairy farmers, and the tax code is welfare for big oil. The whole damn government is welfare. Nothin' wrong with that. That's what government is supposed to do."

"What about suicide, if things were bad enough?"

"Peter?" Crumley looked perplexed, then shook his head. It was the first time he'd called him by his first name. "Not a chance. Man has too much sense. Sure, he's hornier than a two-peckered goat. But men who can't keep their peckers in their pants don't commit suicide. They tuck it in for the next time. I've seen lots of suicides, none of them Peter's type."

"What about murder? Any one of them could have killed him."

Crumley stared at him, ran his hands through his short, wiry, gray hair, closed his eyes, and opened them again.

"Sounds like we're playin' twenty questions here. What'dya got, Przewalski?"

"Nothing. Just surveying the possibilities. Most of them had reason enough to want him out of the way. Jacobs acting in the name of God. Simeon not wanting his scientific theories overturned. Calvert not wanting any other woman to have him. Diana finally tired of playing second scientific fiddle to him. Don't know about Burke—he's gay and Marchand certainly isn't. Bruckmann—well, you don't know this—Marchand thinks that Bruckmann's been hawking the museum's fossils to overseas buyers. Maybe Marchand confronted him. Maybe Bruckmann popped him to keep from being found out. Then there are the wives and girlfriends in the area. Marchand's probably bedded his share over the years. Could be one of the husbands finally came after him. Could be Karlsen himself. Or someone he hired. Like I said, just surveying the possibilities."

Crumley sat back, rubbed his boot-hide face again, and smiled at him. "Possibilities, my ass. Where'd you learn to think, Przewalski? Hell, I'm beginning to believe you can't track a wagon through a mud puddle. You keep playin' detective that way, you won't pay much rent. There ain't many murders in these parts. Those that happen are usually in a bar over a woman—right out in the open, a hundred witnesses. Or a drug deal gone wrong. Or a domestic ruckus. But here you got Marchand disappearin' in the middle of the night. No shots, no blood, no screamin', no body, no nothin'. Hell, no one drove into camp at four in the morning, killed him, and carried him off while the rest of 'em slept like zombies."

"No," Harry jumped in, "but someone could have gotten up at four in the morning, followed him out of camp, killed him, and stuffed his body in a ravine."

"Sure, and gone square dancin' to boot. Pig shit. Listen, Marchand stuck to the dirt road when he walked out that night. He didn't hoof it over barbed wire fence, sagebrush, cactus and gopher holes in the dark. That country's too rough, even in the light. So if someone put him to bed with a pick and shovel, it was on the road. Then they would've had to drag him down into the ditch, out again, under a five-strand barbed wire fence and then on a piece. There's no open pasture, just good, tight fence wire on both sides of the roads. Deputy and I checked when we were out there. We'd've found a body if there was one. Or the range hands would've spotted somethin' by now, ridin' the fence lines. Anyhow, none of 'em has the strength to pull that off, except maybe Bruckmann. That Cornell professor is heavy enough, just a foot too short. And none of 'em out there has the stomach to kill. Facts say it's pretty simple. Most cases are. The man took off, driven by a woman or a change in his own weather. Till you get evidence otherwise, all this talk ain't worth a milk bucket under a bull."

Crumley got up, walked around the desk, turned off the coffee machine, and opened his door to the staccato of the police band radio.

"Mornin', Geri," he said to a deputy in the outer office, a woman with short, blond hair in a gray shirt, black tie, and black pants. Her thick, black belt was a chandelier for a holstered gun, nightstick, cuffs, keys, a two-foot flashlight, and a can of Mace. There was a black plastic badge pinned to her shirt pocket: G. JONES. She nodded.

"This is Harry Przewalski, a PI from Pittsburgh. He's here to find the bonehunter, Marchand. I told him everything we know, which is damn little. Then again there's damn little to know."

He turned to Harry. "Geri here helped me run up and down 20-26 and the dirt roads in the Badwater area. Anyway, if I hear anything, I'll get word to you. But it ain't likely. Go back to Pittsburgh. Marchand's been gone two weeks. He'll come out of his hole before the end of the month, more than likely back there than here."

"I'll stick around. At least till Wednesday, when they pack up camp and leave."

"Suit yourself," Crumley shrugged. "Just don't go botherin' the ranchers around here spreadin' wild stories. You might just get your ass dead in the gully."

"I'll keep it in mind."

It was noon. A line of Winnebagos, Airstreams, and camper-topped pickups plodded US 20-26 through Shoshoni. The exhaust coated the blistering, tight heat. A few were angle-parked outside a faded blue, two-story clapboard building. The sign read "Yellowstone Drug, Best Malts in the West." Beside it, a shuttered café and taxidermy shop hid behind dust-blown panes.

The highway split in the middle of town. US 26 continued west over Boysen Reservoir to Riverton. US 20 wound north through the Wind River Canyon, hugging the east side of the Bighorn River to Thermopolis. Both routes led to Yellowstone. Billboards lured the traffic west or north. Most turned north. Harry wondered which way Marchand had gone.

He headed east out of Shoshoni toward Waltman, windows down, hoping the wind would help the air conditioner in the Bronco get the upper hand. The strong brume of desert sage boiled up in the heat. Poison Creek meandered dry along the left side of the highway, the chocolate brown mudflats sprinkled with a sickly white lime. Higher up, on the scrub flats, dust devils spun like gaunt, mad scarecrows boring into the earth. It was a hard place to hide in. Or run from.

CHAPTER 17

WALTMAN IS A single dilapidated building with a small general store, café, and post office. It sits on US 20-26 at the junction with the gravel road that runs north through Arminto and on northeast toward Kaycee and Buffalo. Outside, there's an old gas pump and a phone booth; in back, a few extinct corrals.

Harry pulled in beside the gas pump. A few years ago, the whole town was for sale, but there weren't any takers. Eighty million years earlier, this place was the Earth in upheaval. To the north, the Bighorn Mountains rose and began sweeping down like a roundhouse left hook. To the east, a vast inland sea covered much of the continent. Its surface waters teemed with billions of microscopic protozoan creatures, each one-celled and encased in a tiny shell. When they died, the shells settled to the sea floor, decomposed into a white sludge, and were compressed into polite, orderly layers of chalk. The sea nurtured a nightmarish ecosystem of giant bony fish, monstrous turtles, voracious forty-foot mosasaurs and killer sharks. Pterosaurs hovered overhead like black, web-winged vultures waiting to eviscerate the rotting fish on the beach. The first pulse of the Rockies drained the sea, leaving a cemetery of extinct reptiles and fish, their carcasses embalmed in the chalky ooze of the ocean bottom. The second pulse of the Rockies sent rivers of silt, sand, and mud eastward, until the debris buried the sea floor, filled the basins, leveled the land, and laid down the Great Plains. Now, Harry thought, Waltman was just a shard of history, decaying in the windblown grit of modern times.

An air conditioner groaned in the store. It wasn't much cooler inside than out. The café was five red stools and a counter that separated the store from the kitchen and living quarters. Two of the plastic seats were ripped, spilling out stuffing like a decaying piece of taxidermy. A metal stand in the middle of the store was stacked with candy bars, peanuts, and Slim Jims. Cans of baked beans and chili, layered over with Wyoming dust, lined a shelf on the rear wall. Beside it stood a struggling cooler with pop and milk. A sign hung on a wooden window next to the counter:

US Post Office
10 AM – 3 PM Monday to Friday,
10 AM – 12 PM Saturday

Harry checked his watch. Two-thirty. It was Saturday. The window was closed.

"Whatcha need?"

A sandy blond in a sleeveless tan smock and sandals had appeared behind the counter. She was skinny, almost anorexic, with a tired voice. A network of blue veins crept up her arms and legs. She had been a looker once, Harry thought, but the hardtack years had beaten her down like a scarecrow on the windswept plains. A baby started crying in the back.

"Iced tea, please."

"Sugar's over there," she pointed to a canister at the end of the counter, beside a gallon jar of pickled eggs and a smaller one of pickled spicy sausage. Both seemed to be fermenting in the same yellowish marinade. It reminded Harry of the dead frogs preserved in formaldehyde at the museum.

"Thanks. The post office?"

"It's closed. Sign says we close at 12 on Saturdays, and we close at 12."

"Yeah, I see," Harry acknowledged. "I'm not here for stamps or mail. I need to know whether a certain letter arrived here in the past month or so."

She brushed a bit of hair off her forehead, weary yet somewhat curious. Her eyes, smoldering and deeply set, looked like two cave fires. She turned to the sound of the crying infant and decided to ignore it.

"Oh yeah? The letter for you?"

"No, not me. It's for Peter Marchand, one of the museum bonehunters working out here. The ones camped up by Badwater. They get their mail here, right?"

She nodded.

"He was expecting a letter from Europe. Sometime in the past month. It would have had foreign stamps on it."

Her eyes narrowed, suddenly indignant. "You don't say! We're not village idiots out here, mister. We know that letters from Europe carry foreign stamps. Same with letters from Asia, Africa and South America. We also get them from Canada and Australia."

"Okay, I didn't mean t—"

But she had turned and disappeared into the room behind the kitchen. Almost immediately the crying stopped. She returned cradling a plump, blond-haired girl about seven months old.

Harry restarted. "Listen, I'm sorry. I need to know whether Peter Marchand received a letter here from France in the past month. I'm hoping you remember. You know he's disappeared?"

She nodded. "Yeah, I heard. About two weeks ago it was. Who are you that wants to know?"

"Harry Przewalski." Harry took out his wallet, fished out a card, and handed it to her. She looked at the card, then back to him.

"It says you're a private detective. Never met one before. But you don't look it. How do I know you're legit?"

Harry showed her his PI license. "I'm legit. Marchand's museum hired me to find him. The letter from France . . . it's from a museum in Paris. It might explain why he left. Maybe where he is. Do you remember him getting the letter?"

She scanned his face like a lie detector. Finally, she shrugged. "Even if I did, I couldn't tell you. Mail is confidential. Anyway, I don't get it. What'dya care about that stupid letter? Everyone knows he ran off with that woman to Montana." Her voice had gone bitter, her eyes forlorn, as if she wished she had been that woman, whisked away from the burnt brush flats of Waltman.

"What woman?"

"Roberta—Roberta Karlsen. Everyone knows they were having this thing."

"How do you know they went to Montana?"

"Don told me. My husband. He works for the Karlsen Ranch. Cowpunching. Says everyone knows."

"Your husband around?"

"Nope. He's out on the ranch, baling. Won't be back till dark."

"Did your husband tell you where in Montana?"

"Didn't have to. Red Lodge. Karlsens have a place up there."

Harry drank some of the iced tea, felt his teeth curdle, and grabbed the sugar canister. Roberta Karlsen could have gone to Salt Lake City, then traded Utah in for Montana.

"About the letter," Harry prompted her.

She looked down at her daughter and stroked her head. "Yeah," she finally nodded, "he got one. From that museum in Paris. It has an impression of the building under the return

address. We don't get many like that. I asked him to save the
stamp for a kid in Powder River."

"Did he bring back the stamp? Or the envelope?"

"No. I didn't expect he would. Too highfalutin for us folk."

Harry nodded. Maybe highfalutin enough to get him
hounded out of the territory. Or killed. "I might come back
later to talk to your husband."

"Suit yourself." She shrugged, turned and walked slowly into
the back room, seemingly dreaming of Red Lodge and the cool,
crisp evergreens growing up the side of the Beartooths.

Harry took the gravel road north out of Waltman, past a
large cemetery of junked cars and trucks. In the distance, at the
base of the Bighorns, he could make out swatches of red cliffs
vibrating in the shimmering heat, iron that had rusted in an
ancient soil. The last pulse of the Bighorns had been violent,
regurgitating past epochs from deep within the earth. Masses of
rock strata were thrust up and bent until they stood jackknifed
in the ground like a twisted totem. After eighty million years,
the ancient forests in which the dinosaurs had scampered were
heaved up to the surface—carbonized tree trunks, mineralized
dinosaur bones, enameled fish scales, exploded turtle shells,
fragile jaws and teeth of tiny mammals.

Eight miles north, Harry crossed the railroad track at
Arminto. He pulled in alongside the pile of scorched stones
below the bent metal sign for the Bighorn Hotel. It had died
twice, Harry thought. The hotel had once sat in Wolton, a
railroad town seven miles west that went to dust in 1914. The
building had been ripped into two sections, hauled by horse
teams to Arminto, and reassembled. Locals said Arminto was
named for Manuel Armenta, who owned the nearby Jack Pot
Ranch and was a suspected horse thief. The town then bustled
with more than a thousand people. Arminto Station was the
end of the line for the Chicago, Burlington & Quincy Railroad.

From here, rail cars loaded with cattle and sheep headed east. Now the trains whistled past Arminto and stopped elsewhere. A dozen or so ramshackle buildings were left. There was a sign at the edge of town: "Population 11." The two glass Esso pumps still stood across the road, art deco curios.

Harry wondered when the hotel had burned down. He remembered the sweltering summer evening when it hosted the first sheepherders' fair and rodeo. Hundreds had descended on Arminto from surrounding towns and ranches. Marchand had gone, piling Harry and the rest of the Carnegie crew into the old Chevy Suburban. When they arrived, the length of bar was already three deep in cowboy hats and the dance floor a forest of boots.

In the crowd, there was a newly wed Roberta Karlsen. George was at the bar when Marchand brushed against her. She became his partner, dancing to a tune from the jukebox. And, later, Harry thought, perhaps his partner in bed.

Maybe Crumley was right. Marchand had likely just fled his life. As Harry himself had after Nicole's murder. The desperation of the landscape was making him imagine something more sinister. So was this pile of bricks in Arminto, all that was left of his time here. The burnt remnants of the hotel were now being swallowed by the scrub desert. It was a hell of a memento for Marchand and Roberta, old passions buried under charred rubble and sagebrush and blown earth.

Harry cursed himself. He'd allowed the past to become sentimental, the worst kind of history.

CHAPTER 18

IT WAS TEN degrees cooler in camp, courtesy of the altitude. A fresh breeze from the Bighorns was waving the cottonwoods in the meadow in front of the old homestead. The sky in the west had grown dark, blotted by an enormous cloud of ink. The storm would hit the center of the basin in a few hours. To the east and south, a thick haze still suffocated the plains. Harry tried to spot Waltman through the vapor, but couldn't. It was like the geography of a love affair gone murky, trying to find a landmark in amorphous terrain.

Harry heard them in the mess tent unloading groceries and squabbling. Simeon was admonishing Diana that she needed to do something before the camp lost its psychological anchor. She told him to shut up, pick up his precious psychological anchor, and drop it off a cliff.

Harry decided not to chance being told where to take his anchor. He went around the stone foundation and ducked into Marchand's tent. It smelled of a long field season, and looked it: a thick foam pad, a rumpled orange and blue Slumberjack sleeping bag, a pillow that was leaking feathers, a pile of laundry stuffed into a pillowcase, and a backpack and Bean duffle. Both were open; both had been searched. Their contents were strewn over the floor.

For what it was worth, Marchand wore colored bikini briefs, gray tube socks, blue Penney's work shirts, Sears painter pants, and University of Pittsburgh sweatshirts. His sandals were in the corner. Also a pair of worn Nike running shoes. Near the bed, he kept his bag of toiletries, a roll of toilet paper, a dirty Pirates hat, a Waterman fountain pen, a 10x Hastings field lens on a leather thong, a manila envelope, a green trash bag and two paperbacks: *Famous Last Words* by Timothy Findley and *Rats Alley* by William Garner. He'd been reading them at about the same rate. Both were dog-eared in the middle. The manila envelope contained bank statements, utility bills, and credit card notices, all addressed to his house in the 15208 zip code in Pittsburgh and forwarded to Waltman. There were no field notes, no envelopes, no letters from France, and no maps with a red circle around Red Lodge or Salt Lake City or any other chosen destination for a new life.

Crumley was right. Marchand's belongings were mute except for the obvious. He walked out of camp wearing his field boots and watch. He took his wallet, but left his field lens and field hat, alimony for his divorce from the profession.

Harry put the clothes back into Marchand's duffel and dumped the trash bag on the tent floor: old candy wrappers, used tissues, a pair of gray field socks with big holes in the heels, five crumpled envelopes. Four had glassine windows for billing addresses. The fifth had a red and blue border stenciled "*PAR AVION.*" It was addressed by hand to Docteur P. Marchand, Carnegie Museum. An outline of the building was embossed below the return address: Prof. René Leclerc, Paléontologie et Anatomie, Muséum National d'Histoire Naturelle, 2 Rue de Buffon, 75005 Paris. The envelope was empty. Crumley either hadn't seen it or didn't think it important. Until this morning, he hadn't known Bruckmann could be hawking Carnegie Museum fossils.

Harry folded the envelope, put it in his back pocket, and left. The mess tent was closed. Camp seemed deserted. It was time to inject a dose of disquiet. He found Lynn lying down in her tent, thumbing through an issue of *Science*. She'd washed up. Her hair, still wet, dangled down over her shoulders, tempting a lover to cool his face before the fervor of embrace. Marchand had apparently quit being tempted.

"Talk to me about Peter."

She sat up, crossed her legs, and put down the magazine. Harry noticed the pile of toiletries by the bed. There were enough cosmetics to coat Mount Rushmore. One of the empty boxes caught his eye.

"Don't take this the wrong way," she declared. "Ordinarily, I'd tell you to piss off. But I want Peter found. So, I guess I don't have a choice."

"Here's the choice," Harry said. "I'm the only one you've got that's looking for Marchand. Otherwise, you can wait for him to turn up. Or wait for the police to find him. You'll keep waiting, because they're not looking. And they won't start looking until they smell a crime."

"Yeah, I got that."

"Good. Of course, you might not want to know where he is. Especially if he's with another woman. So I can understand how you feel."

"Bullshit! You have no idea how I feel! My life with Peter is my fucking business. It's my emotional space. I don't need you to psychoanalyze it. Anyway, what did you mean by 'crime'? Surely, it's not a crime for Peter to disappear for awhile."

"It's a crime if he disappears permanently."

She stared at him with big-eyed innocence. "What do you

mean?" Harry couldn't tell whether the naiveté was real or a cold-blooded con.

"'Permanently' means dead. Accident. Suicide. Murder. The first two aren't very likely. Remember, he walked out of camp."

Lynn froze, her face ossified. Slowly, she doubled over until her body became a bronze cocoon rocking back and forth on the sleeping bag.

"Tomorrow," Harry continued, "in the badlands, show me where you and Peter went in the evenings."

She stayed folded over, a molting instar shedding her old life. Harry waited. He heard yelps from the bathing pool, Burke and Jacobs dipping into the frigid water. Finally, Lynn unfurled her body, a chrysalis rising. Small tears ran into her lower lashes.

"Okay," she whispered, her lips quivering. "We went there the last time we . . . before he left. We went there all the time." She wiped her eyes. "I can't believe he might be dead. Why would anyone kill him?"

"Lots of reasons. Disgruntled student. Jealous husband. Professional rival. Spurned lover."

"Fuck you. I didn't kill him, for God's sake." She tugged at her hair. "I love him."

"Cemeteries are full of love turned to murder."

Lynn shook her head. "He's not dead. You're just saying that to unnerve me."

"You're right. How long have you and Peter been an item?"

"We're not a fucking item!" she yelled, indignant. "We've been together for nine months. We live together. I have my own place but I'm almost always at Peter's. Here . . . in the field . . . he insists on separate spaces."

"Why would he leave you now? In the middle of Wyoming?"

"I don't know," Lynn protested, raising her hands in helplessness. "I've thought about little else since he walked out.

Was it my fault? I go to bed replaying the last few weeks . . . every moment together . . . every conversation. I don't know."

"How was he in the days before he left? Something on his mind?"

She bit her lower lip. "He seemed preoccupied. Even . . . you know . . . sex. It seemed to be more mechanical."

"Any mention of a letter from a paleontologist in France?"

She shook her head and began fooling with her hair, as if the strands were veiling the truth.

Harry took in the pharmacy by her bed and gave it a shot. "When did you tell him you were pregnant?"

Lynn bolted up. "How did you know I was—" She stopped, hugged her shoulders and sagged back down to the sleeping bag.

"The box for the pregnancy test kit. It's right there." Harry waited for the news that the rabbit had died.

"Okay, I'm pregnant," she blurted. "It was bound to come out."

"Who else knows?"

"I haven't told anyone. Except Peter. Meredith might have overheard us. And Peter probably told Diana. He tells her everything. It happened the first week out here. I did the test last month. I joked about it with him. 'Here's the news, Peter: Baby turns blue litmus pink.' I thought he'd laugh, be happy. He used to lament going through life without kids, a family. Christ, I kept the stupid box as a souvenir."

She buried her face in her hands. "But when I told him, he . . . he recoiled. He lashed out at me. Said I'd trapped him, ruined his life, that he'd never marry me. He ordered me to get an abortion. 'Fly back to Pittsburgh, get to Magee-Women's Hospital and lose the goddamn kid.' That's what he said. He shunned me, especially at night. I revolted him, as if those few cells growing in me suddenly made me repulsive. I pleaded with him. We fought."

She looked straight at Harry, eyes callous, narrowing to hate. "You want to know why he left? He couldn't face seeing my belly grow big. He couldn't face anyone else seeing it either. I was just a fucking convenience from the beginning. Literally. A fuck receptacle. Now I've been discarded. It was all about him. It was always all about him. Diana warned me. I should have listened."

"Is that when he took an interest in Roberta Karlsen?"

"That old bitch!" she hissed. "They're two of a kind. Users. They don't give a shit about anyone else. He ate up her attention. I told him she was just playing with him. He told me I was jealous. You know what the bastard said? That she was mature and sophisticated enough to know not to get pregnant." Lynn clenched her fists. "God, I wanted to kill him for that."

"Did you?" Harry asked, matter-of-factly.

She didn't have to think. "No. I meant what I said before. He might be a bastard, but . . . I love him. I'm carrying part of him."

She closed her eyes and hugged her knees into her chest, a mold for the fetus in her. Her talking was done.

CHAPTER 19

OUTSIDE, THE STORM clouds had covered half the sky, a sorcerer's black cloak billowing madly across the basin. The winds had picked up. The tents ballooned like open parachutes, groaning against the poles and corner pegs. Harry felt the temperature drop a dozen degrees.

"Przewalski!" Simeon bellowed at him from in front of his tent. He put down his *Time* magazine, which promptly blew up slope and disappeared into the Bighorns.

"You've been here three days. Learn anything yet? Perhaps from our intrepid sheriff?" Simeon asked.

"Not much. Maybe I can learn something from you. How long have you known Marchand?"

Simeon snorted. "He was a student in a sophomore biology lab at Princeton. I was a beginning assistant professor. He was a wunderkind of sorts, but intellectually scattered. I worked with him into graduate school . . . honed his analytical thinking. I taught him that science is more than what bone goes where. Paleontology, geology, zoology—they're not like physics and chemistry. They're not about prescribed, rule-driven methods . . . cookbook, experimental science if you will. They're less about pure reason and more about the aesthetics of a problem, as much art as science. They're about the implied reality and reconstruction of phenomena. Great scientists operate on what Polyani called 'tacit knowledge.' I learned this long ago. Have you read Polyani, detective?"

Harry had, years ago. But he knew it was a rhetorical question, born out of Simeon's conceit, not curiosity. "How did Marchand measure up?"

Simeon shrugged. "In the end, he didn't. He left Princeton in his second year of graduate work. At most universities, brilliance is a rare commodity, so the brilliant get a free pass without much work. But at Princeton brilliance is common. To stand apart requires old-school focus, sweat and discipline. It also requires a fraternal commitment to . . . what shall I say . . . social place."

"What do you mean?" Harry knew what he meant. He just wanted to hear how Simeon would put it.

Simeon inclined his head, raised his eyebrows and shot a secretive look at Harry. "He refused to be one of the boys, part of the fraternity. We were refined. Cultured. Urbane. And circumspect. Unlike nowadays."

"I see. So, he preferred the company of women. Fortunately, that's not a crime. Happens to most of the population. Where did he go after Princeton?"

"Michigan . . . where he finished. He's not the genius everyone thinks he is. In my estimation, he takes credit for work others have done—graduate students, other scientists. We're a small community, we paleontologists. Chicanery doesn't stay hidden very long. There are more than whispers about where Peter got his newfangled theories. I've checked into it."

"And found what? You deliberately avoid the word, but you keep intimating plagiarism."

Simeon narrowed his eyes and quickly glanced at the other tents. "Quiet, detective. These walls are cloth, not brick. I'm being precise. I'm referring to intellectual theft, the plagiarism of ideas, not the wholesale copying of someone else's words. Peter's theories are not original with him, although he passes them off as such."

"Did you confront him?"

Simeon thought for a moment. "Yes. You might say we confronted each other."

"Let me guess," Harry said. "He threatened you with some disclosure. What was it? Did it date back to the Princeton business?"

"Not directly, no."

"Okay, he discovered that you and Burke are part of the fraternity—continuing the Princeton tradition. Perhaps Burke also went there."

Simeon's hairless pink face flushed a deep red. "How dare you invade my private life? Or Morris's? If you must know— as you already seem to—yes, Morris and I are brethren of a sort. But no, he did not go to Princeton. I imagine Peter told Diana. And as would be expected of her crass character, she did not respect the confidence and shared it with you. The truth is that Peter is vehemently bigoted about . . . uh . . . alternative lifestyles, as ugly as that phrase is. No doubt you also judge and disapprove."

"I couldn't care less, professor. The only lifestyle I judge is my own, and it's not much of one. How did Marchand find out?"

"I'd rather not go into it, detective. Suffice it to say, it was the most unfortunate circumstance to have occurred here this summer. Perhaps worse than Peter up and leaving the expedition."

Harry wondered if Marchand had caught Simeon and Burke *in flagrante delicto* in the badlands.

"In any case," Simeon continued, "he threatened to expose our relationship and have Morris fired from the museum. I suggested a simple gentleman's agreement. Mutual deterrence. I would not broadcast his plagiarism if he would not broadcast my private affairs—or terminate Morris. But—"

"Did he agree?"

"No, detective. As I was about to say before you interrupted, he did not. He was too angry to agree. Peter knows my professional reputation is unassailable. So, he threatened to spread innuendo, perhaps at the annual meeting of paleontologists in October. As it happens, we'll be convening in Pittsburgh this year at the Carnegie Museum."

"So you're not sorry that Marchand has disappeared."

"Nice try, Przewalski. Your intimation is obvious, so I'll respond with the obvious. No, I had nothing to do with his disappearance. And neither did Morris."

"But it would have been worth killing him to preserve your reputation, or Burke's career."

"My reputation is secure, thank you, no matter my private proclivities. Peter, for all his fame, is a lesser man than I in the profession. And surely, detective, your experience has taught you this lesson about the world of university professors. They kiss up, and piss down—excuse my language. Which also means they kill up, not down. Marchand is downstream from me." Simeon smacked his lips, satisfied with his summary of academia.

"Marchand wasn't worried about your threat to expose his plagiarism?"

"No. He was undeterred. He insisted I was delusional. That I was envious of his stature and desperate to hold on to mine."

"What about Diana? Does she kiss up and piss down?"

He shrugged. "Yes. She's a flash in the pan. She's riding Peter's coattails. Everyone thinks she's bright and I'm sure they're not mistaken. But I wouldn't have her on my staff. Diana tries too hard to show that her deportment doesn't matter.

Sloppy old shorts, big hat, no make-up, disheveled hair. It is much more difficult for women out here, an understandable difficulty given their menses and the demands of bodily vanity. It's just the nature of the female condition. They don't belong on these expeditions. Diana's place is in the museum, in the laboratory, not here. I'm afraid this view is very old school and not politically correct. But it is correct! I can read people from their deportment."

Simeon looked up at the Bighorns, perhaps hoping his *Time* magazine would come flying back down the mountain. He got up, grabbed a towel and walked his deportment toward the creek.

CHAPTER 20

ACROSS THE BASIN, the massive bank of black storm clouds had stopped churning. Its underside hung low in the air, a dark vise slowly descending to Earth. Harry walked up the rocky meadow to a Springbar tent that was set closest to the fence line, farthest from the rest of the camp. Two rows of rocks, carefully laid out and spray-painted Day-Glo orange, led to the tent door. It looked like a landing strip.

"What did that butt-wipe have to say?" Bruckmann was sitting in a camp chair behind his tent, smoking and reading a large folio book. His khaki shirt and pants seemed recycled from yesterday. "I saw you talking to the professor."

"So you did. It wasn't complimentary. He said you'd never make it into graduate school at Princeton. Or Cornell." Polite banter was wasted on Bruckmann, Harry thought. "Marchand accepted you because he too is second rate. So is Pitt."

Bruckmann drew violently on what was left of his cigarette and exhaled a cloud of smoke. "Don't buy that shit, detective. It's actually the other way around. Marchand publishes lots of papers. Gets big research grants. Simeon doesn't. Hell, he doesn't even apply any more. He hasn't had an original idea in years. All he can do is crap on others. He's like the fossils out here. Dead. Petrified. He's jealous of Pete."

"Enough to kill him?" Harry baited.

Bruckmann mashed his cigarette into the ground, lit another, and sucked in his cheeks. "Sure! If he could. He pretends he's concerned about Pete being gone. But that's so much bullshit. I bet he hopes Pete's lying dead in some hole in the badlands. Maybe he put him there himself. Everybody out here hates Marchand. They're all a bunch of bullshitters if they tell you different. No one would miss him, dead or alive. Everyone's glad he's gone. If you haven't picked that up by now, you're not much of a detective."

"What about you? You hate him?"

Bruckmann took his time. "I can't afford to hate him. He's my major professor. I need him for the next few years to get my Ph.D. But he's a bastard. A smart bastard, but still a bastard."

"A smart enough bastard to figure out that you were ripping off the Carnegie Museum. Selling its fossils to dealers. That's hard jail time, Bruckmann. That worth murder?"

Bruckmann smiled, took a long drag, and started hacking. It sounded like the overture to a funeral. "A misunderstanding, detective. I have my own private collection of fossils. I've been buying and trading stuff for years. And selling. It's my part-time business. It'll be full-time once I graduate."

He chuckled, dropped the book to the ground, stood up and spit a gob of greenish-yellow phlegm into the dry grass. "You can keep these fucking museum jobs. They pay shit. And you have to deal with all these assholes. Like Peter. Or Simeon. That's the lesson I've learned about academia, detective. Here. And in Germany. Assholes fuck other assholes for professional gain. Or fun. Either way, they just make the asshole bigger."

He ground the cigarette out with his field boot. "Anyway, a Ph.D. is worth shit. Any idiot can get one. All it takes is *zitsfleisch*. Or good looks." He nodded at Lynn's tent. "I'm getting mine as a business investment. Greater credibility as a fossil dealer. I'll make a fortune."

"More likely you'll be making license plates," Harry bluffed. "Marchand had you cold. Those specimens you sold to overseas buyers. They had Carnegie catalogue numbers on them. He had René Leclerc at the Paris museum check it out. Leclerc confirmed it." Harry pulled out the envelope, waved it at Bruckmann, and stuffed it back in his pocket. "I've got his letter."

Bruckmann sat back down and scoffed. "You've got shit, detective. No evidence. No invoices. No bills of sale. Nothing with my name on it. Leclerc is old and crazy. Now, detective, if you don't mind, it's my afternoon off. I was reading."

Bruckmann picked up his book. It was a catalog of skulls and skeletons from an upscale emporium in New York City.

CHAPTER 21

THE STORM FRONT had reached Cedar Ridge south of camp and pushed the temperature down a dozen degrees. Harry rolled his shirt sleeves down and headed down the rocky slope to the old homestead. Each of them wanted Marchand missing: Simeon to salvage his private life and reputation; Calvert and Bruckmann to salvage love and larceny; and Jacobs to salvage Christian virtue. Diana was less clear. Maybe she wanted Marchand's job. Maybe vengeance, if Marchand had told her of Lynn's pregnancy.

Harry found Burke alone in the mess tent, immersed in his field notebook, referencing numbers on the quarry grid map against his list of plaster jackets. Burke exuded the patience of the particularist, that gratifying indulgence in fastidious order. It was a curatorial personality shared by collection managers and stamp fanciers. Likely predisposed by genetics, Harry thought. But not predisposed to murder.

Burke glanced up from his orange notebook. "Hey there. So I heard you used to work out here with Peter. That's pretty neat. Any sign of where he went off to?"

"No. Maybe he didn't go anywhere. Except to ground."

"You mean deliberately disappear?"

"No," Harry corrected, "I mean deliberately killed."

Burke dropped his pen. It was a fine technical drawing pen, a Koh-I-Noor. He picked it up and checked the needle-like ink stylus.

"This might not be comfortable," Harry continued. "What was Marchand's reaction when he caught you and Simeon being friendly and—"

"Hhhow … dddid … you find out?" He stared at Harry, aghast.

"Doesn't matter. Marchand threatened to expose both of you."

Burke put the pen and notebook down. "Okay," he breathed deeply. "Peter became a changed person when he found out about me and Edwin. He was shocked. Disgusted. He said it was a matter of loyalty. I don't know … maybe he meant loyalty to manhood. He'd never let on that he was a homophobe. Anyway, he said that I'd betrayed him, that he couldn't bear to work with me any longer. Here in the field … or in the museum, in the lab. He said if I was smart, I'd resign. If I didn't, he'd get me fired. Ruin my reputation. He said he'd give me six months' grace to find a position at another museum."

Burke slumped back in his chair, then added, "Frankly, it's almost a relief to talk about it."

"Why not move to Cornell? Work in Simeon's lab."

Burke shook his head. "Unfortunately, Edwin doesn't really have a lab, or any positions—no grant funds, no budget for me from the university. Anyway, Cornell doesn't have fossil vertebrates. What they do collect, which isn't much, they send to the Smithsonian. Simeon is winding down there. You've probably gathered that."

Harry went over to a cooler, grabbed two Olympia bottles, popped the caps, and gave one to Burke. "So, you don't mind Marchand being gone. Even better if he doesn't return."

Burke wiped the top of the bottle and took a swig. "I hope

he's left for good...from here...from the Carnegie. As much for Edwin as for me. He treated us like freaks, like social outcasts. Anyway, who the hell is Peter to pass judgment on us? He swipes his science from other researchers. He sleeps with any skirt that comes along, then dumps her. At first, when he disappeared, I thought he'd be back in a few days. Like the last couple of years. It was usually a two-day drunk. Or a weekend shack-up. This time I thought it might have been with the Karlsen woman."

"How come?"

Burke shrugged. "Just local gossip. Do I think something's happened to him? Maybe."

"Such as?"

Burke smiled sheepishly. "Edwin and I have talked about it. You'll think this is funny. He was worried that I did something to Peter. And I thought he had. We wondered if he was dead. He should have turned up by now. Maybe an accident. When he walked out of here that night, he could have tripped, broken a leg or something. If so, he's out there being picked over by the buzzards."

"What if he was lured out of camp, killed and buried? Someone with a grudge."

He squinted at Harry as if he was trying to fathom the implications. "No, I don't think so." He put the beer down and picked up his pen. "Listen, I need to finish this tally before tomorrow. Thanks for the beer." He buried his face in his notebook.

Harry climbed up the path behind the homestead, found a large granite boulder that had tumbled down from the Bighorns a thousand years ago, and rolled a cigarette. There was a flash of lightning in the distance, then the dim roll of thunder. The storm had finally swallowed the sky over the basin. To the south, a silent havoc roiled eastward across the plains. Sheets of rain slashed towards the earth, curtains of thin, steel needles feathering out just above the ground. Electric arcs licked at the prairie under the moving clouds, but the faint after-rumble made the scene disembodied and safe.

From here, Harry thought, the massive storm front was silent cinema. He felt like a voyeur at a nature peep show, detached from the violent fury of the event.

CHAPTER 22

L OST CABIN SITS north-south. The paved road through it is
short, about 300 yards, and lined with old cottonwoods.
At the north end of town, the road crosses a cattle guard,
turns to gravel, and heads north through the Badwater valley
and over the rocky, saltbush hills of the Bighorns to the Orchard
Ranch, Nowood, and Tensleep. The Orchard Ranch is lush,
Nowood is treeless, and Tensleep, for Indians on horseback a
century ago, was "ten sleeps" from Fort Laramie, Yellowstone
Park, or the Indian agency in Stillwater, Montana.

Harry raised a long trail of dust early Sunday morning as
he barreled past the Nowood turnoff and rattled across the
cattle guard into town. At the south end of Lost Cabin, the
road crossed Badwater Creek, lost its pavement to gravel, and
turned east across the dry sagebrush flats for Arminto. US
20-26, the lone strip of two-lane asphalt between Casper and
Shoshoni, ran parallel to the Lost Cabin-Arminto road eight
miles further south. Between the highway and gravel road, the
tracks of the Burlington and Northern Railroad bisected the
scrub prairie.

Harry figured that Marchand had hiked south in the early
morning light of July 22. Maybe he made it to the highway.
Maybe he hopped a passing freight train. He could also have

gotten picked up on the Badwater road below camp. Either way, he would have come through Lost Cabin.

The town had nine houses arrayed along the west side of the road. Five were ramshackle trailer jobs; three, weather-beaten stuccos. The ninth rose from the scrub like a fevered hallucination, an elegant Victorian mansion wrapped in big-block, ochred limestone. It had four floors, a windowed tower, an expansive veranda that girdled the house, a tall, wrought iron gate, and a winding driveway. Locals called it the Okie house. It was owned by George Karlsen, who also owned the town and most of the Badwater valley.

Harry drove the Bronco through the open gates. Karlsen himself opened the thick oak doors as Harry climbed the stairs to the veranda. He beamed a broad smile and thrust out his hand.

"Good morning, I'm George Karlsen. I take it you're the detective that called yesterday."

He had a deep voice that took charge, as any future governor of Wyoming would. He was shorter than Harry had imagined, and rounder, showing the remnants of a solid build. His black hair was brushed straight back and oiled down. His face had started to sag around his deep-set eyes, heavy black eyebrows and large ears. It lent him the kind of gravitas people expected of a politician. All except for his nose. It had been broken multiple times, hadn't healed right, and had grown bulbous with liquor. A former football player gone soft, Harry thought. Or prizefighter.

"Right. I'm Harry Przewalski. Thanks for agreeing to see me. I hope this doesn't disrupt your Sunday morning."

"Not at all. Come in." Karlsen was dressed for church—for praying and campaigning. He was sporting a dark blue suit with faint red pin stripes, a pinkish shirt with pearled buttons, a bolo tie, and black cowboy boots.

He led Harry into a cavernous, paneled living room. The stone fireplace at one end was large enough to roast a moose. Trophy heads of African zebras and antelope stared down onto the parquet floor. Each head was mounted above the rifle that had ended its life. A bear rug covered some of the parquet squares. It looked like a grizzly to Harry. Its mouth was frozen open in a ferocious snarl, as if it were about to pounce on the processed wood.

"Sit, please." Karlsen motioned to a rectangle of four leather couches that surrounded a massive coffee table. A thick expanse of Plexiglas on top of the table was embedded with polished stones, fossil ammonites, arrowheads, and petrified wood, symmetrically arranged into circles. Rooms were museums, Harry thought, exhibiting the personas we wanted on display. This was Karlsen's. Harry wondered what Roberta thought of it. And what hers was like.

Karlsen sat opposite Harry and propped his boots on the table, blotting out a big, pearled ammonite.

"We've got about an hour before I leave for church in Shoshoni. Do you know about this house? No, you wouldn't. It's the sweat and grit of the Wyoming pioneer, a capsule of the American dream." Karlsen sounded as if he were beginning his stump speech.

"It's the old Okie house," Harry said.

Karlsen furrowed his eyebrows, surprised that Harry knew anything about the mansion. "Yes. John Okie built it at the turn of the century. 1898. It cost him $100,000, when a dollar was real money. The Indians called it Big Tepee, because back then most of Wyoming was living in sod-roofed shacks. Okie started as a penniless cowboy and became a millionaire. He bought up land, livestock and general stores. He built the first steam sheep-shearing plant in the United States, right here in Wyoming, in Casper, in 1894. He had his wife inaugurate the plant. She steam-sheared the first sheep in less than five minutes. It was good theater. He made a fortune."

Karlsen waved a hand at the window. "I bought the whole town a few years ago, such as it is. It's a bad comedown from Okie's day—not much left, really, except for this house. Two hundred sheepherders used to work for him. A thousand people lived here. And he brought in the finest goods. You see that old brick building across the road when you drove in? The one falling down? That was his general store. It carried the latest fashions from Paris for the ladies. It was also his Oasis Hotel. Served fine food. And had a dance pavilion with fine music, and a roller skating rink. Hell, he installed electric lights in Lost Cabin while the rest of Wyoming was still living by kerosene. He put modern plumbing in this house when most of the state was still running to the outhouse. This room," Karlsen pointed at the trophy heads, "was his library."

He moved his left leg off the coffee table, took a handkerchief from his pocket, licked it, wiped a smudge from his boot, and propped his leg back up on the ammonite.

"Outside on the grounds Okie had a petting zoo. He imported animals from Africa, South America, and India. He took great pride in what he'd built. This was his domain—his town, his hundreds of sections of land, his ranch hands. You saw the tower when you came in? Well, he put a powerful brass telescope up there so that he could command a view of his piece of Wyoming. I imagine he saw that it was good. Kind of biblical."

Karlsen raised his hands, as if signaling "THE END" to a stirring biopic of Okie. "Coffee, Mr. Przewalski?"

"Thanks."

Karlsen got up and disappeared through a set of double doors to the right of the fireplace. Harry knew Okie's more seamy side that Karlsen had left on the cutting room floor. In

1907, Okie began a torrid affair with Mrs. Clarice Lovett and promptly abandoned his sheep-shearing first wife. Clarice had recently arrived in Casper from California. She was acclaimed to be the most beautiful woman in Wyoming. And she didn't believe in wasting time. One morning in 1908, she was granted a divorce from her husband; by sunset, she was Mrs. J. B. Okie.

On a cloudy November day in 1930, Okie left his mansion to go duck hunting near Lost Cabin. He never came back. Two days later, his body was fished out of the town reservoir. Officials ruled it an accidental drowning. Locals knew he was murdered by one of his business or personal enemies. Okie was buried in the Lost Cabin cemetery, an open windblown field just north of town that he used to survey with his telescope.

Karlsen came back with two mugs of coffee and a plate of cinnamon rolls with a crumble frosting.

"I'll get right to it, Mr. Karlsen," Harry said. "You know Peter Marchand, from the Carnegie Museum. He disappeared more than three weeks ago. I'm here to find him. He and his crew have been camping on your land above the Badwater Creek road. They're excavating on your section in the Buck Creek badlands. Do you have any idea where Marchand is? Or why he left so suddenly? Maybe Sheriff Crumley has already gone over this with you."

Karlsen frowned, ran his fingers through the oiled hair, and returned his face to the stump smile. "No, I haven't spoken with Crumley. Or he with me. No reason he should. I don't know anything about this business. I don't have any information, either for Crumley or for you. Of course, I'm sorry that Peter has left the expedition. I imagine he had a good reason to take some time off. Maybe personal. Maybe professional. Leadership brings pressure and anxiety. I can tell you that from experience."

"When did you find out that Marchand was missing?"

Karlsen re-oiled his fingers in his hair. "I might have heard about it in passing from one of my foremen. Maybe a week after Peter left. But I'm not sure. One of Peter's assistants, Diana, came out to the ranch to find out if anyone had seen him. She was worried that he might somehow have become incapacitated in the badlands."

He drank some coffee and reached for a cinnamon bun. "We have a saying out here: a man that was born to drown will drown out in the desert. But Peter's not the drowning kind. Just the getting-away kind. He did it for a few days last year. Wish I could get away for awhile."

He leaned over and bit into the bun, taking care not to get any of the crumble frosting on his trousers. "Anyway, I wasn't here. I was out campaigning in the western part of the state. I'm running for governor."

"Yes, I know. Have you talked about Marchand's disappearance with your wife? She might have an idea where he might be." It was a polite shot to the groin.

Karlsen didn't blink, showing the control of a consummate politician. "No, Roberta and I haven't discussed it. And there's no reason we should. I know what you're hinting, so I might as well tell you how the cow ate the cabbage. In these parts that means I'm going to speak my mind. I've heard the gossip about Roberta and Peter. Isn't that what you're driving at, Przewalski? My campaign people aren't happy about it."

Karlsen seemed less worried about his wife sleeping with another man than what the publicity about the affair might do to his gubernatorial campaign. He sipped some coffee, took another bite out of the cinnamon roll and wiped his mouth on the handkerchief that he'd used to polish his boot.

"The business with Roberta is just so much belly wash. Wyoming has big-minded spaces but small-minded people. If a man and woman dance together and don't trip over each other's feet, they're suspected of having an affair. Hell, if they drive past each other on the Badwater Road and wave through the dust they're having an affair. In Wyoming, we say that suspicion ain't proof."

"Mr. Karlsen," Harry answered, "suspicion might not be proof, but detectives make a damn good living at suspicion. So do paleontologists, like Marchand. People think that he and your wife did more than dance or wave to one another on the Badwater Road. Even some people who work for you."

"Crap," Karlsen bellowed. "Every jackass thinks he has horse sense, and there are a lot of jackasses around here. Some even work for me."

"How well do you know Marchand? I notice you call him Peter."

"We're friendly folk out here. We don't believe in formalities. Peter's been coming out to Badwater for many years now. He stops by when he first arrives in June. He checks on using the old homestead for their camp site. He checks on working the breaks down by Buck Spring and over by Alkali Creek. That's smart, because this is Wyoming, Przewalski. Like I said, we're friendly folk. We love our enemies, but we keep our guns oiled. Go over the wrong fence, or drive through the wrong gate, and you can find yourself on the wrong end of a double-barreled shotgun."

"What about looking at the wrong woman?" Harry asked.

"That too." Karlsen eyed him pointedly. "Happens every Saturday night in Casper. Fools get shot for looking at the wrong pair of legs. Women's lib in Wyoming isn't what it is out East. We're possessive about our land and our women. We put 'em both behind fences and shotguns."

"Is that why he just walked out of camp one night and hasn't come back? Any idea who might have picked him up?"

Karlsen paused to rub his ear. He took his feet off the table and leaned forward. "I didn't know he walked out of camp. You can't cover your back with your belly too long in these parts— sleep out in the open. No, I have no idea why Peter left, except what I said before: pressure of the job. And any ranch hand or tourist on the road could have picked him up."

Karlsen abruptly stood up, went over to the mantle and came back with a large hunk of dinosaur bone. Harry recognized part of a sauropod femur.

"I didn't know Peter well," Karlsen observed, rubbing the smooth surface of the bone. Weathering had polished it to a blue-black sheen. "He once took me to the dinosaur site . . . let me dig out one of the bones in the quarry. I helped him out with some heavy equipment. We scraped that track along the wash below the dig to haul the bones out."

Karlsen looked at the rest of the cinnamon roll, shook his head, and finished his coffee. "Peter and I would talk sometimes. We debated the politics and economics of his digging here. It's an issue that's important to me as a candidate for governor. We need to balance these scientific excavations with the state protecting its unique natural heritage. Right now that balance is way out of whack. Wyoming is the mother lode of dinosaurs. And it's losing them by the herd—to other countries, to other states, to other museums. I know; I'm contributing to this by letting the Carnegie folks dig up and ship out those dinosaurs from my land. But I told Peter I wouldn't back out of the promise that he could excavate at Buck Spring. I made that promise before I decided to run for governor. A promise in these parts is worth more than water. And water in these parts is the price of blood."

Karlsen leaned over and offered Harry the plate of cinnamon rolls. Harry shook his head. "Well, Mr. Karlsen, it's science. Not water, not a piece of land. Wyoming can't own it."

"Oh yeah, why not? In the Old West, a bone-picker made a

living by collecting dead animal bones and sending them east for processing into artificial manure. Marchand and the rest of them are just modern-day bone pickers. They collect dead animal bones and send them east for processing into science."

Harry grinned. Karlsen had the silver tongue of a politician.

"It's simple, Przewalski," Karlsen continued. "We have three major economic resources in Wyoming. We have energy in oil, coal and gas—and we don't give that away. We have beef ranching—and we don't give that away. And we have the best goddamn range of Rockies in the USA—and we don't give that way either. No! We sell the oil to the oil companies, the beef to the beef packers, and the Rockies to the tourists."

Karlsen, animated, waved the chunk of sauropod at him. "Well, by God, we have a fourth resource! Fossils! And damn good ones, too. We've got trilobites. We've got ammonites. We've got fossil fish. And we've got *Tyrannosaurus*. This is about more than state ownership. It's about our economic and educational legacy. Every time a dinosaur skeleton leaves Wyoming, part of the educational future of Wyoming's kids goes with it. Along with tourism dollars for our museums and communities. Hell, Andrew Carnegie plundered Wyoming's dinosaurs back in 1899 for his Pittsburgh museum. Now it's happening again. Don't get me wrong. As a good Republican, I like imperialism, but only when we're doing it to the other guy. We have our own museums in Laramie, Casper, Cody and Cheyenne. What do they get out of this? The chance to buy a plaster copy of our own dinosaur skeletons? Or a high-priced exhibit of rubber dinosaurs from some outfit in Hollywood? As governor, I'm going to ask for legislation to keep our dinosaurs in Wyoming. It's smart educational policy and smart economic policy."

Karlsen leaned back, glanced at his watch, and propped his feet back on the ammonite. He looked pleased, as if he were hearing the roar of ovation from the Wyoming Chamber of Commerce.

Harry yanked him back. "Mrs. Karlsen, is she here?"

"No, she's not. She's on vacation. She doesn't do too well in this heat. She's also resting up for the final campaign push."

"When did she leave? Crumley told me she was in Salt Lake City."

Karlsen sat up, his eyes boring into Harry like the wrong end of a shotgun. "You're crossing the line, Przewalski. I don't see how my wife's schedule has anything to do with Peter taking off. Or your investigation. If you're intimating that Peter's with her, the answer is no. Look under someone else's wife. And I resent you talking about her with Crumley. Now," he rose from the couch, "if you don't have any more questions, I need to get to Shoshoni."

Harry stayed seated. "With all due respect, Mr. Karlsen, it's my job to cross the line. Peter and your wife might have already crossed the line, whether you acknowledge it or not. Lots of folks around here think so. Peter might turn up dead. Then you and your wife will be dragged across the line by local and state police, starting with Crumley."

Karlsen stared at Harry in disbelief and slowly sat down. "Whoa! You're not serious! Peter dead? Do you know he's dead?"

"No, I don't. But Peter isn't talented enough to disappear this long without a trace, even in Wyoming. I don't know what was going on between your wife and Marchand. Or whether they left together. But they talked, so she might have a notion where he went and why. And if you're worried about discretion, I'm probably your best bet. Better than the police. Or the media. You're in the public eye. You need Marchand's whereabouts settled quick. Before the rumors become news stories."

Harry paused long enough for Karlsen to digest the risk. "Now, when did she leave and where did she go?"

Karlsen glared at Harry, then looked up at the head of a gerenuk mounted on the opposite wall. Lost to the rifle and taxidermy was the sensual undulation of its long neck as it bounded across the savannah. Harry wondered whether Karlsen had lost his wife and marriage to a taxidermied life.

"Okay," Karlsen sighed, resigned to the political realities. "Roberta and I have nothing to hide. She left for Salt Lake. In her Jeep. I think it was July 22 or 23. I offered to fly her out earlier that week on the ranch's jet, but she wanted to stay on here a few days. She also wanted wheels. She stayed in Salt Lake for a bit, then went up to Red Lodge. To get away from the heat." He paused, then added, "and the relatives. Can't say as I blame her. They're Mormons."

Karlsen's blood pressure rose at the word. "Utah isn't a democratic state. It's a Mormon state, a theocracy. Their big temple in Salt Lake might as well be the state capitol. Mormons can screw ten wives, half of them still in the cradle, but the real sinners drink coffee. Go figure. You're not a Mormon, are you? No, not with a name like Przewalski. Probably Polish Catholic. Too many of them, Mormons that is, are invading Wyoming. Know what we say? Never approach a bull from the front, a horse from the rear, or a Mormon from any direction. My opponent is Mormon. My wife isn't one anymore," he added, for the record.

Harry waited to make sure the Mormon diatribe was over. "So you weren't here when your wife left."

"No. Like I said, I flew out earlier . . . July 19, I think. To Jackson Hole. Campaigning in western Wyoming."

"Where did Mrs. Karlsen stay while you were gone? Here? The ranch?"

"She stayed here. She usually does when I'm out of town.

More neighbors around." Karlsen gestured north toward the window. "My foreman lives in the pink stucco place a few houses down."

Karlsen was in denial, Harry thought. His mansion in Lost Cabin was perfect for late night assignations. Roberta could have picked up Marchand in her Jeep before daybreak on July 22, stashed him in the house, then left with him for Salt Lake. He'd be under a blanket in the back seat until they made it to Highway 20-26, out of sight of the locals.

"So, Mrs. Karlsen is in Red Lodge?"

"What? . . . Oh. Yes. Not really in Red Lodge. We have a place west of town in the Beartooths. Nice getaway in the summer. Hell, I'd be there now if it weren't for this damn fool campaign. Person who visits the most ranches, shakes the most hands, and steps in the most cow shit will win the election. Right now my opponent has got more cow shit on his boots than I do."

"You fly yourself?"

"Yeah, I like to fly solo. Remember *Oklahoma*? Lazy circles in the sky? I like to do lazy circles over the spread. Sometimes I'll buzz the Basque sheepherders we hire. I know it's illegal, but it's fun. They're lonely up there in the foothills . . . in their sheep wagons. It shows them that I care."

A hell of a Hallmark card sentiment, Harry thought. Hell of a century of progress. Okie surveyed his domain from the third floor tower of his house, sitting in a chair behind his brass telescope. Karlsen now did so behind the controls of a Lear jet, buzzing sheep, sheepherders and sagebrush while humming tunes from *Oklahoma*.

Karlsen laughed, got up, and stuck out a hand, now back to being the politician. "I really need to get going. Voters don't like it if you're late for church."

He walked to the door and opened it for Harry to leave. "Przewalski, my advice to you is to admire a big horse, but saddle a small one. Leave my wife out of this. I know powerful people here. And in Pittsburgh. Like me, they would expect you to respect the privacy of a private citizen."

Harry nodded at the veiled threat. He didn't tell Karlsen he was going to head for Red Lodge early tomorrow morning. He also didn't lay out the murder scenario for him. Karlsen could have flown back to Lost Cabin from Jackson Hole on the twenty-first or early hours of the twenty-second, lured Marchand out of camp, killed him for messing with his wife, buried him somewhere on his ranch, and flown back to Jackson before daybreak. His alibi would be tight. Take off and land at private airstrips. Fly under visual flight rules. Turn off the plane's radar transponder and radios to avoid detection. Drug runners did it all the time.

CHAPTER 23

HARRY HEADED EAST out of Lost Cabin toward Arminto across the dry sagebrush flats. The road lost its asphalt around the first bend to the sand and clay of the plains. Dust rose from behind the truck in the stillness of the late morning air. The Lost Cabin-Arminto Road was straight as a fence line except where it had to crook around buttes of ancient rock that refused to erode to the rest of the earth.

After seven miles, he turned south under a row of high-tension wires and bounced the Bronco above the ruts in the dirt track to the Buck Creek badlands. A few antelope crossed in front of him and high-jumped the barbed wire fence on the left with clearance to spare. Antelope went over fences. Deer went under at a full run, legs folded, backbone flat, a fluid blur below the lowest strand. The deer and the antelope might play today, Harry mused, but evolution had put them on separate paths thirty million years ago.

When he arrived at the quarry, Harry could tell that the crew was flagging. The heat in the ravines had shrunk the air into a suffocating choke hold. Diana fanned herself with the big hat and nodded at him.

"The quarry is a fucking tanning booth. We'll fry if we sit here. We're taking a break. It's cooler if we prospect."

Simeon, Bruckmann, Burke, and Jacobs scattered down the gully into the badlands, heads bent, eyes down, prospecting for bits of dinosaur skeleton or mammal jaw poking through the gray mudstone. Meredith shadowed Simeon, both stumbling along the pebbled slopes.

Harry asked Lynn to show him where Marchand had taken her for their evening trysts. He followed her down the sinuous bends of the dry wash, eyeing the shadows under the overhanging sandstone ledges for rattlesnakes. The buttes were pockmarked with deep hollows, some large enough for a body. Harry remembered crawling into them, sanctuaries from prospecting during the midday heat. Now he was prospecting for Marchand. A killer could have stashed his body in one of these badlands crevices and buried it in the mudstone. Hell of a geologic irony, Marchand buried in the same earth that, eighty million years earlier, had buried the dinosaurs he was now excavating. Paleontology begins when the smell is gone, Harry thought. Murder investigations don't wait that long.

Lynn led him across a flat expanse of badlands strewn with scraps of eroded bone. She stopped at the base of an escarpment and pointed to the top. It was about a mile farther west from the quarries, out of sight from where the trucks were parked.

"You might still see the tire marks up there. We haven't had any serious rain in three weeks. You can get back along the top. Just follow the rim to the trucks. Or come back down and go along the gully to the quarry."

She started back across the mudstone flat, then stopped and turned, her face resigned to an extinct past. "I can't go up there." she declared, bitter. "We had romance up there. Now there's shit."

Harry noticed that her shorts and tank top were loose-fitting, about a half size too large. A coming to terms, he thought. He clambered up the steep slope between the thick ledges of sandstone boulders, each stratum a hundred thousand-year interval. Climbing through time, Harry mused, one of the six impossible things before breakfast that Alice didn't get to do.

At the top of the bluff the wind was gale force, howling past his ears and peppering his face with grit. He shoved his baseball cap into his back pocket before it could blow off and become sediment in a gully. A bank of thunderheads reared up to the west, a white, angry lather erupting across the sun into a blinding blue sky.

Suddenly, Harry's head exploded. He felt himself plunge off the escarpment, smash against the sharp rocks, and catapult downward toward the ravine. Pain shot through his leg and chest. He hit the sand in the dry gulch then slammed into a sandstone boulder. At the last moment, he remembered to wrap his arms around his head before it whiplashed the ground. The darkness in his skull began to spread, a black ink moving across his brain. He saw it stain his life and slowly blot out time. He saw the dark shadow loom behind him; the devil come to collect, silent in the airless seep of consciousness. Then he saw nothing.

CHAPTER 24

HE WAS BACK in the war, knocked flat against the desert pan by an artillery blast. Then he heard her voice.

"Harry, can you hear me?"

No, he was in *Rear Window*. A rapturous face hovering over him, lips close enough to kiss. It wasn't quite right. The hair. Black. Not a shimmering blond.

He tried to speak, but the pain was instant, knifing across the back of his skull. He tried again, this time more slowly.

"You're . . . not . . . Grace Kelly."

"What? Harry, thank God you can hear me. It's Diana. Just lie there. Don't move."

He felt her hands on his head, steadying. He told himself to remember that he liked it. He thought he heard her say something about not bleeding from the ears.

"Now, Harry, slowly, try your toes and fingers."

He concentrated on sending the wiggle message to his feet. Then the hands. They obeyed. "Okay," he whispered.

"Now your arms and legs? Do it slowly."

It took a moment to twitch them. Harry winced at the pain slicing up his right leg.

"Good. Now your neck. I'm holding your head. Just move it slightly side to side."

Harry turned his head and felt the pebbles scrape his scalp. His hair wasn't much of a cushion. He noticed other faces hovering over him. Simeon, Bruckmann, Burke, Lynn, Meredith. No Jacobs.

"That was a bad accident," Diana said. "You've had a nasty blow to the head. Some bleeding. Talk to me." A tinge of empathy, Harry thought.

"Okay," he groaned, after a moment. "Remember *Rear Window*?"

"What? Very funny. You're not Jimmy Stewart. Clearly the bump on the head could have been worse. Your leg is banged up, but fortunately not broken. Your shirt and pants are torn; your ribs took a beating, and I bet your skin is pretty badly grated. But the rest of you seems to be okay . . . including your smart mouth. This is the only time I'd say it was a good sign."

Harry smiled. There went any pretense of empathy.

"I sent Jacobs to get the pickup. He's bringing it to the escarpment above here. If you think you can move, we'll get you back to camp."

Bruckmann and Burke pulled Harry up. The badlands began to weave in front of his eyes, dizzying, tilting the earth out of kilter. They helped him limp up the cliff face and climb into the truck. Near the top of the escarpment, he saw something he wanted to pick up, but thought better of it. His leg ached badly. So did his ribs. Breathing was suddenly painful. He felt like throwing up.

"We'll put ice on your head as soon as we get back," Diana shouted above the wind. "Damn glad we have that refrigerator. You passed out. But not for long. You're lucky nothing's broken. No bleeding from the ears. There's a bit of a gash on the side of your head. Your ribs—it's gonna hurt to laugh." She paused, and turned to look at him with concern. "You gave me a scare, Harry. That's the first serious accident in years of field work here."

Harry gingerly felt the wet spot on the side of his head. His fingers came away red with blood. He wiped them on his jeans.

"It . . . wasn't an accident." The words came out slowly, methodically. "One of your people . . . tried to kill me. Might even have been you."

Diana jammed the brakes, stalling the Chevy and vaulting Harry into the dashboard. The dust trail overtook the truck and filled the cab. Harry felt his brain beginning to drown in a black swamp. He waited for the hammering behind his eyes to ease long enough to speak.

"There you go," he rasped. "Getting whacked on the cliff missed killing me. But the drive back will finish the job."

Diana took off her hat, her face alternating between anger and disbelief. "I'll apologize later. What the fuck do you mean I tried to kill you?"

"Simple. Someone tried to bash my skull in. Then pushed me off the cliff. There's a big rock with my blood on it still lying there. I noticed it on the way up to the truck. Big rocks make handy weapons. Badlands are full of them. Humans have been using them to bash in skulls for two million years. And australopithecines before them."

Diana wasn't amused. "Save me the archaeology jokes. I don't believe this." She started the truck. "Who the hell was it, Harry?"

"Don't know. I didn't see them. Didn't hear anyone either, with the wind."

"You're bullshitting me. You know who it is but you're not telling me."

Harry rearranged his throbbing leg. "I wish it were bullshit. There are some things I hold back, but not this."

"Goddamn you!" Diana yelled at him. "This is my field

expedition! I need to know what you know! Did someone follow you?"

"Could be. Lynn showed me where she and Marchand went at night. You know the spot."

Her eyes spewed poison. "Thanks for the reminder."

"Anytime. But I didn't mean it that way."

"Okay. Did she do it?"

"I don't know. Possibly. She could have doubled back. But anyone else out prospecting could've done it. Simeon, Burke, Jacobs, Bruckmann. Follow me at a distance, scramble up the cliff out of sight. Whack me from behind." Gingerly, he turned his head to look at her. "You, too."

"You can't be serious, Harry," she said in a pained voice. "Why the hell would I want to kill you?" She put her hat back on, hiding her face and emotions in the shadow of the big brim. "You wouldn't think that if you knew how I felt when I saw you lying there in the gully." It was almost a whisper.

Harry stayed on business. "Were you the one who found me?"

"Yeah. I was prospecting in that direction, about halfway up the exposures, following that gray-blue horizon that the quarry bones are in. Why would anyone want to kill you?"

"Think about it. It'll come to you." Harry grabbed a cigarette from her pack of Pall Malls and lit it. "When you found me, did you see anyone come down the cliff?"

"No. I was concentrating on you. I yelled for help and blew that goddamn whistle I carry around. First time I've ever had to do that. Jacobs must have heard me first. I sent him to get the pickup."

They didn't speak again until the Chevy climbed over Cedar Gap, crossed the hay meadows along Badwater Creek, and bumped up the dirt track to the barbed wire gate below camp. Diana got out and jiggered it open. Harry slowly slid across to behind the wheel, made his foot hit the accelerator, winced, drove through the gate, and winced again when he hit the brake. Diana got back in, her face creased in anguish. She stared at the clump of hair and blood on the side of his head.

"Harry," she said, earnestly, taking her hat off. "Look at me. It wasn't me who tried to kill you. You need to know that."

Harry didn't answer.

CHAPTER 25

THAT EVENING, THE table looked like a bottling plant. Simeon, Calvert, Bruckmann, and Burke had demolished a case of Olympia. Diana nursed Scotch in a coffee mug. Jacobs kept dividing his attention between his Bible and Lynn's chest. Meredith, in a camp chair off to the side, eyed the crowd and wrote notes. They were tight-lipped and twitchy, like prostitutes in church.

One of them had picked up a big rock, whacked him on the side of the head, and shoved him off the cliff. The odds had increased, Harry thought, that Marchand might be dead. He'd played with the idea of driving back to the escarpment, retrieving the rock, and delivering it to Crumley on the off chance it might yield the fingerprint of a gravedigger.

But he was too stiff and sore. He'd put ice on his head and swallowed four Advils. Diana had cleaned the blood from his scalp and taped his ribs. He thought her fingers had lingered, almost a caress, when she gently felt each rib to see if it was fractured. More likely it was his willful delusion.

He propped his bruised leg up on a Coleman cooler and rolled a cigarette. It was the last of his tobacco. Simeon got another Olympia from the cooler, poured half into his glass, and broke the tension.

"Peter has skedaddled. Mr. Przewalski here had an unfortunate fall in the badlands. But, Diana, it is no reason to panic and cut the field season short. I smell a frightened rat."

"Edwin, stuff it!" Diana barked. Alcohol made her pugnacious. She'd put a serious dent in a fifth of Macallan, and wasn't sharing the bottle. "If I had my choice, I'd stay out here for another two weeks and pull all the goddamn bones out of the ground one by one with my own hands. But the fact is, we're out of time, and we're out of money."

She picked up the Macallan, saw that her glass was still half full, and put it down. "We've got a decent enough haul to carry the research this winter. And more than enough for Morris to prepare: four skulls, parts of six animals, a few isolated limb bones. Edwin, I know you want to section and study them."

Simeon flexed his eyebrows, eyed the glass of beer, and pushed it aside, as if he had lost all thirst.

"Today is Sunday," Diana continued. "There's a pelvis and a few ribs still to plaster out. We'll finish it Tuesday. The rest of the skeletons are under too much overburden to take out this season. Morris has mapped what's exposed on the grid. We'll bring in the flatbed semi along the gully Wednesday morning and load up the plaster jackets. Karlsen is lending us his forklift."

Burke interjected. "It better stay dry if we're going get the semi in and out of the wash." He was still wearing his blue bandana. None of them had changed out of their field clothes.

Diana nodded. "Let's hope. We'll cover the quarry with back dirt and tarps. It'll be here next year. So be it. Something to come back to." She sounded as if this were a separate life to escape from.

Simeon began to bluster. "Diana, you—"

She ignored him. "Wednesday morning we'll pack up camp,

close the quarry, and haul ass out of here. Edwin, tell Morris which limb bones you want him to prepare for sectioning. He'll start on those jackets first thing when we get back."

"Balderdash!" Simeon exclaimed, indignant, heaving up his bulk. "There's a pile of unopened plaster jackets from last year and the year before in that Big Bone Room. They're stacked three deep. Hell, you've still got unopened jackets from 1915. From Utah . . . Dinosaur National Monument. Old Andrew was still alive then and signing the checks."

His voice turned conspiratorial. "The skeletons from here are too important to wait that long . . . to keep in the ground . . . or under wraps."

"What's this crap about 'under wraps'?" Diana asked, becoming impatient. "They'll have priority in the lab." She glanced at Burke. "Right, Morris?"

Simeon scoffed. "Save the niceties, Diana. I think you and Peter have something to hide." He looked pointedly at Meredith and Harry, advertising that he had just lobbed a grenade.

Diana scowled at him. "Watch it, Edwin! You're plastered. You don't know what you're saying. What the hell could we possibly have to hide?"

Simeon sat down and pointed to his unfinished Olympia. "I have all my faculties, thank you. It's not the way Peter would have done it."

"I don't give a fuck how Peter would have done it," Diana snapped. "Peter isn't here. The bastard walked out. He left with the money. And he left me holding all of you and all of this. He has no voice here. The only person who does is me. I'm in charge. And I've decided we're going to finish up by Wednesday. That's it. If you don't like it, tough. You can kiss my ass. I don't want to hear about it."

Diana lit a cigarette and stared angrily around the mess tent, daring anyone to challenge her. Harry grabbed a mug. She leaned over, poured him some Scotch, and tossed him her pack of Pall Malls.

"Professor," Meredith closed her notebook and smiled at Simeon, "let's not play Twenty Questions. What could they have to hide by not preparing the bones?"

Simeon sat back, reached for his glass of beer, drained it, burped, and licked his lips.

"First, hiding the evidence that their theories about dinosaurs are wrong. Second—and worse—theft." He looked accusingly at Diana. "Plagiarism!"

Diana picked up the bottle of Macallan, slammed it down on the table, and leaned menacingly toward Simeon.

"Goddamn you, Edwin! How dare you. I've heard you fling this crap before. Out here it passes for drivel from a drunken gas bag. But back at the museum, it'll be slander. I'll haul your fat ass into court faster than you can lose a hard-on. Which I imagine these days is pretty fast. That's if you can get it up at all."

Alcohol had made her raw, Harry thought. He noticed Burke beginning to squirm.

Simeon's face reddened. "Now, now, there's no need to get personal and prurient."

"Prurient my ass. We all know what you do and who you do it with."

Diana looked at Meredith. "Maybe everyone doesn't know. Well," she announced, waving her hand, "Professor Simeon likes boys." She glanced at Burke. "Even one of the boys in camp. That's fine. Each to their own. Isn't that why you're really here, Edwin? It's not the dinosaurs, it's a piece of ass, to put it crudely."

She downed her Scotch and chuckled. "And it's not Pete's ass. For all of his faults, he's a straight two-X man. Pete told me about it after he caught the two of you rutting in the badlands. Made him vomit."

Burke got up, tripped going around the table, and stumbled past Harry out of the tent. Simeon watched him leave and scowled at Diana.

"Congratulations. You've managed to abandon all prudence and civility in this company. You've revealed your true coarseness in making my private life public. And Morris's. I've got no choice but to do the same. When Peter returns—if he ever does—I will destroy him personally and professionally if he besmirches me at the meetings in Pittsburgh in October. Or if he has Morris dismissed from his position at the museum. Tell him that. I will expose his blatant plagiarism."

"Wait a fucking min—" Lynn exploded, but Simeon cut her off.

"Keep out of this, Calvert. You're an amateur. There are other words to describe you, but I'll leave that to Diana's revealed talent for tawdry salaciousness. Meanwhile, it's time you found another bed on which to graduate."

"You fucking fat faggot piece of shit!" Lynn screamed, picked up her beer bottle and threw it as hard as she could at Simeon's head. It missed by a foot, splattering beer on the canvas tent wall behind him. Infuriated, Lynn got up, grabbed a second bottle, an empty, and hurled it at him. It sailed past his right ear and clunked against the two-by-four post holding up the end of the mess tent.

Bruckmann giggled between drags on his cigarette. Jacobs shrank deeper into his seat, as if the sexual references were sinking him into iniquity. Diana poured herself another Scotch, winked at Harry, lit a cigarette and sat back. She was in her corner of the ring, between rounds, resting, ready to come out swinging.

Simeon turned back to Diana. "Now then, Diana. Peter's

threat to dismiss Morris is outrageous. As I told Przewalski here yesterday, what Morris and I do in our private lives is none of Peter's business. I will lodge the strongest possible protest with President Stewart. He will listen to me. He is an old classmate from Princeton and fraternity brother. He would never condone such retribution."

"Okay, Professor," Meredith pressed on, "why are Marchand's theories so controversial? And if he stole them, who from?"

CHAPTER 26

SIMEON SIGHED. "THE problem is larger than Marchand and his theories. As Plato said, the beginning is half the whole. The problem begins with Peter's disregard of established knowledge. He's vainly trying to overturn half a century of progress. Including, I might add, my own theories. Disraeli once advised that the most dangerous strategy is to jump a chasm in two leaps. That, I'm afraid, is what Peter has done."

Simeon paused, began to open another beer, then stopped. "Leap one is his theory that most dinosaurs were cold-blooded. It's merely a modern rehash of the old, traditional view of them as slow, lumbering, dim-witted beasts. Peter accuses the hot-blooded revolution of making good headlines and good movies but bad science. He says that the pattern of growth rings in the limb bones of large dinosaurs, such as *Tyrannosaurus*, or the herbivorous *Alamosaurus*, show that they grew slowly, at rates similar to modern cold-blooded reptiles. That's one of the reasons this site is so important. The bones preserve exquisite growth rings . . . better than others I'm aware of. They can tell us whether his cold-blooded theory is full of hot air . . . so to speak."

Meredith wrote quickly in her notebook.

"Are you getting all this?" Simeon asked.

"Yes."

"Good. Peter's second leap involves the Earth being hot and tropical from the Arctic to Antarctica during the Jurassic and Cretaceous, when dinosaurs flourished worldwide. He thinks the big species, like *Diplodocus* or *Camarosaurus*, didn't need to generate their own heat--be warm metabolically. Their volume was so big and their surface area so small that they would have retained external heat. Only the smallest, chicken-sized predators might have been lukewarm-blooded. The newest skeletons from China indicate that they had feathers for insulation."

"Sounds reasonable to me," Meredith said.

"To a reporter, perhaps, but not to most dinosaur paleontologists, including myself. We interpret the evidence differently. In the sociology of science, my dear Ms. Shue, assertion becomes fact when a critical mass of colleagues becomes convinced. Wouldn't you say that's so, Diana?"

"So far, so good," Diana agreed, tipping the Scotch glass. "I'm waiting for the plagiarism punch line. We have all night."

Burke came back into the mess tent, got a beer from the cooler, and sat down at the table near Simeon. Harry noticed he had been lurking outside, eavesdropping on the conversation. Now the talk was about science, not sex.

Simeon nodded at Burke and continued. "The bigger issue is Peter's explanation of how the Earth became a tropical greenhouse during the Jurassic and Cretaceous. He claims it was a massive change in the tilt of the planet beginning 200 million years ago." Simeon paused and looked around for dramatic effect.

"Science has drawn many lines in the sand--the speed of light, gravity, evolution, and so on. These verge on natural laws not to be crossed. One of those lines is the tilt of the Earth's axis of rotation. It averages 23.5 degrees off vertical. It's the reason we have four seasons. The Earth actually wobbles from 22 degrees to 25 degrees every 41,000 years, which might have caused the coming and going of the ice ages during the past two million years. A Serbian named Milankovitch deduced that in the 1920s. I'll return to him in a minute."

"How do you spell that?" Meredith asked. Simeon patiently spelled "Milankovitch" for her, pleased that his sermon was being recorded for the *Pittsburgh Post-Gazette*.

"In any case, the greater the tilt, the greater the difference between the seasons. The smaller the tilt, the more the climate is the same from season to season and from pole to pole. Peter has postulated that the Earth's axis during the last part of the Mesozoic was not tilted at a 23.5 degree angle, but was perfectly vertical. If so, virtually all areas of the Earth received the same amount of sun and heat, reducing seasonality to almost nothing. Peter says that explains how palm trees could grow in the Arctic eighty million years ago. And why it was uniformly tropical from pole to pole."

Harry had to hand it to him. Simeon was pompous, but he held an audience. Jacobs, Calvert, Bruckmann, Burke, and Meredith were rapt. Even Diana was listening with begrudging respect, despite just having called him a fat, impotent gas bag.

Meredith looked up. "What's wrong with that?"

Simeon grunted. "Physics, my dear lady—that's what's wrong with that. There is no physical force that could have knocked the Earth's axis to a vertical position eighty million years ago from whatever it was before, or knocked it back to the 23.5 degrees it is today. Consult any astrophysicist. The Earth is too massive to change its tilt axis. It would violate one of the basic laws of planetary mechanics, the conservation of angular momentum. There is no external force large enough in the solar system to have tilted the Earth and accomplished what Peter says happened. He—"

"Wait!" Meredith interrupted. "How does Peter counter the physicists?"

"How? Blithely! He says they are just wrong, plain and simple, which is preposterous. It's like saying Newton was wrong about the three laws of motion. Or Einstein about relativity."

Diana interrupted. "That's bullshit, Edwin. You're exaggerating. Get to the crux of Peter's theory—actually, our theory—the ground-breaking part."

He looked at her and raised his eyebrows. "Well, I have other adjectives for it." He turned to Meredith. "Peter maintains that plate tectonics was the force that caused the Earth's axis to tilt. Are you familiar with plate tectonics, Ms. Shue?"

"Yeah. Floating, moving continents."

"Good. Alfred Wegener, a German geophysicist, came up with continental drift in 1912. So did others before him. They recognized that the map of the world was a jigsaw puzzle. Three hundred million years ago, all the land masses formed one supercontinent. Wegener called it Pangaea. At the beginning of the Mesozoic, 220 million years ago, it began to splinter into enormous plates—continental masses—that slowly drifted apart, creating the Atlantic Ocean, for example. This drifting, says Peter, caused a drastic redistribution of mass on the surface of the Earth. That made the rotating Earth change the tilt of its axis, first to the vertical in Mesozoic, and then gradually to today's 23.5 degrees."

"That sounds brilliant . . . at least to a reporter," Meredith said, wryly. "If you move blobs around a rotating basketball, it will tilt in different directions. It's one of the physics displays at the Carnegie Science Center."

"I imagine it does," Simeon answered, still condescending. "The trouble is that the Earth is not a basketball, and the continents are not blobs. Physicists don't buy it. No matter how much mass those continental plates have, no matter how much they've drifted about the surface of the Earth, it's not sufficient to change the planet's rotational momentum or tilt."

"So what gave the Earth its 23.5-degree tilt originally?" Meredith asked.

"Good question. Physicists don't know. They hypothesize that the massive bombardment of the early Earth by meteorites four billion years ago knocked it into its present 23.5 degree angle."

"So why couldn't the meteorite that hit the Earth sixty-five million years ago knock it off its axis?" Meredith asked.

Simeon raised his eyebrows, surprised by unexpected knowledge. "Good try. Bad timing. An end-Triassic rather than an end-Cretaceous meteorite impact would be needed to tilt the axis to affect Mesozoic climate on Earth. In any case, physicists discount that as well."

"Okay, wrong or right, who cares," Meredith countered. "That's the stuff of science. All this sounds original. Where's the plagiarism?"

"Remember Milankovitch? He deduced the Earth's wobble and its connection to the advance and retreat of the ice sheets. In the 1920s and 1930s, he was working with Russian scientists on Earth's orbital mathematics—how it might have effected past climate change, including the ice ages. They had the radical idea, long before Peter did, that Earth's climate zones would change drastically if its axis of rotation went beyond its natural wobble—less than 22 degrees or greater than 25 degrees. All they lacked was a force, a mechanism."

Meredith finished writing, and looked up. "Did they find one?"

Simeon folded his hands on his stomach, leaned back, and pronounced, "In fact, they did. They happened across Wegener's book. They seized on continental drift as the mechanism for changing the Earth's tilt angle. They even calculated the effects over the past 200 million years."

"So?" Meredith asked, still puzzled.

"So," Simeon said, raising his voice, "they published their thesis in Russian, in an obscure Russian physics journal. The paper stayed buried there, unnoticed. I came across it quite by happenstance. Peter, I contend, also found it. He stole the idea from that article. He never cited it or credited it in his work. There you have it. Case closed."

The silence was long and awkward. Simeon leaned forward, poured some beer, drank half the glass and sat back, satisfied. Burke opened his orange field book to the gridded quarry map and began marking the bones they would excavate tomorrow. He'd likely heard it all before from Simeon. Bruckmann got up, smirked at Harry, and sauntered out of the tent. His own crimes were no worse than Marchand's. Jacobs began rocking.

Diana put the cap on the Scotch, sobered by the revelations. "Edwin, these are very serious accusations. I need to digest this. I didn't know about the Russian work when I wrote those papers with Peter. Needless to say, I think you are wrong. Give me the journal reference. I'll check the Russian paper and get it translated. If you're right, I will divorce myself from Peter's projects, officially retract the paper, and join you in reporting the plagiarism. If you're wrong, you will apologize to Peter and me at the annual meetings in Pittsburgh in front of the whole society, all 1400 members."

Simeon thought for a moment. "That's fair, Diana, but premature. I will not reveal the Russian journal to you until Peter returns. He deserves the chance to explain this on his own. I owe him that much. Despite his plagiarism, Peter deserves his due for trying to stand science on its end. Milton wrote in *Paradise Lost* that it is better to reign in hell than serve in heaven. Had Milton lived in Wyoming, he'd have said it's better to be the head of an ass than the tail of a horse. Peter has tried hard to be the head of an ass. He's succeeded. It took months of digging to find the Russian article. You are welcome to have at it on your own. Perhaps Przewalski here will help you. He might be better at finding literature than missing persons."

Harry moved his leg off the cooler, got up, put some weight on it, and winced. He debated letting the cheap shot go, and lost.

"You and I are in the same profession, Professor. We dig up bodies from the past and the dirt that buried them. Yours have no consequence. Mine do. It's also time to change the vocabulary. I might no longer be looking for a missing person. Odds are better I'm looking for a missing corpse. And a killer. Maybe even you."

Harry limped out of the tent into the still, cold night.

CHAPTER 27

O<small>N THE GEOLOGIC</small> map of Wyoming, the Wind River Basin is a large taupe blob smack in the center. It looks like a giant amoeba trying to flow in two directions at once, one arm creeping northwest into Yellowstone, the other lapping southeast against the Granite and Laramie mountains. The basin covers 13,500 square miles. Only two highways cross it.

Harry was on one of them early Monday morning, US 20, heading north out of Shoshoni across the taupe blob toward the Wind River Canyon and Thermopolis. On the right, the sun was just rising on the horizon, littering the road with long running shadows of poles and fences. On the left, Boysen Reservoir was beginning to turn pink, as if it were a sanctuary for flamingos.

Harry remembered driving with Marchand across the map, one of his first field lessons. The taupe color indicated rocks that were between sixty million and forty million years old, which covered most of the basin. By then, the dinosaurs had vanished. Volcanoes kept erupting in the young Rocky Mountains, spewing tons of volcanic ash into the atmosphere and trapping the sun's heat. Wyoming became a greenhouse, a hot, humid jungle teeming with furry, hairy ancestors: the first horses, tarsiers, lemurs, hedgehogs, shrews, tapirs, rhinoceroses, and rodents.

The areas on the map with older rocks at the surface were colored teal, blue, red and purple; those with younger rocks were yellow, orange, brown, and chocolate. When Marchand drove to the escarpment overlooking the Buck Spring badlands, he pointed to a small splotch of green on the map: rocks dating to the Cretaceous and the last dinosaur gasp on Earth.

Harry didn't know who had come up with this color scheme but it had long been blessed by the U. S. Geological Survey. Bunches of black lines slashed across the colored swatches on the map. Each marked a geological fault, where huge chunks of earth had heaved up, plunged down or jerked sideways, throwing the neat stone strata into a mangled mess. Geologic maps, Harry thought, were the art of the terrain, a polychromatic history of the surface of the earth. They belonged in museums of modern art, abstract expressions in furious color of four billion years of chaos and calm.

Roberta Karlsen didn't know he was coming. Harry could make the 200 miles to Red Lodge in three and a half hours if the traffic to Yellowstone was light. He'd left camp at five in the morning to avoid the endless stream of motor homes that lumbered west every day like a migrating herd of behemoths. It only took a few minutes behind one of them to wish for a howitzer mounted on the hood.

Harry slowed the Bronco. Ahead, at the entrance to the Wind River Canyon, the road narrowed sharply and twisted under a leaning wall of rock. It was a messy piece of geography. The Wind River, flowing north, had cut a 2500-foot gorge through the Owl Creek Mountains into the Bighorn Basin. The river owed its name to a U.S. military expedition, which had mapped it arising in the Wind River Mountains to the west. Unaware, Lewis and Clark, coming down from the north to the canyon entrance, christened the waters "Bighorn River" for the wild sheep in the Bighorn Mountains. One river, two names, Harry thought; one segment artificially evolving into the other, like a single species changing through time. For the Shoshone Indians, the entrance to the gorge was the "Wedding of Waters."

Traffic in the canyon was light. The road wound north along the east side of the Bighorn River, hugging the sheer vertical wall of the gorge. Burlington Northern train tracks ran along the west side. The Wyoming Highway Department had openly defied the state's adherence to strict biblical geology, erecting large road signs that proclaimed the name and age of the exposed layers of rock: Gros Ventre Formation, 500–600 million years old; Phosphoria, 225–270. At the sign for the Chugwater, 185–225, the canyon suddenly opened into an expanse of blood red bluffs, as if the road had wandered onto an alien rusted planet.

At Thermopolis, Harry took US 120 west and north through the Grass Creek Basin, an optimistic name for a grassless scrub desert. He stopped to fill up at Meeteetse, the old name for the Shoshone "meeting place" on the Graybull River. It was now a one-horse town with a bar, mercantile, and gas station. The coffee was weak and light brown. It might as well have percolated through a cow chip.

Harry hit Cody at eight o'clock. Main Street was already clogged with a long, slow procession of motor homes headed to Yellowstone. William "Buffalo Bill" Cody founded the town in 1896, built the Irma Hotel, named for his daughter, and moved in. It was now a thriving anachronism, feeding tourists his gun-slinging lore. The Irma Hotel staged an Old West gunfight every evening, Monday through Saturday, June through August. After sixty years, Harry thought, it was the longest running play off Broadway, a one-act fable of swagger and bravado, giving the crowd the Old West it wanted.

North of Cody, Harry raced the Yellowstone River along US 120 across the Badger Basin to the Montana line, turned west at Belfry, and slowed down through Bear Creek, Washoe and other ghost towns blackened by coal mining. Historical markers beckoned the sparse traffic to stop and relive rural extinction. Ten miles later, he climbed three switchbacks and descended into Red Lodge.

It was almost nine. Harry pulled into a 7-Eleven next to an old opera house and got out into the cool, hard morning light. He looked up the address for the Karlsen place and got directions from the clerk. Nine miles west into the foothills of the Beartooths, he found the Karlsen mailbox.

The house was a large log A-frame with an extension and porch. It sat in the middle of a grassy meadow surrounded by a thick forest of pines and spruce. Solar collectors on the south roof glinted in the sun before absorbing the rays. A red Jeep was parked outside the garage. At the foot of the porch, Karlsen had anchored a cast-iron replica of the Wyoming bucking bronco. A cow bell clanged in the soft morning wind blowing down the mountain. Harry thought of rolling a Drum. Instead, he let the sharp, bracing air singe his lungs.

CHAPTER 28

HARRY GRABBED THE horned bull on the big brass knocker and thumped. Roberta Karlsen answered the door. It was for women like her that the word statuesque was coined. She filled the doorframe, tall, striking, big-boned and fit. Thick auburn hair erupted out of her head like a lava flow and spilled down to her shoulders. Her face was a broad landscape: broad forehead, broad blue eyes, broad jawbones, even broader cheekbones, and a broad, sensuous mouth with full lips that spoke of the last long smoldering kiss. Only her nose was thin.

It was nine-thirty in the morning, but she was dressed and groomed: a large men's white shirt hanging off one bare shoulder, blue jeans, bare feet, no jewelry, no makeup. She was honest about the creases in her face. Harry could understand why Marchand had chased her. But not why George Karlsen chased skirts on the campaign trail.

"Can I help you?" She gave Harry the once-over. He suddenly felt naked, as if he were being appraised by a porno talent scout. Her voice was husky and coarse, grated that way by years of smoking.

"Mrs. Karlsen?"

"That's right. But I'm not interested in what you're selling." She started to close the door.

Harry propped himself against the door jamb. "I'm not selling, Mrs. Karlsen. I'm detecting. Tell me whether Peter Marchand is holed up here with you. If he is, I'll quit detecting and leave."

Her eyes narrowed for a second, then went back to broad and blue. "And you are?" She was cool, confident, unflappable. If he'd hoped to rattle her, he'd failed.

"Harry Przewalski. The Carnegie Museum in Pittsburgh wants its star paleontologist back. He went missing three weeks ago." Harry took out his wallet, handed her a card, and flashed his license. "It's a long drive from Badwater. I'd have more faith in western hospitality if you'd invite me in and offer me some coffee."

She studied the ID, comparing the picture to the real thing. "C'mon in," she said, and stepped aside.

The A-frame was one huge room soaring to a skylight. An enormous stone fireplace anchored one end, a kitchen the other, with white appliances and counter tops that blazed in the sunlight. The table near the kitchen was a huge hunk of rough-hewn wood resting on an industrial chrome base. Over it hung a large, round chandelier with flat hoops of wrought iron from an old hay wagon. An archway led to the extension off the A-frame. Stairs on the other side rose to a loft that hung over half the room.

Roberta Karlsen pointed Harry to a couch near the fireplace, went to the kitchen and came back with two large mugs of coffee. She walked slowly, with a deliberate grace, holding her left arm slightly out from her body, as if she were going to signal a left turn at any moment. Harry noticed a canvas propped on a painter's easel near the couch. It was shrouded by a length of beige linen.

She slid into a sofa chair, reached for the open bottle of Booker's bourbon on the side table and poured a healthy slug into her coffee. "You were saying, Mr. Przl—"

"Przewalski. Like the Mongolian horse, named for the Russian who discovered it. He's dead; the species almost is, but I'm hanging on. Call me Harry. It's easier."

She chuckled. "Okay . . . Harry. I like horses. I haven't ever known a man named for one. But I'm sure you didn't come here from Pittsburgh to talk horses. What's this about Peter?"

"He disappeared on July 22 and hasn't surfaced since."

"Really? Where did he disappear? Casper?"

"No, from his field camp. At the old homestead. You know where it is."

She didn't twitch.

"Seems he walked out around four or five in the morning. He left his green Chevy in camp. And, maybe, his life. A few hours earlier he'd returned from his usual late-evening sojourn to the bluff near Buck Spring. You know the green Chevy, Mrs. Karlsen. And you know the bluff."

"Go on, Harry," she said, raising one eyebrow.

"Could be you picked him up at the gate near camp. Or below, on the Badwater road. Could be you took him to your place in Lost Cabin—the Okie house. Maybe he was hunkered down in the back when you drove your Jeep to Salt Lake—at least till you were past Shoshoni, or Riverton. Then you came up here. I'm hoping Marchand took off with you. The alternatives are less pleasant." Harry paused, took a gulp of coffee, and pointed up to the loft.

"Tell me he's up there. Or out there." He motioned to the extension through the archway. "If I were Marchand, I'd be here. You're a beautiful woman, Mrs. Karlsen. Beauty is the purest of temptations."

Roberta inclined her head, drank some coffee, and added a

lick more bourbon. "Thank you. I'll allow myself to be flattered. I hope brains are also a temptation, although perhaps less classical. You know, if George, my husband, were here he might have shot you for that speech. Fortunately, he's not here."

"Who? Marchand or your husband?"

She grinned. "Neither. What did you mean by the alternatives being less pleasant?"

"Simple. Promiscuity isn't fatal. Murder is."

She stopped grinning. "What do you mean?"

"Odds were decent that you and he had taken off. Now the odds are that he's more than missing. Maybe dead. Maybe killed."

She pulled her fingers through her thick hair. "I imagine you're trying to shock me, detective. It won't work. But it's a good excuse for a bit more bourbon. You might think it's early, but it isn't. Would you like some?"

"No. I'm not trying to shock you. Do you know where he is?"

"No. I didn't know he was missing. He's not here. He's never been here. And I don't know where he is. Last time I saw him was a few days before I left."

"Where was that?"

"None of your business."

"Right," Harry nodded. "I don't care about your business. Or anyone else's. Until it smacks into my business. Marchand is now my business. Like I told your husband yesterday, it's in your interest for me to find him—alive. Otherwise, the police will make it their business, starting with Crumley in that building in Shoshoni. Lousy coffee, no bourbon."

She looked at him, pensive, pulled her hair back and tied it behind her head. It made her face even broader.

"There's no East Coast bullshit to you. Refreshing. Not like the Washington pols advising my husband."

Harry leaned over and reached for the bourbon. "Pittsburgh is not the East Coast. It's still a blue-collar steel town twenty years after steel went downriver. Where did you and Marchand get together?"

She took another sip of coffee, put down the mug, and clasped her hands in her lap. "What the hell. Like I said, a few days before I left we spent part of the night on that bluff in the badlands. Talking!" She jabbed a long finger at him for emphasis. "Just talking. George was away on the campaign trail. I wanted company. And Peter can be amusing. I haven't seen him since."

"Has he called you?"

"No."

"What did you talk about that night? Any hint of why he might disappear? Or where?"

She thought for a moment. "No, nothing along those lines. Mostly about the course of life—his life, where it's been, where it's headed. He felt he'd lost the controls. That other people and circumstances were steering it."

"Who?"

"His current amour . . . what's her name?"

"Lynn Calvert. The one who threw a fit at the fair."

"Yeah. I see you've heard about that."

"Badwater fodder."

"No doubt." Roberta poured more bourbon. Harry doubted there was much coffee left in the mug. "Anyway, Peter told me he'd ended it. She bored him. He said the sex could make her immaturity tolerable only for so long."

Lynn wasn't too immature for Peter, Harry thought, just too pregnant. Either Roberta didn't know, or wasn't letting on. "Were you the maturity he was looking for?"

She laughed. "He thought so. Do you know Peter? No, of course not. There are two things he fears: A real woman. And a life alone. Go figure that contradiction. Women exist for the serial stroking of his self-esteem. For a while, he convinces himself and the woman of the moment that it's the last great American love story. It's his make-believe. It's the raw ego of an adult dressed in teenage romantic mush. Mush doesn't last too long, Harry. Neither do the women."

"It's make-believe until the wrong woman is dumped."

"Surelyyoudon'tthinkthatLynnorhisex . . . Diana . . . might have harmed him. I know women, detective. Neither is the type."

Harry frowned at her. "Graveyards say otherwise. Are you the type?"

Roberta threw her head back and hooted in laughter. "I might be, but it would take the right man. Not Peter. Like I said, we talked. I didn't say 'made love.' I said 'talked.' He can be flattering, entertaining and conversant. Not many around Lost Cabin can do all three. There's an old Wyoming saying that applies to Peter. He can talk the hide off a cow and the pants off a woman. But not this woman. I like men who have no delusions about themselves. Peter is all delusion. He lies well— mostly to himself."

She paused, reached back and untied her hair. It might just have been a nervous gesture, but it made her breasts rise, thrusting her nipples against the shirt. If she was wearing a bra, it was thin. Against his will, Harry felt himself suddenly wanting her.

She picked up the mugs, went to kitchen, and came back with more coffee. "I've left room for the bourbon. Pour me some, will you Harry?" She picked up her mug and clinked it against his. "You drove a long way to talk to me. Here's to your finding Peter, whatever bed he's in." She chuckled.

"What's the joke?" Harry asked.

"Oh, I just remembered a line he threw at me that night.

He asked me why in the hell George wanted to be governor of Wyoming when he could be governor of my body." She chuckled again.

Harry shook his head. "I don't want to know the answer. None of my business. And the bourbon might tempt me to make it my business." He pointed at the covered easel. "Tell me about the painting."

She got up from the sofa and pulled the cloth from the canvas. She was naked, leaning against the fireplace. Her head was slightly bowed, the eyes looking up, wanton, waiting for the man who would govern her body. The auburn hair matched the fever, a Hopper woman, smoldering yet alone, shoulders high and square, breasts full and heavy and beginning their sag, nipples pink and erect, strong jutting hips, a thick waist, soft thighs, a light silky-haired triangle, long legs crossed at the ankles, red nails.

"What do you think?" Roberta asked.

Harry kept staring at the painting. "Someone wrote that Democritus plucked his eye out because he could not look at a woman without thinking of her as a woman. If Democritus had seen this portrait, he would have torn himself to pieces."

She thought about it. "I like that. It's a self-portrait of what can't be governed. But one can try. Are you married, Harry?"

"No."

"A lady back in Pittsburgh?"

"We're taking it for a test drive."

"Good. Floor the accelerator. Keep the tank full. You don't want to run on fumes."

She motioned to the portrait with almost a sensual mirth. "It's destined for the governor's mansion in Cheyenne. The counterpoint to the traditional portrait—y'know, the first lady in gown and tiara that hangs in the downstairs parlor. This one will hang upstairs in my private bedroom."

"You're not the Mormon your husband talks about," Harry quipped.

"No," she said bitterly, "I'm not—and never was! Don't get me started. He's got this obsession about Mormons, like they're pathogens invading the state. He's Catholic. He conveniently forgets about the thousands of priests who've been buggering the altar boys in the name of serving the church. Remember Bing Crosby in *Going My Way*? Yeah, going to the rectory to bend over."

Her face was inflamed. A crimson splotch spread down her neck to her chest where her shirt was unbuttoned. "Y'know Harry, when I studied history, I came across a quote that burned itself into me. It was in the will of a Parisian who died in 1733. 'I should like to see—and this will be the last and most ardent of my desires—I should like to see the last king strangled with the guts of the last priest.' I plan to put that on my tombstone."

Harry let Roberta Karlsen feed him lunch, a roast beef sandwich with horseradish and a beer. She told him of growing up in Salt Lake City, meeting George Karlsen at a ranchers' political convention, the first lonely winters in the Badwater valley, and rebelling against a life of male politics and pretense. For Karlsen, everything was political, including luring Roberta to Wyoming. She was the necessary accoutrement, the political accent. Life on the campaign trail meant performing for oil men and bankers with more money than personas. Most of them, she thought, were pathetically machismo in their ten-gallon hats and pointy boots, pretending they were cowboys in a John Wayne film.

The subject came back to Marchand. She refused to think that he was dead. He was just acting out his desperate need to keep reaffirming his manhood, either with women or academic feats. He was probably shacked up in Casper or Riverton with someone he'd met in a bar. Likely, the woman had picked him up that night on the Badwater Creek road.

Harry didn't tell her about getting bashed on the head and hurled off the cliff. Or Lynn carrying Peter's child. Or Diana's resentment at being dumped, Bruckmann's brokering of Carnegie's fossils, Jacobs' Bible punching, the Simeon–Burke amour, or the changing angle of the Earth's axis of rotation eighty million years ago. He didn't tell her that one of that bunch probably made Marchand go to ground with his teeth up.

CHAPTER 29

THE DRIVE BACK from Red Lodge was uneventful. A mirage kept shimmering on the baked tarmac a few feet in front of the Bronco, a pool of mercury he would chase forever. It was like chasing intimacy, he thought. Illusive. Ultimately illusionary. Truth was, being a detective was emotionally safe, a solitary confinement of his own making. He could float in and out of commitment with each case. The Marchand business was an opening into emotional engagement. The close would give him safe exit.

Harry pulled into Cody at four in the afternoon under a wretched sun. The heat had turned the streets into a ghost town. He drove the length of the strip, randomly stopping at bars and motels to flash Marchand's picture at bartenders and clerks. He was going through the motions on the off-chance that Crumley hadn't looked hard or looked at all. An hour and a half later Harry did a replay in Thermopolis. If Marchand had stayed here or in Cody, he'd either had plastic surgery or shaved his head.

The sunset began to fool with the light and the landscape, flooding the brown scrub desert in a wet, luscious green. Harry plunged into the darkness at the northern end of Wind River Canyon. The sun was blotted out except for a thin, yellow ribbon strung along the top of the eastern canyon wall. Across the river, a long line of freight cars loaded with coal chugged south along the base of the massive cliff, a toy train dwarfed by the terrain.

He reached Shoshoni at seven-thirty. The lights were still on in the municipal building. Harry pulled a U-turn and parked in front. Crumley was shuffling papers behind his desk, getting ready to leave. Harry checked the picture of the governor of Wyoming. The guts of the horsefly were still sitting on his left earlobe.

Crumley looked up. "Well, Przewalski, found your missin' bonehunter yet? What's it been, two days?"

"He's not missing. He's probably in the ground."

Crumley raised his hands, exasperated. "Don't start down that gopher hole again. I don't have time to shoot the bull, unless you've got evidence. You got a corpse?"

"No, no corpse. Just seven people who wanted Marchand to be one. One of them tried to make me a corpse yesterday in the badlands. Picked up a rock, bashed me on the head, shoved me off the edge of the cliff. "

Crumley shook his head in resignation. "Okay, who was it?"

"Don't know. Could've been any of them."

Crumley rubbed his face. "You sure you didn't just slip and fall and thump your head? Those breaks can get slick. I've seen surefooted antelope slide on those hills and take a tumble. You're hankerin' to make Marchand murdered, not missin'. It's goosin' your imagination."

"Listen, Sheriff. Dump the hayseed act. We've both been around enough to smell death when it's happened. It smells the same in Pittsburgh as in Wyoming. I've got a hunch where Marchand is. But I'm not ready to talk about it. And you're not ready to listen. That's fine. I just stopped in to see if anything new had surfaced on him. I suspect not." Harry turned to leave.

Crumley's voice rose. "You suspect right, Przewalski. I've got better things to do then sit up straight every time you barge in here with a hunch about a body. You got anything concrete? Fork it over so we can check it out. Otherwise, your hunch ain't worth a sack of wet chicken feathers. Sure, some stuff surfaced about Peter. But it's about you pesterin' a respected citizen like George Karlsen. And then goin' up to Red Lodge to bother Roberta."

He poked a finger at Harry. "Yeah, we know. The country here might be big, and you easterners might think we're hicks, but we've got it covered. George told me about your little chat, spreadin' fool gossip about his wife and Marchand. He was madder'n a rained-on rooster. You're lucky he's got bigger things to think about—a governor's race to win and a cattle ranch to keep afloat. Hell, another week without rain and he and every rancher in this area will have jerky on the hoof."

"Can't be that bad. The creek's high. Lots of rain the other day."

"Just gully-washers. They settle the dust and make mud. They don't do a damn bit'a good in the hay meadows or the upper pastures. Growin' grass is like charmin' a woman, Przewalski. You need long, slow rain—days of it." Crumley smiled, almost sheepishly.

"Give me a pen," Harry retorted, sarcastically. "Let me write that one down. Yeah, I talked to Karlsen. Last I heard, it was still allowed under the Constitution. He's good at bluster, but he suspects his wife of dallying with Marchand. I know you don't want to hear this: Karlsen was in Jackson Hole the night of July 21. He could have gotten in his jet, flown here, taken care of Marchand, and flown back without anyone knowing. The campaign trail is a perfect cover. Marchand's not in Red Lodge with Mrs. Karlsen. I just got back from there, but you already know that. She's quite a woman. Too much for Marchand.

Too much for George, too. Anyway, Diana and the bunch are packing up camp and leaving the day after tomorrow. I'm flying back to Pittsburgh on Thursday. I'll call you when Marchand turns up, because I'm giving odds you'll have a body in your jurisdiction."

Crumley nodded. "You do that, Przewalski. I'll be sittin' right here by the phone. But right now you've got nothin' under your hat but hair—at least you've got a good dose of that." He stood up. "It's closin' time. Don't hit any antelope on the way back to Badwater."

Harry did another illegal U-turn on US 20-26 in front of Crumley and slowly headed east out of Shoshoni. There was a large church sign near the edge of town, warning that the road to hell was washed in alcohol. The railroad had built Shoshoni in 1904. By 1906, it had 2,000 people and twenty-three saloons. Now it had shriveled to one bar and 487 people, too late and too few souls for a new temperance movement.

At Moneta, Harry turned north. The headlights played tricks. The black pavement streamed toward him between two white lines. Shadowy silhouettes of jagged buttes converged on him from either side of the road, looming and vanishing like geologic wraiths. He rumbled across the railroad tracks at Lysite, sped past the old Okie mansion in Lost Cabin three miles later, and churned up the dust on the Badwater Creek road toward camp.

Suddenly, Harry slammed on the brakes. He remembered the town dump. He jammed the gear in reverse, backed up a hundred yards, and turned off the road onto a worn track that led behind a thicket of saltbush. He left the high beams on, got out and checked the pile, a jumble of animal carcasses skinned and tossed there months ago, now eaten to the bone. It had been a good year for the trappers. Beetles could strip a beaver down to a skeleton in a week. A bear would take two; a cow three. Harry wondered how long it would take the bugs to pick Marchand clean. There were lots of species in the dump: beavers, coyotes, foxes, muskrats—*Castor, Canis, Vulpes, Ondatra*. But no *Homo sapiens*.

CHAPTER 30

IT WAS AFTER eleven when Harry bounced up the rocky track into camp. A light in the mess tent made it glow like a white alien vessel. He hoped Diana was still awake. After the dump, he was ready for the promise of Scotch, a cigarette, and her angular face. But it was Simeon, beer in hand, reading a novel, and Jacobs, nose in a large Bible with red script down the outside margin of each page. The portable radio was crackling, white noise interrupted by a word now and then. Jacobs leaned over and turned it off.

"Anyone else moving?" Harry asked.

Simeon lifted his head and shook it. "No, the others turned in about an hour ago. They're fatigued. It was stiflingly hot in the quarry and Diana kept us out longer than usual. She still insists on wrapping everything up by Wednesday. The truck will be there in the morning to load up the blocks and transport them to Casper."

"Marchand turn up while I was gone?" Harry quipped. He opened a beer, lit a cigarette from a pack that Diana had left on the table, and settled into a camp chair.

Simeon harrumphed. "No, detective, he didn't."

"And we don't miss him," Jacobs added snidely and waved to clear the smoke.

"He rode you pretty hard, didn't he?" Harry tried to sound sympathetic and failed. "At least that's what the others tell me. About your religious beliefs."

Jacobs straightened up. He was physically unassuming—short, plump, wispy blond-brown hair, a round moon face, white skin, strawberry lips. It belied his assertiveness.

"Yes, Peter did. He called me a Jesus freak. I'm not ashamed to admit it. Proud, actually. I am one. I don't try to hide it." He closed his Bible and lifted it up, as if it were an exhibit for the jury. "Peter had all kinds of misconceptions about us. So do most people."

"Had?"

"I'd like to think I made him see born-again Christians a bit differently. At least I hope so. He didn't like me talking about religion . . . or having a personal savior. I think it embarrassed him."

Jacobs was showing an earnestness that Harry hadn't sensed before. Perhaps because, without Lynn nearby, there were no temptations of the flesh. Or because there was peace in knowing that, in the eyes of his God, he'd rid the world of Marchand, a malefactor.

"Why should it embarrass him?"

"Because, at heart, he could not fool himself. He knew he was a sinner. With Lynn, with Mrs. Karlsen, and God knows who else. I was his conscience. I told him he had transgressed against women, against love, and ultimately against himself. I also challenged evolution—Darwinism. It irritated him. I tried to talk to him about intelligent design theory as an alternative. He scoffed. He said it wasn't worth an intellectual nanosecond."

"You don't hold with evolution, but you're studying to become a paleontologist. That's like an atheist studying for the priesthood. Or a vegetarian vying to work in a slaughterhouse."

Jacobs smiled at Harry and Simeon. "It's not a contradiction.

It's deliberate! Gentlemen, I aim to learn enough about evolution to expose its unproven assumptions and falsehoods. To bolster the evidence for an intelligent design in the history of life. Evolution is a theory in trouble. Biologists admit it in their papers and textbooks. It violates laws of mathematics and chance. It conflicts with the written word of every culture on earth. It is the new religion of secular humanists."

Simeon grabbed the bait. "Bah. Science and religion have different cognitions of the world. Science, by definition, prohibits supernatural explanations for natural phenomena, whether it's life on earth, the motion of the planets, the drifting of continents, or a change in the weather. That's a one-sentence history of the Enlightenment, Jacobs. You have heard of the Enlightenment, haven't you?"

"Yes, of course," Jacobs acknowledged.

"Good! It's why we no longer invoke Thor to explain thunder, the primum mobile to explain all motion in the universe, or the devil to explain bubonic plague. To cite scripture as science insults both. Do you really want to subject scripture to the merciless microscope of scientific accuracy? Do you really want to expose all the errors in the Bible? A flat earth? A sun that stands still in a geocentric solar system? The zoological flapper in Leviticus whereby a bat is classified as a bird instead of a mammal? Jacobs," Simeon bellowed, "your religion is done no service when the claimed word of God is made to look stupid!"

With that salvo, Simeon got up, grabbed his novel, and left. Harry guzzled the rest of his beer and lit another cigarette. In five days, he'd gone from quitter to chain smoker.

"Listen, Jacobs; I don't care about your religious ideology. Tell me, why did Marchand accept you as a student, knowing your beliefs?"

Jacobs clasped his hands and beamed. "He didn't know. I didn't tell him. I am what you might call one of a corps of stealth Christian students. We're invading geology, biology, paleontology and other sciences in universities across the country. We're academic missionaries. We will pervert science into revealing and reinforcing the word of God. We will graduate. There are hundreds of us. We will get professorships in universities and colleges and museums across the country. We will start changing the liberal, secular humanist dogma that students are being taught. We're organized, we're committed, and we're well-funded."

Jacobs sat back and folded his arms. He had a zealot's certainty, Harry thought, a conviction born in credo, immune to doubt.

"Did you sing Marchand this new version of 'Onward Christian Soldiers'?"

"Yes, I did," Jacobs said, pointedly. "Part of our duty as academic missionaries is to sow doubt in the minds of the faculty and their students. Once we're in the program, they can't kick us out. Not if we keep up our grades and pass our graduate exams."

"How did Marchand react?"

"At first he was incredulous. He couldn't believe that he'd been fooled into accepting a creationist into his paleontology program." Jacobs started crossing and uncrossing his legs, then abruptly shot up and charged out of the tent.

Harry heard him run up to the outhouse and slam the door. A minute later, Jacobs returned and sat down by his Bible.

"What was I saying? Oh yes . . . it's poetic justice. Actually, biblical justice. Peter thinks creationists are fools. And here a creationist made a fool of him. He was furious. He accused me of committing fraud, of applying to graduate school under false pretenses. He vowed to kick me out unless I transferred out of paleontology to some other discipline, like religious studies."

"Did he try?"

Jacobs folded his arms again, defiant. "He can't. He has no such power. The university won't let him drop me. Their lawyers know it would expose them to a religious discrimination suit. It would put Pitt's federal research funding in danger. Also Marchand's grants. I told him we'd studied the law in this area. Precedent is on our side."

"I'm sure Marchand welcomed that legal update," Harry said, drily.

"He called me 'a sack of puke.' That's verbatim. He told me he's not bound by university rules and regulations because he's courtesy faculty at Pitt, not regular. He said my doctoral work at the Carnegie Museum was happening only under his sufferance. He swore that I'd graduate over his dead body."

"How prophetic. Did you accommodate him?"

Jacobs giggled. "If you're asking whether I killed him, the answer, of course, is no. Of course, I wouldn't tell you if I had. Not that God wouldn't have forgiven me for taking a life. Just as he's forgiven the killers of abortionists. Peter is, as the prophets put it so well, a whoremonger. And from what we heard the other night, he is also a prevaricator."

Fanatics kill, Harry thought. Worse, Jacobs was a fanatic with a motive—his ordained role in the Christian takeover of academia.

Harry got up, put the beer bottle in the case of empties by the side of the tent, and left Jacobs with his Bible and mission. The cold night was glinting in from space. It was long after midnight. His eyes felt like teeth tired of chewing. His head felt like a tumbleweed unraveling on the rocks as it rolled across the badlands. He imagined Jacobs would say the Lord put tumbleweeds here to show which way the wind was blowing. It was blowing towards Pittsburgh.

CHAPTER 31

WEDNESDAY, DIANA MADE good on closing camp. The last dinosaur block was chiseled loose, jacketed in burlap and plaster, lashed to the wooden raft, and lowered gently to the gully floor. Karlsen brought in the ranch's flatbed truck and front-end loader. Burke methodically recorded the field number of each plaster jacket as it was stacked and cinched down. They buried the quarry under backfill dirt, packed up the tarps, brushes, chisels, hammers, picks, glue and acetone, and climbed out of the badlands for the last time. By next spring, the quarry's gaping lesion would weather and smooth into the contour of the bare gray bluff. It was like the geology of our emotional wounds, Harry thought, the skin grafted over the scars.

Harry found Ken McCarthy, Karlsen's foreman, repairing an irrigation ditch in a hay meadow along Badwater Creek. His smile looked like a horror flick. Years of putting a pinch of chewing tobacco between his cheek and gums had rotted the works.

Yes, he told Harry, he'd heard all the stories about Marchand—taking off with Roberta Karlsen or lying low until she could join him. No, he didn't believe them. He hadn't seen anything unusual on the Karlsen spread in the past three weeks.

And no, he hadn't heard an airplane land or take off from the Lost Cabin airstrip the night of July 21 or early morning of July 22. But one of the ranch hands told him he thought he'd seen Roberta Karlsen in her red Jeep around three that morning returning to the big house in Lost Cabin. She'd come in on Arminto Road from the east, from the direction of the Buck Creek badlands.

Harry followed up with the ranch hand. The red Jeep might have been a Ford truck. Or a Chevy. He wasn't sure of the color. It might have stopped in Lost Cabin or kept rolling. People saw what they wanted to believe and believed what they wanted to see.

At the Lysite general store, the owner, Ella Mae Ransom, told Harry she thought she remembered Marchand making time with a tall brunette who'd stopped to get gas. She was "not from around these parts." No, it wasn't Roberta Karlsen, but everyone knew they'd run off together.

That evening, in Casper, Harry found Diana in the motel bar. There was a C&W band near the front, over amplified, surrounded by oilfield workers, drowning the heat and dust of the day in beer and sentimental lyrics of lament. Diana was closeted in the farthest corner nursing a Scotch. It was a sanctuary, she said, from the tunes the old cow died of.

She told Harry that Burke, Jacobs, Bruckmann, and Calvert would set out in the morning for Pittsburgh in the Carnegie Jeep. If they left early enough, they'd get back Saturday night. She'd booked Simeon, Meredith, and the two of them on United's early morning puddle jumper to Denver, then the connecting flight to Pittsburgh.

Her jet-black hair was parted on the side. It hung over her face every time she bowed her head, tempting Harry to brush it back. The hair went with the dark red camisole. A single white pearl hung in the hollow of her throat. Her fingers were wrapped around the Scotch tumbler, long, thin, almost bony, no rings. She drank, smoked and talked, a personal monologue, pausing every now and then to push the hair off her forehead and throw a glance at Harry to see if he was still with her. The Scotch seemed to release her melancholy, the smoke and peat of her past.

She began with her father. She'd adored him. He'd been a famous paleontologist at Harvard who made his name in the 1950s in the area of the Gobi Desert that extends into northern China. Thirty years earlier, Roy Chapman Andrews led his American Museum of Natural History expedition to the Gobi in Mongolia to find relatives of Peking Man. Instead, Andrews stumbled upon spectacular graveyards of horned dinosaurs, unearthing skeletons of babies, juveniles and adults. Plus the find that electrified the public: nests of petrified eggs. Overnight, the image of huge hulking dinosaurs morphed from cartoon monsters into real reptiles. Like crocodiles in Florida, *Triceratops* had sex, made nests, laid eggs, and brooded their young.

Her father went one better than Chapman. In the Gobi badlands in China, he found a tiny dinosaur skeleton that rewrote the tree of life. It had the unmistakable imprint of feathers along its arms, legs and short tail. It was a dead ringer for *Archaeopteryx*, the earliest known bird from Bavaria. But its collar bones had not yet fused into a furculum, the telltale bird wishbone. It was thumping proof that dinosaurs had sired the world's birds before succumbing to extinction sixty-six million years ago. Evolution had bestowed feathers on birds and dinosaurs, either for flight or hot-blooded metabolism. Only birds survived. Her father's Christmas card that year featured a feathered dinosaur in a pear tree. His conclusions were jeered by science as outlandish. Now they are standard issue.

Diana waved at the barmaid for another Scotch. "Yeah, it's

my third!" She hurled the words at Harry like a preemptive strike. "If I can still count, I can still drink!" She stood up and wound her way through the tangle of bar tables to the bathroom. Harry watched the men stare after her, leaving a wake of desire. When she returned, the Scotch was on the table. She lit two cigarettes, one for her, one for Harry, and slipped back into memoir.

As a child, she accompanied her father on his last two expeditions to the Gobi. Her mother stayed home. They were breeds apart, her parents. She was a Beacon Hill socialite, moving among the fashionable. He was plebeian and unfashionable. She held polite sympathies for Lindbergh and his America First movement. He was an unabashed FDR liberal. Shortly into the marriage, the chemistry of opposites began to repel. They lived separate lives. Diana lived a separate life with each of them.

She had a childhood immersed in bonehunting, but she wanted to study art. Science, she said, put a stethoscope to the world, to sense its rhythms, its incessant beating. She looked to art to tell her how to read the pulse. Then, unexpectedly, her father died. Here at breakfast, gone by lunch. She was seventeen, overwhelmed, suddenly somehow shackled by an obligation to his life.

She scuttled the art, went to Yale, and studied paleontology, a field in which women were rare, and attractive women were preyed on. In graduate school, she had an affair with her mentor, a professor of paleobiology, a charmer, married with two children. They worked long evenings. They traveled together— professional meetings, field expeditions. It recaptured her childhood with her father, except her professor went home to someone else. It was her first in a series of dispiriting affairs.

"I hope I'm not boring you, Harry," Diana said, spitting a piece of tobacco onto the floor.

He shook his head. "No." He thought of his own emotional

contusions. Blue, yellow, purple, Nicole. His personal de Kooning, the scrapes festering on the underside of the skin.

She did a postdoctoral stint as a research scientist at the museum at Oxford. Academic life in England was like its weather—cold, airless, oppressive. The affairs were less about love and more about keeping warm in damp, unheated flats. They ended as perfunctorily as they began.

Marchand hired her at the Carnegie Museum. She wanted to work with him—he was a hell of a good scientist. She also knew his reputation. His apartment had a revolving door. If she chose to open it and go in, she was confident she'd be the woman to close it. She was smart, worldly, and tough. And his match in bed.

Harry stopped her. "Listen, I know the rest. You don't have to go into this."

Diana shook her head. "I want to. It's been more than a year. Time to get it out. But I need another Scotch. And more cigarettes."

At the bar, he got them two tumblers of Talisker, a pack of Pall Malls, and brought them back to the striking woman with the black hair secluded at a far corner table, excavating her past.

The romance with Marchand lasted five years. They lived apart but bedded together. Fierce. Turbulent. Intense. She thought it was a keeper. Until he began to pull back. Until one afternoon when she decided to play, to have him find her lounging naked and wanton on the stairs when he got home. She let herself into his house. Two champagne flutes were on the kitchen counter. Upstairs, two people were in bed. Peter and Lynn, a new student.

She remembered the sequence in slow motion. She'd climbed the stairs to the bedroom, crossed over to him, and whispered into his ear, "You are, after all, a fool." On the way out, she punched the stereo to life, loaded the Ella Fitzgerald-

Count Basie CD, pumped up the volume, and hit track five, *After You've Gone*. She could hear the words as she walked to her car at the curb:

> *After you've gone and left me cryin'*
> *After you've gone there's no denyin'*
> *You'll feel blue, you'll feel sad*
> *You'll miss the best lovin' you've ever had.*

The fool, she realized, needed women to feed the pubescent tumors of his conceit. There was a famous journal article on dinosaur extinction: "In With a Bang, Out With a Whimper." It was a summary of their affair. At least she hadn't gotten pregnant, although she'd wanted a child with Peter.

"We became history," she said ruefully and lit a cigarette. Her voice turned adamant. "No. Strike that. We became collegial, that sophisticated euphemism for hate. In the end, Peter engenders hate. They'll probably find Peter on the open prairie with a pitchfork in his back. You know, American Gothic on Judgment Day."

She brushed the black swoop off her forehead, looked up at Harry and gripped his hand. "Okay, Harry. Don't let this go to your head. You're easy to talk to. You're the first man I've felt a stirring for in a long time." She squinted hard and tightened her grip.

"But you need to understand this. I'm tired of this goddamn pattern, this fervent explosion at the beginning, the dead quiet at the end. Y'know, it's like the fucking birth and death of species. I study it, but I don't want to live it."

Harry stopped himself from leaning closer to her face. He wanted to dip his finger into the Scotch and brush her lips. "I'm going to sit here while you get up, walk out of the bar, go up to your room, and bolt the door. It'll keep until this Marchand business is done."

She nodded, poured her Scotch into his glass, tossed him a cigarette, and left without a word.

In the morning, they left the evening unspoken. They boarded the flight to Denver with Simeon and Meredith and eleven other passengers. The turboprop vibrated down the runway, lifted off to the west and banked up and over Casper Mountain. They tracked Interstate 25 south, two long-running chromosomes coding the landscape. Interstates were the DNA chains of commerce, Harry thought, towns strung along them like genes, some good, some dormant, some mutant. Snow fences zigzagged along the west strip of the interstate.

Coming into Denver, the sky was huge and blue, except for a rust-haze warning around the horizon, like a noose about to strangle them all. Four hours later, they emerged from the terminal in Pittsburgh into a thick, hot, murky fog. If we could blanket an enemy country with this air, Harry thought, we would be accused of chemical warfare.

"Look me up," Diana said. "Even if you think I killed him."

CHAPTER 32

THE POLICE FOUND Meredith Shue at ten-thirty Monday morning, her body as still as stone. She'd been dead in her walk-up on Pittsburgh's North Side for almost twelve hours. On the coffee table, under a pile of newspapers, they found a copy of an article from a Russian journal stapled to a typed translation. She'd scribbled marginal notes in red:

PM theory? Plagiarized?

On her computer they found a draft of a piece for the *Pittsburgh Post-Gazette* about Marchand's disappearance and scientific high-jinx. The article quoted an unnamed senior paleontologist. The police questioned Simeon and Diana, then issued an arrest warrant for Peter Marchand for the murder of Meredith Shue.

On Monday afternoon, the police called Harry. He was in his office catching up on a week's worth of mail. Catching up meant aiming it at the wastebasket. Solicitations from credit card companies, the Allegheny County Republicans, the Pittsburgh Chamber of Commerce, even the Carnegie Museum. Liza probably had put his name on the mailing list to bug him. There was a big envelope with a color brochure from a local Catholic boys' school pleading for a building addition. Harry thought of Roberta strangling a priest with a coil of guts.

He'd avoided the office since getting back from Wyoming. Thursday, at the airport, he'd cursed that no one had stolen the Corolla. All that was missing was a bit more yellow paint from the roof. On Friday, he'd briefed Samantha Mayer, then Preston Stewart, who was dismayed that he hadn't found Marchand. Harry told them he was following a hunch about Marchand's whereabouts, either in Wyoming or Pittsburgh. If he didn't find him, the institute could keep his fee.

On Friday evening, he'd thought of calling Diana, but resisted. Instead, he'd walked along the south bank of the Monongahela watching the sun fade in the haze and the street lights of Pittsburgh sag in the humid air. He retreated to the jazz solitude of his house on Orkney Street, smoked, drank Highland Park, wondered about Marchand's whereabouts, and listened to Ellington play "Cop Out."

When he woke Saturday, half the morning was gone. He was falling off the couch in the living room, still dressed, tumbler on the rug, a lick of Scotch left in the bottle. His mouth felt like a flamethrower. The ashtray had bred cigarette butts. He stumbled to the kitchen, started the coffee, climbed the two flights of stairs to the bedroom, and stood in the shower until he could think. He had the breakfast of champions, if the champion was a rabbit: granola, yogurt, two bananas and three cups of coffee. He put on bib shorts, a cycling jersey that advertised his father's shop, *Velo Europa*, threw his road bike, helmet and biking shoes into the back of the Corolla, drove north and east to Mahoning, and rode the sixty-mile loop along the Clarion River. After the dry desolation of the badlands, Pennsylvania felt like a rainforest.

That night he went to the ball game, one of 9,000 loyal fans lost in Three Rivers Stadium watching the Pirates lose to the Montreal Expos. Afterward, he met Megan in a bar in the Strip District. It was time to bury a relationship that had long been on the coroner's table. He didn't have to say much. She told him she'd already ditched him for someone more corporate to her liking. She wanted the comfort of predictability he couldn't muster. Or master. Improvisation was okay, she said, but life wasn't bebop.

Harry finished tossing the mail in the trash. Outside, a barge hooted on the Monongahela. His office window hadn't become any clearer since he'd left for Wyoming. It still muddied the river and blurred the skyscrapers rising from Pittsburgh's downtown golden triangle.

He figured he knew why the police wanted to talk to him. They'd found his card in Shue's notebook and his name in her notes. He took the Smithfield Street bridge to the Allegheny County Judicial Complex on Ross Street. The building was an 1880s architectural wonder, a neo-medieval mélange of Syrian arches, Byzantine columns, French Gothic dormer windows and French Renaissance roofs. High brick walls surrounded a courtyard, an outdoor fountain, a red granite jail, and a courthouse with a 300-foot tower. Connecting the jail and courthouse was the Bridge of Sighs, the architect's homage to the Venetian original that linked the Doge's Palace and the jail.

The Bridge of Sighs was infamous. On January 31, 1902, the coldest night in the coldest winter in Pittsburgh history, the warden's wife, Katherine Soffel, helped two prisoners, the Biddle brothers, break out of death row and cross the bridge. She'd smuggled in saws and guns, got the brothers past the security gates, and promptly ran off with them, abandoning her husband and four children. Hollywood turned the scandal into a sloppy melodrama starring Diane Keaton as Kate Soffel and Mel Gibson as the brother who gets the girl.

In real life, the threesome stole a sled and fled north. A posse hunted them down the next day, shot and killed the brothers, and seriously wounded Mrs. Soffel. A steel-ribbed corset saved her life, deflecting the bullet above the heart. During the trial, she crossed the bridge twice a day between courtroom and jail, now as inmate rather than warden's wife. She was convicted, served two years, changed her name, settled on Pittsburgh's north side near Shue's walk-up, and died of typhoid fever six years later. Feminists in the 1970s painted Kate Soffel as a victim plotting to escape the prison of a cruel, male-dominated marriage. People, Harry thought, wanted crime to be more than it was—cheap, dingy, dime-store stuff.

The detective's squad room had been painted with leftover cans of hospital green. It smelled as if the air conditioning was only recycling sweat. The metal furniture was state surplus. Harry was ushered to a scuffed gray desk with an inbox marked MAZEROSKI.

Detective John Mazeroski glanced up, put down a manila folder, and took off his reading glasses. "Okay, Przewalski, long time no see. Not since you got us that pervert." He started laughing. "Remember that security guard at the Carnegie Art Museum? He's having a fine time in the pen."

"Yeah, I remember," Harry answered. Every night the guard would have relations with a giant Philip Pearlstein *papier maché* sculpture of a naked woman with pendulous breasts, sagging buttocks and curly pubic hair. The museum called in an art conservator to clean the paper sculpture. She was stumped. She said—with a straight face—that there was no literature on the subject.

Mazeroski was a revered name in Pittsburgh. In game seven of the 1960 World Series between the Pirates and the Yankees at old Forbes Field, Bill Mazeroski was the first batter in the bottom of the ninth, score tied 9-9. The first pitch from Yankee hurler Ralph Terry was a ball. We'll never know what the second pitch was because Mazeroski smashed it over the left-field wall, winning the game and the series. The home-run ball landed in Schenley Park, a few hundred yards from Carnegie Institute.

John Mazeroski was in his late fifties, balding, portly, and looking forward to retiring with a case of Iron City and season tickets to the Steelers. He avoided baseball, tired of being Bill Mazeroski's kin. With Harry, he never brought up Nicole's murder, or the incident at the rural barn north of Pittsburgh. Mazeroski had gotten there first, met Harry when the Corolla skidded to a stop, cuffed him, and thrown him into his police car to keep him from executing a psychopath. It never made the police report or the papers.

Despite the heat, Mazeroski was wearing a sport jacket over a rumpled tan shirt, probably to hide the sweat stains under the armpits. He took a toothpick from his desk drawer and began cleaning his teeth.

"Okay, Przewalski," he said, tapping the folder, "this thing is out of your league. Your tune is chasing perverts, crooked accountants, and alimony cheats. Not murder. Let me have what you got on this guy Marchand. We talked to the people at the Carnegie." He pronounced it 'Car-NAY-gie,' as did the rest of Pittsburgh, rather than 'CAR-negie,' as did the folks in New York who ran the music hall. "We know he's been missing for almost a month. You've been hunting this guy for the past week out there in Wyoming. Where's he at?"

Harry stuck to the straight facts—what he knew, not what he suspected. "Don't know. Looked around. Came up empty. No sign of him. No idea where he's hiding. The sheriff and the locals are giving good odds that he's wandered off somewhere with a woman. At least for awhile. If he's holed up out there, the police will find him. It's what they're good at. It's the kind of detection that takes an army, not one gumshoe out in the middle of a sagebrush desert."

Mazeroski pointed a finger at him. "Listen, none of you

found him cuz he's been back here the whole time, what with this Shue woman. What do you make of this plagiarism business?"

Harry shrugged. "Not much, till I see some evidence. Sounds like we've heard the same stories. You've been talking to Simeon."

"Yeah, but we got more than stories. We got evidence. Marchand bopped her. She got back from Wyoming on Friday. Same as you. We figure she somehow got in touch with Marchand. Or he with her, after he saw her pieces in the *Post-Gazette*. Anyway, she tells him she's working on the plagiarism story, wants to talk to him about it. He says okay, he'll come over. The stupid broad lets him in, tells him what she's got. He grabs this big flower pot, this vase, bashes her head in, and it's all over. We have an arrest warrant out for him."

Harry couldn't believe that Marchand was wandering the streets of Pittsburgh bumping off newspaper reporters. But an arrest warrant takes hard evidence. Maybe he'd been wrong all along. Maybe Marchand had skedaddled back to Pittsburgh, read Shue's reports in the *Post-Gazette*, figured she was being egged on by Simeon, and killed her before she could publish Simeon's proof of scientific fraud. If so, Simeon could be next.

"Sounds like you have his prints on that vase." Harry was fishing.

Mazeroski fingered the folder and disregarded the question. "Okay, here's a head start on tomorrow morning's *Post-Gazette*. Shue's reporter friend, this Cynthia Ballard, found the body this morning when Shue didn't show for work. Ballard had a key to the place Shue had given her. The door hadn't been jimmied. The big vase was on the floor. It had dead grasses in it. They were all over the body. Shue knew her killer. She let him in."

"Prints?" Harry persisted.

"Can't talk about that yet."

"That means you don't have any prints. What did you find at his house?"

Mazeroski glared at him. "What do you think this is, Przewalski, giveaway night at the ballpark? We just got through with his house. He hasn't been home in a few months. Newspapers and flyers piled up by the neighbor. No one's seen him since he left in June. Car hasn't moved. Mail still being redirected to someplace out there called Waltman. We're talking to his neighbors over there in Point Breeze. The Palantier woman checked his place on Saturday. Also the Calvert woman on Sunday. They didn't see him. He's too smart to go home. Probably has a woman somewhere in town. Probably using her car to get around. We're checking the motels."

The phone on Mazeroski's desk buzzed. He listened, grunted, said nothing, and hung up. "You want a fingerprint? Here it is. Shue had some papers from a Russki journal. Also notes about this plagiarism. We showed them to Simeon. He said they were the ones Marchand had swiped his ideas from. Shue was at the Carnegie Library on Friday, checking out this journal and making copies. She had a Russki prof at Pitt translate the articles. Even paid him. We have the translation."

Harry knew Meredith could not have tracked down those Russian articles on her own. Simeon, the conniving bastard, must have slipped her the journal name and dates.

"Let's say Marchand killed her because of the articles. Why would he leave them behind?"

The chair groaned as Mazeroski shifted his weight. "Okay, that's easy. The Russki stuff was buried on the coffee table under a stack of old newspapers. He doesn't see it; she doesn't show it to him. She tells him she's got the goods; he can read all about it in the *Post-Gazette* in a couple days, what's his side of it?"

Mazeroski paused to wipe the sweat above his mouth. "A good reporter, but dumb. No, naïve. Why the hell didn't she meet him at a bar or restaurant? Anyway, he probably searched the place but never thought of checking under a pile of old *Post-Gazettes*. This Ballard woman says Shue was a slob, stuff stashed everywhere. I believe it from the look of the place. Lucky for us. Otherwise Marchand would have found the articles and we're shit out of luck."

"Did Shue tell anyone she was meeting him?"

"Okay, we asked Ballard that. She had dinner with Shue last night at that fancy Frenchie place on the South Side—"

"Le Pommier," Harry broke in.

"Yeah, that's it. I don't know what she and Ballard make, but they must pay reporters a damn sight more than cops. Anyway, if she'd already arranged the meet with Marchand, she didn't tell Ballard. Could be he followed her, rang the bell, and she let him up."

"I don't buy it. What about prints?"

"You don't have to buy it. Shue and Ballard have their prints all over the place. There's also a goddamn set of aliens on that ceramic vase. Along with Shue's hair and blood. This guy's an amateur, even for an academic. We'll run the matches. Ten to one they're Marchand's."

A piece of paper came floating by the desk, courtesy of a high speed fan rattling in the corner. It was doing a better job of blowing papers around the room than dropping the temperature.

"I'm going to leave before you throw me out. Your case stinks worse than this sweat room. No witnesses, no prints. All you got is a couple of articles from a Russian journal that Shue dug up. And some stories from a Cornell professor." Harry stood up. "Forget Marchand. Start checking alibis for the rest of them."

"Okay, big shot," Mazeroski exclaimed, pushing his chair back. "We called the sheriff . . . what's his name . . . Crumley.

Funny guy. Doesn't think much of your abilities as a PD. I'm starting to think he's right. We got a body, a weapon, a reason, and a damn good suspect. You want me to check alibis? Let's start with you, Przewalski. What the hell were you doing last night. And who with?"

Harry looked directly at Mazeroski. "I was with a lady friend. She's now an ex-lady friend. Her name is Megan Bannion. Call her. She's in the book."

The phone on his desk buzzed again. Mazeroski picked it up, listened, grunted, and hung up. "I'm not telling you this, but we got Marchand's prints on that vase that bashed her head in. Give it up, Przewalski."

Harry wound through the maze of desks in the squad room and out the building. In the courtyard, he lit a cigarette, rehashed Shue's murder and Marchand's fingerprints, crossed the Bridge of Sighs, and tossed the butt in the fountain.

CHAPTER 33

THE COROLLA WAS a small blast furnace. He'd left the windows up. Otherwise, he'd have come back to half a dashboard. Pawn shops on Liberty Avenue were crammed with lifted car stereos, CD players, and fuzz-buster units. A client once hired Harry to retrieve a cassette tape she'd recorded at a concert. It went missing with the player that was pried out of her Honda Civic.

He took Forbes Avenue east out of downtown through the Hill District, a tough, low-income neighborhood that had inspired the television cop show *Hill Street Blues*. He hit every red light through the seven-block stretch of the University of Pittsburgh's urban campus. Litter, fast-food joints, a theater showing the cult favorite *Rocky Horror Picture Show*. And twin, tall dormitories that an architect had inexplicably fashioned after a cleanser canister. Students called them Comet and Ajax. Pitt's gothic Cathedral of Learning sat on the only square block of green space. Across Forbes, the stately entrances to Carnegie Institute's Music Hall and Natural History Museum were anchored by Andrew's noble quartet—bronze statues of Shakespeare, Michelangelo, Bach, and Galileo.

Harry parked by the art museum, alongside the thick, smoked glass that enclosed the rear entrance. Inside, the exhibit staff was putting the final touches to the Carnegie International. The institute billed it as the premier North American showcase for the world's finest contemporary art and artists. Andrew Carnegie started the International to acquire what he called the "old masters of tomorrow." Every four years, it drew critics and glitterati from the art scene in New York, Los Angeles, and overseas. Harry looked at his watch. Three o'clock. The gala opening was in four hours.

A semi-trailer was backing through the rear tunnel into the courtyard of the natural history museum. The dinosaur blocks, Harry thought. He climbed the two flights in the rear stairwell to his old haunt behind a dark oak door stenciled "Vertebrate Paleontology" in gold leaf. The suite was lined with built-in mahogany and glass specimen cases. Among them were the drawers holding the fossil primates and marsupials from the Wind River Basin that he'd once collected and studied. Marchand's office was at the far end of the suite. Diana's was near the front.

"Harry!" She rose from behind her desk. It was covered with piles of receipts from the field. "I've been calling you all day. I'm so glad you're here. The police . . . I can't believe Meredith is dead . . . killed . . . by Peter. I . . . I don't know what to think."

"It doesn't matter. The cops are doing all the thinking. Calvert around?"

Diana hesitated, then shrugged. "Yeah . . . she's in the basement. In the Big Bone Room. The truck with the plaster jackets just arrived. We're rolling them in. She's . . . she's jangled. Trying to stay occupied. Wondering why the fuck Peter's in Pittsburgh. And where the fuck he is. So am I. So is everyone." She raised her eyebrows. "Why Lynn?"

"It's about Marchand's place."

"What about it?"

"The police said you'd gone by there on Saturday."

Diana frowned. "Yeah, I told the detective . . . what's his name—"

"Mazeroski."

"Right. I called Peter's place on Thursday. After we got in from the airport. Also on Friday. All I got was his answering machine. So I went by Saturday to check if he was holed up there. He wasn't. Lynn told me she did the same on Sunday. She and the others got in late Saturday night."

"Notice anything unusual? Out of place? Missing? Anything to show he'd been there?"

Diana thought back. "Uh-uh. The place looked dead—sorry, bad choice of words. I don't think he's been there since June, since we left for Wyoming. The windows are still closed. The air conditioning is off. It's hot. And the place smells. Where are you going with this, Harry?"

"Up blind alleys. I'll tell you when I find one that isn't."

"Damn it, Harry; you're holding out on me."

"You're right."

Diana glowered at him. "Okay then, you owe me. The Carnegie International is tonight—the opening. I'd rather not go, given what's happened . . . you know . . . with Meredith. But I have to. Preston Stewart has ordered all the senior scientists to show up. Especially us."

"Let me guess. It's for show. All must appear normal in paleontology at the natural history museum."

"You've got a talent for this private eye thing," Diana mocked. "Yeah, it's for the media, the Institute's board, the Women's Committee, the elite donors. They're all going to be at the International. Luckily, it's only been on the radio-- Meredith's murder, the police looking for Peter. It won't make the TV news until six tonight. Or the *Post-Gazette* till tomorrow morning."

She took his hand, squeezed it, and flashed him a beguiling

smile. "Come to the opening with me. I don't want to go alone. I could meet you here. Or you could pick me up. At seven. I'm in Shadyside, on Bellefonte, off Walnut."

"Hmmm. This means a suit."

She laughed. "There's that detective thing again. Please, Harry, it would mean a lot. And, hey, I promise you will be the only PI there with a great-looking woman on his arm."

Seduction as plea, Harry thought. "I'll pick you up. Seven."

"Wonderful!" Diana beamed and gave him an impromptu hug. "While you're here, let me show you a memory from this place."

The door at the back of her office opened onto an elegant balcony with a marble floor and ornamental filigreed railing. It circled above Dinosaur Hall, providing a dramatic view of five hulking, full-mounted dinosaur skeletons marching north: *Diplodocus, Apatosaurus, Stegosaurus, Allosaurus, Tyrannosaurus rex.* The bones were real, stripped of flesh millions of years earlier by beetles in a Jurassic graveyard in Utah and a Cretaceous one in Montana.

"It's been awhile," Harry reminisced.

"It's all about power—this museum, this hall," Diana stated. "You know the story?"

He did. As a student, he'd worked weekends giving public tours of Dinosaur Hall. Nicole had winked at him on one of them. *Diplodocus carnegii* was the first sauropod in the world to be mounted in a museum—eighty-four feet long, sixty-six vertebrae, tiny head, serpentine neck, long whip-like tail, massive limbs. Carnegie Steel forged the rods and armatures to support each bone. The skeleton became the centerpiece of the museum and wowed the world. King Edward VII asked Carnegie to "get one for England." The rest of European royalty got in line for copies behind the king. Carnegie obliged. He imported Italian sculptors to make exact plaster replicas of each bone. He sent teams to mount the skeletons in the grand halls of the national museums in London, Paris, Berlin, Vienna, Rome, and St. Petersburg. Carnegie's dinosaur became immortalized in a tavern tune.

"Yeah, I know the story," Harry said. "Even remember the ditty:

> "Crowned heads of Europe
> All make a royal fuss
> Over Uncle Andy
> And his old Diplodocus."

Diana laughed. "I'm impressed. Of course, Carnegie was just sticking it to them. Imagine *him*, a dirt-poor kid from Scotland, riffraff, banned from libraries, baths and parks, lording it over the king of England, the president of France, the kaiser of Germany, the emperor of Austria, the king of Italy and the czar of Russia. Now he could gloat. He was the big shot. He had the real goods, not them. All they were getting were plaster copies. It must have been sweet revenge."

Harry looked down at the *Diplodocus* skeleton, the agent of vengeance. A thick bony spine jutted up from each of the massive thoracic and lumbar vertebrae. In life, the spines supported the bundles of muscles, nerves, blood vessels, ligaments and colorful folds of skin running along the dinosaur's back. Now, for support, each spine was anchored to a vertical iron spike welded to the skeleton's steel backbone armature.

"Not many get up here." Diana pointed to the wooden barricade at the end of the balcony. "The city inspectors made us close the balcony to visitors. It's not safe. Especially this railing. They're afraid some tourist will lean on it too hard and fall through. It's historic . . . y'know, the marble and ironwork . . . from 1907. Some board members want to restore the balcony and railing. Others say it's too expensive, chuck history, tear it down, and build a new one."

Harry wiggled the railing. The ironwork was coming loose from the marble flooring.

"Yeah, we wouldn't want anyone falling on the *Diplodocus*," Diana observed. "Or the *T. rex*. Christ, it's the type specimen, Harry, the one Barnum Brown collected in Montana for the American Museum. Most don't know how we got it from New York. Their official line is that they shipped it to us in 1941 to safeguard the *T. rex* in case the *Luftwaffe* bombed New York. What lying sacks of shit. The truth is less patriotic. The paleontology department at the American Museum was broke. So they sold their most valuable asset to us for $7000. I have the correspondence to prove it. The crates arrived here on December 4, 1941, three days before Pearl Harbor."

They made their way down a rear stairwell to the basement. A forklift was ferrying the plaster jackets from the semi-trailer down the hallway to the Big Bone Room. Bruckmann and Jacobs guided each jacket to a soft landing. Burke checked the field numbers on each jacket against the ledger in his notebook. Simeon sat off to the side on one of the old crates containing the Jurassic dinosaur bones from Utah, the ones he'd complained about to Diana in the field. It had yet to be opened, eighty years after the bones had been collected.

Harry found Lynn outside, leaning against the semi. A loose yellow sundress hung off her in the limp air, keeping her pregnancy discreet.

"Thank you for not telling anyone," she said softly, putting a hand on her belly. Instinctively, she checked the courtyard to see if they were being overheard or observed. "I don't understand what's happened. Meredith. Peter. The cops came to see me. I told them to fuck off. He didn't do it. I'm waiting for him to call me."

She paused, then looked up at Harry, desperate, almost beseeching. "He didn't, did he?" Marchand's nightmare had become hers.

"No. I don't think he did."

"But if the police want him, that means he's here, in Pittsburgh, alive. In Wyoming, you hinted he might be dead."

Harry shrugged. "I've been wrong before. You went to his house Sunday morning. Was anything missing? Or out of place?"

"No . . . I didn't notice. I didn't stick around. He wasn't there. He must be hiding out somewhere else."

The forklift returned to the courtyard, belched blue exhaust, loaded the last jacketed block of dinosaur bones and drove it into the museum. In the Big Bone Room, Diana uncorked a bottle of red wine, summoned everyone to the pile of plaster jackets in the middle of the room, and passed out glasses. Harry stood back.

"It's close to five," she announced, glancing at her watch. "We've got the opening of the International tonight at the art museum. Morris, you don't have to go. You do, Edwin. Preston insists on us—on paleontology—presenting as normal a face as we can under the circumstances."

She looked at Calvert, Bruckmann and Jacobs. "Students, I'm afraid, are not invited. Consider yourselves fortunate. Detective Przewalski has kindly agreed to escort me."

Burke shoved his field notebook into his back pocket. "Just as well. I'll be back here after dinner. I need to check some of the field numbers." He turned to Simeon. "Remember the *Alamosaurus* femur you wanted shipped to Cornell instead of here? Then you changed your mind? It made me screw up the numbering in the field."

"Whatever," Diana interjected impatiently. She held up the bottle of wine. "Ever since I've been here, Peter has had the tradition of toasting the end of the field season. This has been an awful day for all of us––a tragic day. Despite that, and despite what the police think Peter did, we're going to continue the tradition. He'd want it that way."

She raised her glass. "Here's to Peter, wherever the hell he is. I'm confident he'll come back to us, that it's all a big mistake. And here's to Meredith. She . . . God bless her . . . can't come back to us. Damn it, she ought to be here."

They hesitated long enough to look uncomfortable, then drank.

Hell of a eulogy, Harry thought. A bizarre sect holding a macabre funeral rite around a pyre of extinct beasts.

CHAPTER 34

HARRY SPENT TWENTY minutes in Monday evening's rush-hour traffic going nine blocks on Fifth Avenue, then took the Birmingham Bridge across the Monongahela to East Carson and wound up the maze of side streets to Orkney.

He owned two suits, a light one and a dark one, both wool, both old, both double-breasted with wide lapels. He chose the dark one. It was as close as he would get to a tux. He put on a white shirt with French cuffs, and a black tie that sported a scatter of faint, chalky fingerprints, with one, at the bottom, dipped in blood.

Diana answered the door. Jet-black hair piled loosely on her head. Liquid hot-rouge lipstick. Gold earrings, dangling, flaunting her neck. A tight red dress, slinking down the contours of her body. Two spaghetti straps snaking across her bare shoulders. Red pumps on black stiletto heels.

"What do you think?" She flashed Harry a brilliant smile and held up her arms, inviting inspection.

"What can I say? There is a reason why Victorian bordellos came outfitted in vivid red and black. It works for me. And I bet it'll work for every man tonight."

"That's the right answer," she laughed. "Keep it up."

Harry took Wilkins Avenue to Forbes, cut around the line of cars waiting for valet parking at the Carnegie Institute, turned into the lot behind the art museum and parked illegally in a fire lane. They waded into the crowd in the glassed-in atrium, an urban reef swimming in black satin. A sign warned against food and drink in the galleries. They needn't have worried— the galleries were empty except for the art, an eclectic splash of paintings, sculptures, videos, and installations by forty-six artists from five continents. The art was a pretext for the occasion, Harry thought. The people had come to the exhibition to be the exhibition. And apparently to drink and eat. The crowd was four deep at the bar and canapé table. Crumley would have called it a high-class feed lot.

Diana stopped in front of a huge, foreboding landscape; a barren, disembodied terrain in endless ruin. "It's Kiefer. He's German. His paintings uncover the necrosis in the human condition." She squeezed his hand. "I need a drink."

Harry spent twenty minutes in line at the bar getting two glasses of red wine and another twenty finding Diana. He spotted her in the crush of people moving slowly up the granite stairs to the art on the second floor. She stood out, pulsing red in a mass of well-heeled black. He followed her into one of the galleries, a performance art installation. A naked woman sat in a bathtub half-filled with water. A frayed, live electric cord dangled over the side, seemingly daring the audience to complete the electrocution. It was all about tension, the label explained.

"What crap," Diana snapped. "Fry that piece of shit out of its misery. What a comedown from the early Internationals— Hopper, Pissarro, John Singer Sergeant, Rouault, Eakins, Cassatt."

At the far end of the second floor, they found Simeon at a

bar table with Preston Stewart and the Princeton faithful on the Carnegie Board.

"Diana. Przewalski." Stewart stuck out his hand. "Glad you could make it. Edwin here tells me that you've had a busy day, what with those dinosaurs arriving from Wyoming." He turned to the board members. "Diana Palantier is one of our chief paleontologists. As you may have heard, the other one, Peter Marchand, has gone AWOL on us." He didn't introduce Harry.

"Preston," Diana said, putting on her best public relations face. "I wouldn't be surprised to see Peter make a grand entrance at this affair. It would be just like him."

"Don't count on it," Harry murmured.

Diana stepped on his foot. "Gentlemen, would you like to see the dinosaurs we've brought back from Wyoming?"

"Don't oversell this, Diana," Simeon intoned. "There's not much to see. The bones are still encased in the burlap and plaster for safe transport from the field. The Big Bone Room is also not the cleanest of spaces." He brushed imaginary Wyoming dust from the left sleeve of his tuxedo.

"Well, I for one would like to see them, dirt or no dirt," Stewart announced. "I'm ashamed to say that in all the years as president, I've never been in the Big Bone Room. Show the way, Diana. The rest of you can stay here if you wish."

Diana led Stewart and Harry through the glassed-in mezzanine to the foyer of the Natural History Museum, down the marble staircase to the basement, and along the old narrow gauge rails to the Big Bone Room. She fished her keys out of her small black purse and unlocked the massive doors.

Stewart's face twitched at his first sight of rack upon rack of black dinosaur bones stretching to the far wall. It twitched again at seeing the body sprawled face down on the pile of white plaster jackets.

CHAPTER 35

"HARRY!—NO!" Diana screamed. "WHAT'S GOING ON! THIS CAN'T BE!" She was shaking, almost convulsing.

Harry walked over to the body. Burke was warm, face down in his own blood, his forehead resting on one of the white dinosaur blocks. There was an indentation in the back of his head, a reddish brown mush of blood and hair where his skull had been crushed. Harry was willing to bet that the geological rock hammer on the floor would fit the indentation. Blotches of blood were smeared on the white plaster, obliterating parts of the catalog number that Burke had written in the field.

"Th . . . th . . . that's Peter's!" Diana whispered hoarsely, pointing to the rock hammer. She bent down to pick it up.

"Don't!" Harry ordered. "Don't touch a bloody thing. Stewart, call the police. Ask for Detective Mazeroski. Use the phone in your office, not here. Do it now. Don't touch the door, the knobs, anything on the way out. Keep your hands in your pockets."

Stewart didn't move. His eyes flitted crazily from Burke's body to Harry to Diana to the racks of bones, disoriented, as if he had suddenly been transported into a macabre play. He started to swoon. Harry caught him before he fell, then grabbed him hard by the shoulders and spoke calmly into his right ear.

"Preston. Pay attention. Go to your office. Call the police. Now."

Stewart opened his mouth, promptly shut it, then half walked, half ran, out of the room.

They spent the next four hours being questioned by the police at the museum and the judicial building on Ross Street. Stewart, still somewhat in shock, replayed the discovery of the body. A distraught Simeon recounted his evening with Burke to the minute. Calvert, Bruckmann, and Jacobs were picked up and asked to account for their whereabouts on Monday night.

Diana and Harry were kept till one in the morning at the judicial building downtown, by which time the wrap-up of Burke's murder was over except for the trial. He was killed between eight and nine o'clock. Two sharp blows to the back of the head. His blood and hair were on the square steel end of the rock hammer. He'd been bent over the pile of jacketed dinosaur blocks, had fallen on his face, broken his nose, and bled over the white plaster. It was Marchand's rock hammer. His prints were all over it. At one in the morning, Mazeroski issued an arrest warrant for Peter Marchand for the murder of Morris Burke.

According to Simeon, he and Burke left the museum at five o'clock, drove to Stewart's house to get Simeon's tux, and then to the Holiday Inn in Oakland, two blocks from the Institute. After dinner, at about six-thirty, Simeon went to his room to change for the International. Burke headed to the museum to check the numbers on the plaster jackets against the list in his field notebook.

Calvert told Mazeroski she was home alone the entire evening. Jacobs insisted he'd remained in his student cubicle upstairs catching up on a summer's worth of science journals.

Bruckmann said he walked three blocks to the Big O in Oakland, ate a couple hot dogs and fries, and returned about six-fifteen to finish cleaning a specimen in the preparation lab down the hall from the Big Bone Room. He and Jacobs hadn't run into one another. They hadn't seen anyone else. None of the security guards had noticed anyone entering or leaving the Big Bone Room or the hallway from the courtyard.

Mazeroski was convinced that Marchand was hiding somewhere in the Carnegie Institute's quadrangle of buildings. He sent an expeditionary force to search the art and natural history museums, the library, and the music hall.

"Hey," Harry suggested, not trying to hide the sarcasm, "check out the crawl space under the stage in the Music Hall. Back in the '50s, Philip Morrison, the famous physicist, snuck in and hid under there when he was a student at Carnegie Mellon. He wanted to hear Albert Einstein's sold-out lecture that night."

"Okay, Przewalski, thanks for the information. You're a goddamn useless encyclopedia."

"You're wasting your time," Harry shot back. "Marchand's not the Phantom of the Opera."

Mazeroski called Harry an asshole and threw him out of his office, then politely told Diana she could go.

Downtown was deserted. Harry gunned the motor and headed up Bigelow Boulevard to Diana's house in Shadyside. She put a hand on his arm.

"Harry, I'm scared. I'm scared to go home . . . to be alone." She paused, bowed her head, then turned to him, her voice a plaintive whisper, almost embarrassed. "Tell me I can stay at your place tonight."

Harry studied her face, suddenly waiflike, at odds with the steamy red dress riding up her thighs. Abruptly, he pulled a U-turn on the empty boulevard, sped back downtown, across

the Smithfield Street bridge to East Carson, and accelerated up
Josephine Street to his walkup on Orkney.

Diana took off her red pumps at the foot of the stairs. She
held his arm for support and put her head on his shoulder as
she climbed the two narrow flights to the bedroom. He gave
her a white shirt to sleep in, went down to the kitchen, and
returned with two tumblers of Highland Park. She'd changed.
The shirt hung to her knees. The black hair, now down, hung to
below her shoulders.

They sat on the bed in the dark, smoked, drank Scotch, and
didn't talk about the sleeping arrangements or Burke's murder.
The wail of a siren drifted up from East Carson. Diana shivered
despite the heat. Harry brushed the swoosh of hair off her
forehead, grabbed a pillow, went down the flight of stairs to the
living room, and settled in on the couch for what was left of the
night. The Scotch helped. He was asleep in minutes.

He dreamt he heard her scream. He was in Diana's office. She
was on the other side of the door, on the balcony overlooking
Dinosaur Hall. He tried desperately to get to her, but his legs
felt mired in mud, moving in slow motion. Diana screamed
again.

"HARRY!" He bolted upright on the couch. "HARRY!"
He took the stairs two at a time. She was standing on the bed,
clutching a pillow against her chest, a madwoman, wild eyed,
her hair flying away from her head.

"I had a nightmare. It was awful. Bruckmann was chasing
me . . . in the badlands . . . he had a rock hammer."

He held her and she nestled into him. The first streaks of light
diffused through the blinds across the bed. He felt her exhale
the rigid fright in her body. She buried herself deeper into his
arms, inhaled his skin and slowly, gingerly, began brushing her
lips against his neck, his cheek and then his mouth, running her
tongue along his lips. Suddenly she grabbed his head in both

hands and kissed him violently, feeling his hardness, consumed by a fevered hunger. She moaned when he entered her and lifted her shirt to caress her thighs and her belly and her small breasts. She rose to meet him, locking her legs, burying her teeth in his shoulder with every thrust, rocking her hips against him, until suddenly she stopped breathing, arched high in the air, and cried out.

They were entwined when they woke. A car's security alarm was blaring in the street. She kissed him, slid out of bed and padded to the bathroom. He slipped into a pair of blue jeans, went down two flights to the kitchen, and returned with coffee and two oranges. On the way up, he punched the CD player. Diana emerged from the bathroom to "Jumpin' at the Woodside."

"Nice," she said, "I love Basie."

"You know your jazz."

"I know a lot of things. I know that this night was sweet." She took her shirt off, slowly wet her finger with her tongue, and began rolling the wet tip around her nipple. "Come to bed, Harry. We have time." She came towards him slowly, the ballet of a sexual acrobat.

Harry shook his head. "We'll wait till this is over. Last night shouldn't have happened. If it's good, it'll keep." Harry could see her face deflate, replaying disappointment in yet another lover.

They drank the coffee and ate the oranges in silence. She changed back into her red dress, put the earrings in her purse, and carried her pumps down to the car. Harry drove her home and walked her to the door. She gave him a weak smile and went in.

He called Stewart at home. "Meet me in the Big Bone Room at ten. Make sure everyone else will be there. Mayer too."

Stewart grunted. He was not used to taking orders.

CHAPTER 36

HARRY BOUGHT EIGHT copies of Tuesday morning's *Post-Gazette* at the Quick Shop on the corner of Craig and Forbes, crossed the street to the museum, and headed down the stairs to the Big Bone Room. He ripped away the yellow tape the police had tied across the big steel doors to secure the crime scene. Mazeroski wouldn't miss it. The police had done all the picture taking, blood sampling, and fingerprint dusting last night after removing Burke's body.

At ten they began filing in: first Simeon, then Diana, Lynn, Bruckmann and Jacobs. Harry gathered them around the long library table at the far end of the room. Simeon looked edgy, a cork of magma ready to blow. The pile of dinosaur blocks didn't help. Burke's blood was splattered across the white plaster, an abstract memento of his sudden death.

Stewart and Mayer were late. Harry didn't wait for them. He passed out copies of the paper.

"Here's this morning's *Post-Gazette*. Read it. Front page."

P-G REPORTER, MUSEUM TECHNICIAN, MURDERED
MISSING MUSEUM SCIENTIST SOUGHT

By Cynthia Ballard

PITTSBURGH, Tuesday, August 16 — Police are combing the city and the Carnegie Institute on Forbes Avenue for Peter Marchand, one of the natural history museum's scientists and a curator of paleontology, for questioning in the murders of *Post-Gazette* reporter Meredith Shue and the museum's paleontology collection manager, Morris Burke.

Shue's body was discovered by fellow *P-G* reporter and friend, Cynthia Ballard, Monday morning in Shue's home on the North Side after Shue did not report for work. Police indicated that Shue died of a blow to the head from a ceramic vase. According to reliable sources, Marchand's fingerprints are on the vase.

Burke's body was found Monday night in the Big Bone Room of the museum by Carnegie Institute president Preston Stewart, museum curator Diana Palantier, who is a colleague of Marchand's, and private investigator Harry Przewalski. They had been attending the art museum's Carnegie International opening.

Przewalski was hired by the Institute to find Marchand, who has been missing since his disappearance July 22 from the museum expedition's campsite in the Wind River Basin, west of Casper, Wyoming. Burke and Palantier were members of the expedition which Shue was covering for the *Post-Gazette*. Burke's cause of death is listed as a sharp blow to the head with a geological rock hammer.

Police have listed Marchand as a fugitive, but are not

confirming whether his fingerprints are on the ceramic vase that killed Shue or the rock hammer that killed Burke.

The picture accompanying the story showed Stewart leaving the Carriage Drive entrance of the Institute between two burly policemen. He was trying to shield his face with his hands, the classic shot of a perp hiding his mug from the cameras. Stewart looked panicked, as if his breeding had not prepared him to be thrown into the underworld. Likely, he was anticipating the displeasure of the Carnegie Institute board. A brutal murder had scandalized the opening of the International, the institute's most prestigious event. And its president was being hauled downtown for police questioning.

"I don't see—" Simeon began to object. Harry stopped him.

"Save it, Professor. I should have done this yesterday. That headline would be about one murder, not two. Stewart and Mayer will be here shortly. Detective Mazeroski too, when I'm ready."

Harry eyed each of them around the table. "None of you has an alibi for the time Shue was killed Sunday night. At least three of you don't have an alibi for Burke's murder here last night. Bruckmann, you were in the prep lab alone. Jacobs, you were upstairs in your office alone. Lynn, you were home alone. The professor was at the opening of the Carnegie International in the art museum. So was Diana. I was with her."

Lynn murmured something unintelligible under her breath. She looked stranded, cast into a turbulence she couldn't fathom. The father of her baby was a hunted man, wanted for two murders and suspected of scientific fraud.

The tall doors to the Big Bone Room opened. Stewart walked in with Mayer. He looked as if he'd just come from a Fourth-of-July parade: blue shirt, red bowtie, white trousers, and blue suspenders. Harry hadn't seen Mayer since returning from Wyoming. She looked like a beaten dog. He suspected that Stewart had done the beating.

Stewart stopped inside the doorway and glanced nervously at the pile of dinosaur skeletons jacketed in brown burlap and white plaster. He had recovered since finding Burke less than twelve hours earlier and being grilled by police until after midnight.

Simeon leapt up. "I don't see the need for this. Peter has gone berserk. He is clearly on the loose in Pittsburgh. The police want him for both murders, Miss Shue's and Morris's. She had the Russian articles. She knew he'd plagiarized them. She was going to expose him. He killed her."

"I can't believe it, Edwin," Diana uttered without conviction, her voice dispirited, sounding the tiredness in her face. A maroon t-shirt, jeans and sandals had replaced the red dress and pumps. "Peter is many things. But he's not a murderer."

Simeon shook his head. "Events say otherwise. I don't know why Peter killed Morris. We witnessed his anger in the field at Morris and me. It revealed him to be a homophobe. Perhaps an executioning one. Peter has keys to the museum." Simeon looked at Stewart and Mayer, then added, pointedly, "and to this room. Right Diana?"

"Yes," she whispered.

Simeon turned to Harry. "Whether or not we have alibis, Przewalski, is irrelevant," he stated, heatedly. "We don't need alibis. What we need is police protection! Which one of us is next? All of you can thank me for calling Detective Mazeroski about it this morning."

"Cork it, Professor," Harry said. "Save it for your memoirs." He looked around the table. "Burke's field notebook. Where is it? It's not in his office desk or field gear. Diana checked this morning. It's not in his house—at least the police haven't turned it up there." Blank stares.

"I sense desperation, here, Przewalski," Simeon challenged, glancing over at Stewart, who took the cue.

"Yes," Stewart cleared his throat. "As you can imagine, I am not pleased with this turn of events. The media is feasting on us. In their report, one of the television stations even stooped to the cliché: 'skeletons in the Carnegie closet.'"

He pointed to his picture in the *Post-Gazette* and raised his arms in exasperation. "Here I am, plastered across the front page, being taken downtown by the police like a common criminal. They're swarming the institute looking for Marchand. They have dogs sniffing through the library stacks and under the stage in the Music Hall. They're searching the dressing rooms and the collection rooms. We're under siege. What's worse, they're finding everything but Marchand!"

Stewart reddened. "They found a makeshift room . . . a . . . a . . . brothel, for God's sake. A bed . . . with a curtain . . . in the basement of the Music Hall! It's shocking! The custodial crew has been running a nightly prostitution racket! The police found . . . uh . . . condoms . . . used ones . . . and girlie magazines . . . and stashes of marijuana."

Stewart twitched and pointed at Harry. "Frankly, Przewalski, after discussing this with Edwin, we blame you for this mess. You—"

"Exactly," Simeon, broke in. "You were hired to find Marchand. You didn't. Not in Wyoming. Not here. Now he's gone on this rampage. So much for paleontologist turned detective. Humph. Couldn't make it in science," he snickered. "Clearly can't in detecting. At least you're consistent."

Harry decided to let it go, then changed his mind. "Hang it up, Simeon. You want to rant and pound your chest, go on talk radio. Better yet, Pittsburgh Theater is looking for someone to play Mussolini. Go audition."

He turned to Stewart. "Go ahead, fire me. Now would be a good time. After you do that, go over to that telephone on Burke's desk, call police headquarters, and ask for Mazeroski. Like you did last night. When you get him on the line, tell him Marchand is in the museum. Tell him I know where he's hiding. If he wants Marchand, he should hightail it up here."

Stewart seemed paralyzed, welded to the floor. Finally, he turned, strode to the desk, and picked up the phone.

"Harry, you—" Diana started to speak, and quit. She had wrapped her arms around her shoulders, hugging herself, trembling.

Lynn stared at Harry, wary of the sorcery that might bring Marchand back. Bruckmann kept reaching for his cigarettes, then putting them away. Simeon burbled once and was quiet.

Traffic must have been light on the Boulevard of the Allies. Mazeroski walked in twenty minutes later. He'd brought a couple of uniforms and another detective. The name tag read "R. Nowak."

"Okay, Przewalski, I'm here. This better not be a goddamn goose chase. Where's he at?"

"Over there." Harry motioned to the pile of jacketed dinosaur blocks in the corner of the room.

Mazeroski looked at him, perplexed. "Where? I don't follow."

"He's in one of those plaster jackets. Encased and moldering. Has been for a month. Since the night he was killed in Wyoming. Surprised we can't smell him."

CHAPTER 37

SIMEON SHOT UP, knocking over his chair. He looked around the room, frantic.

"Preposterous! This has gone far enough," he exclaimed. "Don't listen to him, Mazeroski; he's desperate. There's nothing in those blocks but dinosaur bones. We excavated them ourselves. We wrapped them in burlap and plaster. They're catalogued in our field ledgers. Przewalski's been chasing chimeras ever since he arrived in Wyoming. This one wins the fairyland prize."

"OH MY GOD!" Lynn suddenly screamed at Simeon. "If he's in there . . . he's dead! You killed him, you fat pig! That's why you don't want the cops to open it!"

Simeon dismissed her. "Nonsense, my de—"

Without warning, Lynn leapt up and charged at Simeon. Nowak was quicker. He stepped between them, and gently put a restraining arm around her shoulders. Slowly, she lowered herself back to her chair, holding her belly under her loose blue skirt. Diana gave her a puzzled look.

"Okay, people!" Mazeroski barked and looked at Simeon. "Nonsense, my ass, professor—with all due respect. Show me, Przewalski. This better be good. Or I'll haul you downtown, book you, and take your license for breaking a police seal and tampering with a crime scene."

Harry grabbed his wallet, fished out his PI license, and tossed it to Mazeroski. "Collateral."

He walked over to the pile of plaster jackets. "These were unloaded yesterday. Burke did the tally. It didn't jibe with his field catalog. He thought he'd made a clerical error. It bothered him. Yesterday, he said he was going to come back here after dinner to check it out. He discovered the error wasn't clerical. There's an extra plaster jacket."

Harry turned to Mazeroski. "It's the third one from the top. Check it out. Burke marked it with a red Sharpie. I noticed it last night. He'd made the mistake of telling the killer, who crushed his skull with the rock hammer, then smeared his blood over the mark to hide it. Blood dries darker than Sharpie red. Open it up."

Mazeroski gave Harry a long, hard look, his forehead furrowed in skepticism. Then he grunted, walked over to the pile, and bent over to check the red mark, laboring to keep his paunch from getting in the way. He straightened up, grunted again, and gestured to Nowak. "Roman, get some people up here who can open this thing." Nowak spotted the phone on the desk, punched in a number, mumbled something into the handset, and hung up.

"Wait!" Simeon exclaimed. "The museum owns these blocks. You can't just open them up without cause. You need a warrant! Diana? Dr. Mayer? Preston? You can stop this madness!"

"Can it, Edwin," Diana interrupted. She stood up and came over to the pile of dinosaur blocks. "Harry's wrong. Peter's alive. I'm sure of it. So let's prove it. It'll be the *Alamosaurus* limb; Harry will go home; the police will leave us alone, and we'll have gotten a head start on the preparation schedule."

Mayer spoke for the first time. "Yes, Edwin. The jacket and its contents are museum property. As director, I'm the responsible authority. Open it up, Detective Mazeroski." She stared directly at Stewart, daring him to reverse her decision.

"At least get a professional to do it," Simeon begged, gesticulating with his hands. "The jacket needs to be opened without damaging the femur. It's irreplaceable. We've got all the rest of the limb bones in other jackets—tibia, fibula, tarsals, toe bones. All were in articulation in the quarry, with all the muscle markings. It's . . . it's . . . priceless."

Simeon looked over at Stewart, a last appeal, but he seemed transfixed, staring at the dinosaur blocks, as if he could not expunge the image of the hole in Burke's skull. Finally, he walked over to the pile, hesitated, then gently pressed his hand against the white plaster just beyond a blotch of dried blood. He inclined his head, as if listening intently, his palm a stethoscope. In his red, white, and blue getup, he looked to Harry like a carnival wizard about to divine whether the plaster jacket held the decomposing body of the museum's star paleontologist. Finally, he motioned to Mayer, waiving the institute's rights.

"Okay, Professor," Mazeroski declared, looking at Simeon. "We'll handle this now. It's evidence."

The police technicians arrived, two women detailed from the morgue, a tall brunette and a short blond, both with cropped hair. They put the plaster jacket on a fork lift, wheeled it down the hallway to the preparation laboratory, and lowered it into a 10-by-10 sandbox on an elevated table. The blond unzipped a gym bag, pulled out lab coats, gloves and hair caps, passed a set to her partner, and slipped on a pair of safety goggles.

"Looks like a gigantic albino peanut," the brunette joked, tapping the hard plaster surface. "Time to crack it."

Mazeroski threw her a withering look. Morgue duty bred a grotesque kind of humor.

The plaster saw was an electric drill with a six-inch circular blade attached to the shaft. The first cut screeched into the plaster and burlap. It sounded as if they were sawing through bone, dismembering a body that was still alive. Lynn screamed.

"Okay, get her outta here," Mazeroski hollered at one of the uniforms. "Matter of fact, get the lot of 'em outta here. But keep 'em close. Przewalski, you stick around."

The screech of the saw put Harry back in a barn north of Pittsburgh, hearing Mazeroski tell him how a madman had rendered Nicole into pieces that would fit into a fifty-gallon drum.

"I protest!" Simeon bellyached.

"Okay, Professor," Mazeroski sighed, exasperated. "Protest all you want. Just do it on the other side of the door. Find some cardboard, a big stick, some tape, and a thick magic marker. Make a sign. Walk it up and down Forbes."

The uniforms ushered Simeon and the others out of the preparation laboratory. The blond technician continued sawing a horizontal cut around the entire midsection of the block. A cloud of fine white dust rose and fell on her hair cap, arms, goggles and upper lip. Mazeroski, Nowak and the brunette stood huddled around the plaster jacket. Archeologists at a sarcophagus, Harry thought, waiting silently in the augur of death.

After fifteen minutes the blond quit sawing. She straightened up, took off her goggles, and wiped her mouth. "It's done. It's loose. You can lift the top off."

Harry was surprised how little decomposition had occurred. Marchand was wearing a blue Penney's work shirt, Wrangler jeans and high-top Vasque hiking boots. He looked ready to go prospecting in the badlands. He didn't know he'd dressed for his own funeral. There was a large blood-matted wound on the side of his head. His jaws were frozen open in a last, frantic gasp for air. Odds were good that he was still alive when the murderer entombed him in plaster and burlap.

Harry told Mazeroski they didn't need the coroner to tell them the date, time and cause of death. In the early morning hours of July 22, someone put a window in Marchand's skull. Dead or unconscious, he was wrapped in burlap and plaster, given a fake catalog number, and left in the gully below the quarry amid the pile of jacketed dinosaur bones to be hauled back to Pittsburgh and forgotten.

CHAPTER 38

A T ONE O'CLOCK, the police wheeled the plaster jacket with Marchand's corpse out of the preparation laboratory and down the basement hallway to the courtyard. Stewart, almost apoplectic, lost his CEO composure. Mayer tried to calm him, but couldn't. He stalked off, yelling back at Mazeroski that he was incompetent, that he'd be calling the mayor of Pittsburgh, a personal friend. Mazeroski mumbled "go piss up a rope" loud enough to be heard.

Lynn collapsed at the sight of Marchand in his tomb. Nowak caught her and passed her to Bruckmann. He looped her arm around his shoulders and walked her up the stairs to her student office. Simeon was speechless, his face ashen. Diana gaped at Harry, her shoulders hunched, her body stiff, inelastic, suddenly bereft of lovers. One dead, one deferred. She whispered something about needing a cigarette, shoved her hands into the front pockets of her jeans, and headed down the basement hallway to the courtyard.

Jacobs sat in the hallway, his back against a wall, knees hunched up to his chest, rocking, mumbling. He looked bewildered. Harry wondered whether he was floundering in divine uncertainty—satisfied that the wrath of God had visited

Marchand, or terrified that God might somehow have listened to him.

Reporters and television crews descended on the Carnegie like a locust storm. Stewart, Mayer and Diana held an impromptu news conference in the Board Room. Harry and Mazeroski ducked the press and escaped to a bench along the wall in Dinosaur Hall. The skeleton of *Tyrannosaurus rex* loomed over a group of school kids dressed in khaki slacks and royal blue shirts. The mount was badly dated. It still featured three fingers, instead of two, on its stubby arms. And it was posed standing up, like a kangaroo, rather than pivoted on its hips, head forward, tail back, torso parallel to the ground. The kids didn't seem to care. They stared up at the huge skeleton, awed by its violent swagger, eighteen feet high, forty-seven feet long, a mouthful of six-inch dagger teeth, a seven-and-a-half-ton killing machine.

Harry checked the balcony above the skeletons. The door to the rear of Diana's office was shut. Mazeroski fished a toothpick out of his shirt pocket.

"Okay, Stewart stomped off and called the mayor. The mayor called the chief. The chief called the lieutenant. And the lieutenant called me. How the hell could I have issued an arrest warrant for a goddamn carcass? He said the police had enough trouble in city hall without me telling the Carnegie Institute president to 'go piss up a rope.'"

"It doesn't sound as if you'd take any of it back," Harry remarked.

"Goddamn right, I wouldn't," Mazeroski said, indignant. "Przewalski, it's time to rip the head off this chicken. What the hell is going on here? For two days, we've had an army scouring the town and tearing up this place for this guy Marchand. He was a dead ringer for the Shue and Burke jobs––the vase, the Russki papers, the hammer, the fingerprints. We had him cold. Now we find out he's been dead for a month, rotting in a plaster coffin trucked in from Wyoming. The lieutenant is right. We look pretty goddamn stupid. If it wasn't for you, that damn dinosaur jacket would be doing time in the museum basement for the next fifty years. We'd all be dead when it was opened."

"That was the plan," Harry said.

Mazeroski looked at his watch. "Okay, you got fifteen seconds to gloat."

Harry grinned. "You call Crumley yet? Tell him he had a murder in his county?"

Mazeroski nodded. "Yeah, smart ass, I called him. He's okay, but he talks funny. He said you ended up pulling the right pig by the ear, whatever the hell that means." He looked at his watch again.

"Gloat-time's up, Przewalski. Tell me how it happened out there."

"Simple," Harry explained. "Marchand had a late night routine. He'd grab some beers and take off in his truck to a cliff in the badlands near the dinosaur site. Sometimes he took Calvert. Years past he'd take Palantier. The last few weeks he went alone. Or met someone." Harry decided to leave Roberta Karlsen out of it.

Mazeroski rubbed his face. "Okay, that still doesn't get him tucked into a goddamn plaster straitjacket!"

"That night he got killed it did. One of the bunch went with him out there, whacked him, wrapped the body in burlap and plaster, rolled the jacket down to the gully below the quarry, and drove his truck back to camp. Anyone awake assumed it was Marchand coming back from his nightly jaunt. Bruckmann says he heard the truck return around three in the morning. A few hours later, people get up, and Marchand is gone. He's seemingly vamoosed, but the truck is still there. Everyone thinks he walked out of camp after returning in the middle of the night. Only the killer knew different."

Mazeroski shook his head. "Okay, didn't any of the others notice who left camp that night with Marchand?"

"No. He left after everyone else hit the sack."

Mazeroski took the toothpick out of his mouth, examined it, and stuck it back in his shirt pocket. "Any other way to play it?"

"Yeah. Marchand gets whacked in camp that night, maybe while he's bending over the back of the truck, getting ready to leave. The killer shoves his body into the truck bed, drives to the gully below the quarry, does the burlap and plaster job, and comes back. People who hear the truck leaving and returning think it's Marchand on his nightly run."

"Riskier," Mazeroski suggested. "All that ruckus could wake someone."

"Yeah, probably. But they were used to Marchand making a ruckus before driving out. Loading beer, cleaning out the truck bed."

"Anything else?"

Harry shrugged. "A long shot. Two killers. Marchand drives out that night and meets someone. A local. Prearranged. Someone with payback on their mind. A woman he's dumped. Or a pissed-off husband. Maybe the person surprises him there. Whoever it is knows the routines: Marchand's nightly trips, the plaster-and-burlap operation. Maybe they've been to the quarry site and helped out. Like the landowner, Karlsen. They kill him, wrap him up, drive the truck back to camp, and walk back down to a vehicle they've left on the road below. Like I said, a long shot."

Mazeroski shook his head. "Yeah, doesn't square with Shue and Burke. Need a second killer. Remember Shue's notebook? There's some interesting stuff in there. All of them wanted Marchand missing. Now we know one of them wanted it bad enough to make it permanent. Their alibis for Shue and Burke aren't worth a bucket of hot spit. From what you're telling me, the alibis aren't any better for the night Marchand bought it out there."

The school kids began playing a game around the *Diplodocus* skeleton––leap up and touch a rib. The security guard was nodding off at the end of the hall.

Harry shook his head. "No, they aren't. I can predict what's in Shue's notebook. Marchand discovered what hell was like in Wyoming. Calvert, his squeeze, got pregnant and got dumped. Bruckmann was in the business of stealing Carnegie fossils and selling them overseas. Jacobs conned his way into Pitt's graduate school to be a creationist fifth columnist and bring evolution down. Burke emerged from the closet, gay instead of straight, after he and Simeon put on a triple X show in the badlands. Simeon has two strikes. He wanted to stop Marchand from getting Burke fired. And he thought Marchand plagiarized some Russian's theories as his own. Diana wants to run the scientific show. She had a love/hate thing for Marchand— hadn't gotten over being jilted for Calvert. Shue had all the dirt that was fit to print. And she let everyone know it, just to keep more dirt coming. It got her close to a front-page piece in the *Post-Gazette*. It also got her a bashed-in skull."

Mazeroski nodded. "Okay, I figured you knew most of it. You might as well know the rest. But don't let it go to your head. Cops don't share case stuff with a PI. This one's an exception. You were out there. You found Marchand."

He paused, fished a piece of paper out of his breast pocket, and looked at his scribbles. "Shue's got something about Jacobs taking some medicine for high blood pressure. It makes him piss a lot. It happens her father took the same stuff. Also something about Palantier checking out those Russki journals from the Carnegie Library."

"Does Shue say when? Last Friday or Saturday after she got back from Wyoming?"

"No, she doesn't." Mazeroski got up and put the note back in his pocket. "Okay, I've got the bunch lined up to talk to downtown in about two hours. We've got warrants and we're searching their places. I want to see what we turn up. I want the clothes they wore last night. You made a big deal about Burke's field notebook. I want the bastard who squirreled it away. Our people are going over Marchand's body, but I don't expect any surprises. Oh, yeah, that reminds me. They found a letter in Marchand's back pocket from a guy . . . René something."

"Was it Leclerc? René Leclerc?"

"Yeah, that's it, Leclerc. It's about Bruckmann fencing fossils—sabertooths, I think. To a dealer in Montpellier." He pronounced it "Mauntpeelier," as if it were in Vermont.

"Anyway, Przewalski, I want you in the room listening when I talk to them. It's against regs, but the lieutenant cleared it. And keep the trap shut. Now it's meet-the-press time." He headed to the institute's board room.

Harry watched one of the teachers corral the school kids under the *Brontosaurus*. She told them the label was wrong. These beasts, she said, were mentioned in the Bible. They were not 130 million years old. They were only 6,000 years old, when God created the dinosaurs along with all the other plants, animals and us.

Harry got up and wandered over to the group. The teacher, in her thirties, looked at him warily, then smiled. He considered telling her that coming to a natural history museum to prove creationism was like touring a modern maternity ward to prove the stork theory of sex. Instead, he assured her that she was right—the label was indeed wrong. The dinosaur's correct name was *Apatosaurus*, not *Brontosaurus*. Both dinosaurs were discovered and named more than a century earlier. Comparison of the skeletons eventually revealed them to be the same beast. *Apatosaurus* was named first. It had priority.

Harry wandered back through Dinosaur Hall to the main office. He found Liza alone, whacking out a letter on the computer. She looked up, took off her reading glasses, and beamed a smile that extended the shimmer of her blond hair. He could have sworn it was red two weeks ago.

"Well, if it isn't Sam Spade. Maybe Houdini. A pair of gumshoes, an abracadabra, and poof, out pops a corpse." Redhead or blond, Marchand's murder hadn't disrupted her poise. Or wit.

"I know two things about you," Harry said. "Two weeks ago you were a redhead. And two weeks ago you put me on the solicitation list for the Carnegie. I like giving money back to clients before I've even billed them. Keeps currency circulating, the economy afloat, and my reputation as a socialist intact."

She laughed. "Seriously, Harry, you've got my gratitude. Mayer's job . . . you probably saved it. Stewart stormed in here at nine-thirty this morning, went into Sam's office, slammed the door, and went on a tirade. After he left, she was shell-shocked. He'd just fired her. Because she'd hired you to find Peter. And got the *Post-Gazette* to send Shue out there. Stewart—"

"I thought you said I saved her job?"

"Shush. Gratitude doesn't mean you can interrupt. About an hour ago, Stewart and Sam returned here. Right after Peter's body was discovered. He was furious. Not at her. At the police. He told me to get the mayor on the line. He chewed him out about Mazeroski being inept and rude. I thought he was going fire Sam a second time. Instead, he apologized for being out of line this morning. He admitted you had shown up the police. He asked her to stay on as director. Even pleaded. He said the museum needed stability and good sense."

"What did Sam say?"

"She'd think about it. I hope she stays on. She's one of the good people here. Unlike Marchand."

"What was he like to deal with?"

Liza glowered. "He thought women should faint in his wake. He tried his serenade on me. I wasn't tempted or flattered. I told him that only one person could love him completely, and he was already doing an excellent job of it. I'm surprised Diana fell for the guy. Which reminds me: I saw her on your arm at the Carnegie International."

"Escort service," Harry grinned. "Part of the job. Are the two of you friends?"

"No, not really. She takes me to lunch occasionally. When she wants to pump me for information about museum politics. She was just here about an hour ago. She was wondering whether Peter had asked me to send flowers to Shue last June after she interviewed him for a *Post-Gazette* feature."

"Did he?"

Liza eyed him, perplexed. "No."

The phone rang. She listened, nodded at the receiver and said, "Mr. Przewalski is here. I'll tell him." She was a pro, instantly assuming her formal voice.

"Dr. Mayer and President Stewart are done with the press conference. They want to see you in his office." Liza winked at him, put on her reading glasses, and went back to her letter.

Stewart's face twitched when Harry walked in. Mayer was in an easy chair by his desk. "Przewalski. This is a formal apology—a double one." He sounded uncomfortably contrite. "I've congratulated Director Mayer on her judgment in recruiting you. You found Peter, horrible as it is. She advises me that the job is not done, and I agree. It's paramount that the Carnegie Institute end this nightmare. The museum is in a state of fright. Two of our own, Peter and Mr. Burke, are dead, brutally murdered. So is Ms. Shue. The police are bungling amateurs, and I've told them so. They keep intimating that one of our expedition members is . . . a killer. We can't believe it. We know them too well. There must be another explanation. We want you to find it."

Harry didn't understand the talent in CEOs for wishful delusion. "Stewart, murders are pretty straightforward. So are the people who commit them. They sing in the church choir, give to the United Way, and help blind ladies cross the street. They're sociopaths. They pass for normal till they're driven over the edge. The drive is short for some, longer for others. One of that bunch drove over the edge. He or she is quick, canny, and smart. Too smart."

Harry looked at his watch and stood up. Mazeroski was expecting him downtown. "Listen, you might not like what I find. Your people aren't who you think they are. They're time bombs ticking in your building. You need to defuse them. Start with Bruckmann, before he pawns off more of your fossils. Then Jacobs, your stealth creationist crusader, before he papers over Dinosaur Hall with Genesis and attributes your *T. rex* to intelligent design."

Harry crawled downtown in the Fifth Avenue traffic to the judicial complex. He rolled down the window and turned off the Corolla's lousy air conditioner to keep the engine from overheating. By the time he hit Ross Street, his shirt was soaked. He circled police headquarters a few times before beating a big Cadillac with a pair of pink pom-poms hanging from the rear view mirror to a parking spot two blocks away on William Penn.

CHAPTER 39

"**N**o, I don't want to call an attorney. I don't need one."

Mazeroski had started on Diana by the time Harry walked into the interrogation room. Pittsburgh cops affectionately called it the "confessional." It had either been painted a dirty cream or been left off the cleaning detail. The only furniture was a beat-up wooden table and three chairs, two on one side for the cops, one on the other side for the perp. Diana was in the perp chair. There was an ashtray in front of her and a no-smoking sign on the wall behind.

Harry took the chair beside Mazeroski, facing Diana. She lit a Pall Mall, met his eyes, and gave him a glint of a smile.

"That's fine. I've asked Przewalski here to sit in. We want you to help us get to the bottom of this, Miss Palantier." Mazeroski was a fatherly Jekyll and a gruff Hyde. With Diana he played Jekyll. "Did you and Miss Shue happen to get together after you returned from Wyoming?"

"No, Detective. I already told you that yesterday afternoon at the museum."

"That's right, you did," Mazeroski agreed. He opened a folder and checked some scribbled notes. "I thought she might have called you. Maybe to follow up on the article she was writing for the *Post-Gazette*."

"Yeah, as a matter of fact she did."

"Okay, when was that?"

"Late Friday. She wanted to get together and talk about Peter's theory. I begged off."

"That so?" Mazeroski feigned surprise. "Giving up free publicity?"

Diana waved her cigarette dismissively. "Listen, Detective, after a summer together, she and the rest of them were the last people I wanted to see or talk to. I caught up on things at home. Also caught up with a few friends. Had dinner with them on Saturday and Sunday."

"And paid a visit to Marchand's house," Mazeroski reminded her.

Diana stubbed out the cigarette and pushed the swath of black hair away from her forehead. "Yes. Like I told you on Saturday. To check whether Peter was there . . . or had returned. I knew it was a long shot. I didn't stay long. The place was stale and hot. I believe Lynn went there on Sunday."

"She did," Mazeroski nodded. "We'll talk to her shortly. You had dinner with your friends in Shadyside Sunday night. According to them, it broke up around nine-thirty. You claim you went straight home."

Diana narrowed her eyes, first at Harry and then at Mazeroski. "Of course I did. I was tired. And had a bit much to drink. You can check the bar bill with the restaurant."

"Thank you, Miss Palantier, we have. Did you happen to phone anyone after you got home?"

"Yeah, I called Peter's house—another long shot. But surely you already know that. I left a message on his answering machine."

"Yes, we know you did. Close to ten o'clock. You asked him

to turn himself in and clear his name. Good advice. Too bad he couldn't follow it. What then?"

"What do you think?" She raised her voice, annoyed. "I went to bed!"

"Okay, Monday night you were with Przewalski, here, at the Carnegie art show."

"Yes, the International." Diana grabbed a cigarette and pointed it at him. "Professor Simeon and President Stewart were also there. Along with half the population of Pittsburgh."

"Yes, thank you." Mazeroski, the tough street cop, could ooze graciousness. "Were you alone at any time? I realize Przewalski here is pretty irresistible, but you must have needed a restroom sometime during the evening."

Diana laughed and reddened at the base of her throat. "As irresistible as he is, I let him go get us a couple glasses of wine from the bar. We got separated in the crowd. Christ, it was wall-to-wall people. He found me heading to the second-floor exhibits. It's where we ran into Simeon and Stewart."

She glanced at Harry for confirmation, then shot a caustic glare at Mazeroski. "But, hey, Detective, I gotta hand it to you. I did visit the restroom. There was a long line for the stalls. You can always tell a building designed by a male—never enough stalls in the women's john. One of the women noticed that the spaghetti strap on my dress was coming loose. So I had to do a quick stitch job."

"You always carry a sewing kit, Miss Palantier?"

She mashed out her cigarette, shaking her head. "We women are prepared for anything. Even idiotic questions. Yeah, I carry a sewing kit. And a condom." She grabbed her handbag, a woven straw affair from Africa, and dumped it over on the table. "Entertain yourself, Detective."

Mazeroski pawed through the pile: red lipstick, blue ballpoint pen, green notepad, store receipt, Mellon Bank checkbook, wallet, eyeliner pencil, towelette packet, and a small black velvet sack. He yanked the string-tie on the sack and emptied it: a small sewing kit, the complementary kind that hotels put in their bathrooms. It had a needle and five different lengths of thread wound around a cardboard sleeve. One of the threads was red. It had been unwound. Mazeroski felt the sack and shook it again. Out popped a Trojan Double Ecstasy. Harry wondered when condoms and tea bags began to be packaged in the same factory. The hot purple wrapper promised "Ultrasmooth lubrication."

Mazeroski, unfazed, stuffed the condom and sewing kit into the sack, returned the rest of her stuff to the handbag, and pushed it across the table to Diana.

"Okay, Miss Palantier, about how long were you and Przewalski separated?"

"Who knows?" She threw her hands up, exasperated. "I didn't fucking time it! Maybe twenty minutes, give or take. Harry wasn't around when I came out of the washroom. So I started up the stairs to the galleries on the second level. I knew he'd find me. He did."

Diana lit her third cigarette, took a deep drag, and blew the smoke at Harry. "Is that about right?"

He nodded. "Yeah, maybe a bit longer."

Mazeroski got up and strolled around behind Diana. "Okay, run into anyone you know in the restroom?"

"No, but like I—"

Diana froze. She turned in her chair to face Mazeroski, her eyes open in disbelief.

"Wait a second, Detective," she exclaimed. "You don't think that . . . okay, hold on, maybe I do need a lawyer. Are you implying that I ducked out of the International while Harry was getting us drinks, strolled over to the natural history museum, went down to the Big Bone Room, dispatched Morris, calmly strolled back to the art museum, and met Harry on the stairs with romance on my face? Is that what this is about? You gotta be joking. Are you sure I also didn't dash down to Three Rivers Stadium to catch the bottom of the ninth inning?"

"The Pirates weren't in town," Mazeroski said, drily. "They ended their home stand on Sunday."

"Very funny," Diana cracked. "I'll humor you. The woman in the restroom? The one who told me about my dress strap? A bottle blond, forties going on sixty, leopard skin from too much time in the tanning booth, red nails, big diamond, takes her Chardonnay to the can. But I wouldn't know her from Adam . . . Eve, that is. Ligonier crowd, likely. Probably track her down at the Rolling Rock Club."

Mazeroski grunted. "We'll check it out."

"Do that," Diana scoffed. "Anyway, you can't be serious. Why in the hell would I want to kill Morris? I've worked with him for years!"

"I think you know why, Miss Palantier. Marchand came back from Wyoming buried in one of them plaster jackets. The person who put him there counted on it staying that way for the next fifty years. But Burke got in the way. He noticed the screw-up in the catalog numbers. He said he'd come back after dinner to check. The game was gonna be over . . . as soon as he opens the thing and finds his boss in there. So he gets bopped last night. Just like Miss Shue got bopped the night before."

"Not by me, Detective." Diana cocked her head at Harry and then Mazeroski, cool and confident in her innocence. "I had no reason to want Meredith dead. It's beyond me why someone killed her. And I certainly had no reason to want Peter dead. Christ, he was my professional colleague. We did our field work together, got research grants together, published together. Our careers depended on one another. We were a team—a successful one. He was going to be nominated for the National Academy of Sciences. Working together, I might have made it a few years later—it's tougher for women. Anyway, Morris was an essential part of the team. In the lab, in the quarries."

She studied the ash at the end of the cigarette. "If you're looking for people who benefited from Peter's death, there's no shortage. I'm sure Harry has clued you in. I have my own suspicions. The night Peter was killed, he told me he'd dumped Lynn. He also told me he'd confronted Bruckmann about stealing and selling the Carnegie fossils. He said Bruckmann threatened to kill him. I saw Bruckmann hanging around the old homestead when I went to my tent."

She stubbed out the cigarette and immediately reached for another, but the Pall Mall pack was empty. She rummaged through her handbag again, with no luck. Frustrated, she slammed the bag on the floor and clasped her hands in front of her on the table. "Got a smoke, Harry?"

"No," he lied. "Sorry." He had Drum and papers in his pocket. Her jitters might shake something out. "Who packed up Marchand's tent and field stuff last Wednesday?"

Diana thought back. "I'm not sure. Maybe Lynn. Or Bruckmann. Or both. Why?"

"What happened to his rock hammer? Did you see it after he disappeared?"

"Christ, I never even thought about his rock hammer. It was probably at the quarry with all the other tools. I'm sorry, Harry; I don't know. I guess anyone could have grabbed it at the end of the field season. Who would have thought someone would use it to kill Morris?"

"Did Marchand tell you he'd received the letter about Bruckmann from René Leclerc?"

"No." She furrowed her eyebrows. "Did he?"

Harry nodded. "The police found it in the pocket of his jeans."

"Bastard!" she rasped. "He didn't tell me." The red blotch reappeared at the base of her throat and crept up her neck. Either she was lying, or pissed that Marchand had kept it from her.

Mazeroski paced slowly around the table, his hands jingling the change in his pockets. "Okay, Miss Palantier, it would be human nature to want to take over the project from Marchand after being second fiddle for so long. We understand that. It would also be human nature to resent Marchand getting Miss Calvert pregnant not a year after he and you split. We understand th—"

"Pregnant!" Diana exclaimed. She slowly turned to Harry, her face aghast. "When the hell did you know?"

Harry slumped down in his chair. He watched her begin reeling, her body jacketed in shock, her face spewing the hate of betrayal.

"Fuck you, Harry! What else didn't you tell me? I thought we had something." She grabbed the Pall Mall pack and uncrumpled it, her hands shaking. She probed inside, desperate, as if a cigarette would be granted her as a last wish. If it was an act, she belonged in theater.

Her voice turned to a raw whisper. "I'm sorry, Detective Mazeroski; that was a kick in the gut. Lynn pregnant. I would say I'm happy for her . . . but . . . hell, can one be happy for her now?"

She pulled the ashtray over, grabbed one of the mashed cigarette butts, straightened it out, muttered "Crap!" then tossed it back. There wasn't enough tobacco left to smoke. She got the towelette packet from her handbag, ripped it open with her teeth, pulled one out, wiped the black smudges from her fingers, and wadded it into the ash tray.

"Detective Mazeroski," she turned her chair away from Harry, her face steeled into a forced smile. "You're wrong about the dinosaur research. I didn't want my own project. If I did, there are lots to be had at the Carnegie. Like I said, Peter and I were a great team. Sure, I took over the work in Wyoming. Peter disappeared—" she looked down and shook her head, "was killed. I had to."

Mazeroski pulled his chair away from the table, sat down, and folded his arms. "Okay, Miss Palantier. That's all for now. Stick around town. I'm sure we'll have more questions. If you don't mind, we'd like to have the red dress you wore to the art opening. Before it goes to the dry cleaner. If you do mind, we have a warrant."

Diana stood up, grabbed her handbag, took out a store receipt, and handed it to Mazeroski. "I dropped it off at the dry cleaners on Forbes in Squirrel Hill this morning. About nine. If they haven't shipped it off yet, you're welcome to it. I can save your crime lab some time and chemicals. If you find Burke's blood on it, you might as well check the lining for the Holy Grail. When you're done with it, give it to Goodwill. It's a bad memory now." She turned and walked to the door, deliberately not looking at Harry.

"One last thing," Harry said quietly. "You asked Liza this afternoon about Marchand sending flowers to Meredith after she interviewed him here in Pittsburgh in June."

Diana raised her eyebrows at Mazeroski. "Do I have to answer his question?"

"Okay, you don't." Mazeroski was still fatherly. "But then I'll have to ask it."

Diana turned to Harry. Hostility had replaced disillusionment. "Peter told me he was going to send her flowers . . . to thank her for the publicity. She was going to be out with us in Wyoming. He wanted her to feel welcome. I told him it was a sweet gesture. This morning's paper mentioned that Peter's fingerprints were on that vase that killed Meredith. I put two and two together. He probably sent her a vase of flowers in June. So I asked Liza about it. Peter didn't ask her to do it. He probably had a florist send them. Or delivered them personally."

"How long after the interview did you leave for Wyoming?"

She shrugged. "I don't know. Let me think. The interview was on a Monday. Thursday we flew out to Casper: me, Peter, Meredith, Edwin. The others had driven out earlier. Why?"

"Just details," Harry said. "So three days to send the flowers."

"Brilliant detection," Diana snapped, and turned to Mazeroski. "I'm sure the police are intrepid enough to track down the florist shop. Peter was a pretty distinctive-looking guy. Probably paid with a credit card during one of the those three days. Even Harry can check that out."

She slung the handbag over her shoulder and stalked out. She didn't close the door behind her.

"Okay, quite the little lady that one is," Mazeroski remarked. "Wouldn't want to piss her off."

Harry was still slumped in his chair, replaying the nude dance that had beckoned lovemaking in the early morning light. His time with Diana was done. He'd kept Lynn's pregnancy from her out of compassion. At least that was what he wanted to believe. More likely, he knew not telling her would poison the affair, an interlude lost in a rift of trust. It was his exit strategy against imminent commitment.

"Przewalski, you didn't tell me about the goddamn flowers," Mazeroski bellowed. "We'll check it out, but it works. It puts Marchand's prints on the goddamn vase. Whoever Shue met Sunday night lucked out using that pot on her. Made us think Marchand did it. That, and the Russki articles."

Harry nodded. "I found out about the flowers this afternoon. After you left. Yeah, it works. It worked enough for awhile to convict a dead man."

CHAPTER 40

I T WAS THREE o'clock. Nowak ushered Jacobs in. He looked around the room, made a disapproving face at the ashtray, and shoved it to the other side of the table. His interrogation was short and testy.

"Okay, Mr. Jacobs, that blood pressure medication you take . . . that HCTZ. It's quite the diuretic. Doctors tell me it makes you piss all day and night."

Jacobs frowned at Mazeroski. "That wasn't a crime last time I checked. And, with all due respect, that's none of your business. It wasn't anyone's business. Not till that nosy reporter didn't mind *her* own business and broadcast my prescription."

"And look where it got her, Mr. Jacobs. Is that why you killed her? Let's detour back to Wyoming for a second. We have her notes. Miss Shue suspected you of killing Marchand. He made one too many wisecracks about your religious beliefs. She says people heard you go to the outhouse that night. And you went into the mess tent where Marchand was having his private drunk. No one heard you go back to your tent."

"Lies! That's not—"

Mazeroski slammed the table with his hand. "What happened, Jacobs? Marchand bug you too much that night? Push you over the edge? You lose it? Whack him with a rock?

Didn't mean to hit him that hard? Didn't mean to kill him? Just wanted to give him a little tap, teach him God's simple lesson? We understand accidents. Happen all the time. God forgives those who face their mistakes."

Mazeroski's ploy had no effect. Jacobs sat at the table, hands clasped in front of him, grinning, almost taunting.

"Nice try, Detective. I'm well versed in fables. The moral of the one I just heard is that you can't make a monkey type the Bible. I don't believe Meredith wrote any of that stuff. Except the part about going to the bathroom. Only because I did every night. Yes, it's a side effect of the medication I take."

Jacobs folded his arms across his chest and smirked at them. "Now, if you're smart, you'll ask me who *was* in the tent that night arguing with Marchand. I heard them while I was in the outhouse."

"Okay, who?" Mazeroski asked.

"Bruckmann."

Harry broke in. "Why didn't you tell me this in Wyoming? Or the sheriff?"

"Because I wasn't going to make accusations in front of Bruckmann. Or anyone else. Because I thought Marchand was a fornicator, whoremonger, and liar. He deserved his fate, no matter who inflicted it." Gone were Jacobs' doubts about divine intervention, Harry thought. He'd returned to doctrinal certainty.

"So, you knew he was dead?" Mazeroski pressed.

"No, I just prayed that he was. Of course, I had no idea he was in the plaster jacket. I thought someone had killed and buried him in the badlands. Maybe Karlsen, maybe Bruckmann."

"What were Bruckmann and Marchand arguing about?"

"Something about missing specimens. The wind kept drowning out what they were saying. But Peter was yelling. He was drunk or angry or both. I didn't stick around to eavesdrop."

Mazeroski left the room and came back with a Bible. "Okay, Mr. Jacobs, sometimes I think a monkey did type the King James version." He put it on the table and slid it across to Jacobs. "Especially that eye-for-an-eye stuff. That's why you put Marchand down. You were doing's God work. Shue got wise to it, confronted you Sunday night, and you put her down. Then Burke needed handling to keep Marchand under wraps— literally. Probably helped that he was gay. That too was you doing God's work, right? Cleansing the world of abomination, a two-for-one biblical special."

Jacobs stood up, unperturbed, confident. "Are we quite done, Detective Mazeroski? If so, I'm leaving, unless you plan to charge me with something. Please do. Mr. Przewalski can brief you on our organization of Christian scholars. We have a pack of lawyers waiting to sue for false arrest. You have ten seconds."

Mazeroski eyed him as if he were the chicken, ready to have his head ripped off.

"I thought not," Jacobs gloated, and walked out.

Mazeroski flung the Bible after him. It thumped against the door and fell, cracking the spine.

"Goddamn Bible-puker. Give me a cold killer any day."

CHAPTER 41

MAZEROSKI WENT OUT and returned with Simeon and a manila envelope. He stooped to pick the Bible off the floor and winked at Harry. Something had transformed him into one of the good humor boys.

"Okay, this won't take long, Professor. I'm sure you are as anxious as we are to find the person who murdered Burke, your . . . uh . . . close friend."

"My lover, Detective. It's a fine word, used by Shakespeare and abused by cheap romances." Simeon licked his lips.

"Okay, lover it is. As Shakespeare put it, you protested too much this morning at the prospect of opening the plaster jacket with Marchand in it. Why?"

Simeon inclined his head, condescension tinged with grudging respect. "I'm impressed, Detective. It's not every police officer who knows his Shakespeare. They must have broadened the curriculum at the police academy."

Mazeroski let it pass. "Did you know Marchand was in there because you put him there?"

"No! That's preposterous!" Simeon protested. "The reason I objected so strenuously is simple. Even corny. I was desperately afraid that Morris had killed Peter for my sake, to keep Peter from sullying my reputation. When Morris mentioned the mix-up in catalog numbers Monday afternoon, I thought it was a clever ploy—a preemptive move."

"Oh yeah? How so?"

"Just in case Diana or one of the students had also kept a catalog. They too would notice the discrepancy and ask that the block be opened. Morris could then say he'd checked it, that it was his inadvertent numbering error in the field. The plaster jacket would get shoved into the recesses of the Big Bone Room and molder until kingdom come. Marchand wouldn't be found for a generation."

Simeon licked his lips again and looked around. "Could I have a glass of water, Detective?"

"In a minute. You were with Burke before the International show."

"Yes. We had dinner Monday evening in the hotel. Morris was oddly quiet about the catalog numbers. I did not raise the issue. Morris was fastidious about order and precision. It's what makes for excellence in collection managers, librarians and engineers. It's what the modern vulgar vernacular calls 'anal.' You probably don't know that the same kind of fastidiousness possessed totalitarian despots. Stalin. Hitler. Idi Amin. Interesting phenomenon."

Mazeroski grunted at the phenomenon. "Okay, that still doesn't explain why you didn't want the block opened. After all, Burke was dead, his field notes stolen, all to cover up the extra jacket with Marchand in it."

"Like I said, I thought Morris might have done it. Who else would think of jacketing Marchand like an excavated dinosaur limb bone? I was frantic. I wanted to preserve his reputation. In retrospect, I admit that I behaved foolishly. I was overcome by ardor, overwhelmed by allegiance."

Mazeroski shook his head. "Okay, Professor, I don't buy it. Here's what I *would* buy. Burke was protecting you all right, but not by killing Marchand. Burke was covering up what he suspected you did to Marchand. Maybe you told him. Lovers do that. Hell, maybe the two of you teamed up, whacked Marchand that night, piled him in the truck, drove him out, wrapped him up, came back, and tucked yourselves in. Ardor and allegiance are dandy, but you can't stake murder on that for very long."

"Lunacy, Detective, sheer lunacy!" Simeon bellowed.

Mazeroski nodded. "Most murders are, Professor. You killed Marchand solo or together. Either way, Burke was a liability. So, come Monday evening, you head over from the hotel to the Carnegie art show. You stop off in the Big Bone Room to see Burke. Then it's 'so long, lover.' That's not the way Shakespeare would have put it. But it's good enough for the police academy."

"That's . . . that's pre—" Simeon stammered.

Mazeroski cut him off. "Same deal with Shue. On Friday, you find out she's onto the two of you whacking Marchand. You send her after those Russki journals at the Carnegie Library. You figure she'll focus on Marchand's plagiarism instead of his disappearance. Then, Sunday night, you—or you and Burke—take care of her."

Simeon composed himself, scowled at Mazeroski, turned the scowl to Harry, and threw up his hands. "Preposterous. Simply preposterous. You don't have a shred of evidence to support this fairy tale . . . this twaddle." Simeon looked around for a water fountain, sucking his lips in and out. "Now, Detective, may I have a glass of water?"

Mazeroski went to the door, yelled something, and sat down. A minute later, Nowak walked in with three bottles of water. The label said "Pure Pennsylvania Spring Water." More likely straight from the Monongahela, Harry thought.

Simeon guzzled half the bottle, leaned back in his chair,

clasped his hands over his belly, and began slowly twirling his thumbs.

"Now, Detective, pay close attention. As I told Przewalski in Wyoming, neither Morris nor I had anything to fear from Peter. We had nothing to gain from killing him. My reputation could withstand his slander. So could Morris's. Especially with the mutual deterrence offered by Peter's plagiarism. Peter had the most to lose. He knew it. I knew it. Morris knew it."

Simeon downed the rest of the bottle and carefully screwed the cap back on. Then he promptly stood up, marched to the door, and looked down at Mazeroski, eyes narrowed, condescending.

"If I were you, Detective, I'd plow some fertile ground. Bruckmann. Morris overheard something about Bruckmann selling the museum's fossils. Morris and Peter were going to look into it. And Jacobs was intent on undoing Peter's career at the museum and the university. And Miss Calvert—the fury of a woman scorned. That's the ground that's fertile, Detective. Not Morris, who's dead. And not me, who's sterile. Good afternoon, gentlemen." He inclined his head and left.

Mazeroski stared at Simeon's chair, his fingers twisting the manila envelope. "They all puffed up like that, those Ivy League profs? He's a tad too precious for murder." He reached into the manila envelope and pulled out an orange field notebook and what looked like a single-page letter.

"Burke's notebook?"

"Yeah." Mazeroski grinned at him.

"Who had it?"

"Our German friend, Bruckmann. In his office desk, bottom drawer, under a bunch of stuff. Guy's an amateur."

"And the letter?"

"Y'know the one we found in Marchand's jeans? From this Frenchie guy?"

"René Leclerc?"

"Yeah, that guy. About Bruckmann selling Carnegie fossils to this broker in Montpellier. This one's a copy. Found it in Bruckmann's apartment. Stuck in a catalog of fossils from some New York joint. Here, read it. We got him."

It bore the official letterhead of the Muséum National d'Histoire Naturelle in Paris. Harry skimmed it. "Yeah. Marchand gets the letter, makes a copy in Casper, and confronts Bruckmann. Probably in the mess tent the night he bought it. Marchand tells him he's headed for the slammer rather than a Ph.D."

"That's the way I figure it."

"Keep Bruckmann for last."

"I'm ahead of you, Przewalski."

CHAPTER 42

LYNN ARRIVED IN a wrinkled burgundy T-shirt, jeans and open sandals. She looked disheveled, her face anguished, her eyes vacant, the skin around them swollen. It wasn't from crying, Harry thought. More like a woman imprisoned in an accursed dream trying to blind herself. Marchand, her lover, missing for weeks, turns up as a cadaver after suffering the least comfortable of deaths. The unborn child was now hers, not theirs.

Mazeroski told her the questioning would be short. He kept his word. She knew more about the night of July 21 than she had let on. She went to bed at about ten and woke an hour later. She needed water for her anti-nausea pill. Morning sickness from the pregnancy was arriving at night.

"I saw the lantern was on in the mess tent. Peter and Diana were inside. I could hear him yelling. About Simeon. Y'know, the constant baiting about plagiarism, the Russian articles. He swore he'd dig them up, get them translated, prove his ideas were original. She tried to calm him down. But he kept going on about calling Simeon on it. In public. At the meetings here . . . at the Carnegie . . . in October. He'd make him retract his insinuations and apologize."

She began to cry, silently letting the tears flow down her

cheeks. "I didn't go into the tent. He was drunk. I was afraid he'd start yelling at me about the baby in front of Diana. Or tell me how much I revolted him now. So, I didn't go in."

Lynn grabbed the bottom of her T-shirt and pulled it up to wipe her face. It came away with dark splotches. "But I should have. Maybe it would have distracted him. He might have stayed back . . . maybe not gone off that night. He'd still be alive."

Mazeroski nodded, sympathetically. "Maybe. Unless, of course, it was you who went out there with him that night, Miss Calvert. Maybe you had a fight. He said you revolted him, that you and the kid were history. You got so furious you picked up a rock and hit him before you realized what you did. We understand crimes of passion. Happens all the time."

"NO!" She stood up, fists clenched. "Yeah, I hated him at first. But I was sure he would come back to me. I could never kill him—anyone—like that. Not the father of this child." She unclenched her fists, clasped her hands on her belly, and sat down. "I didn't go out to the badlands with him that night. I was nauseated, remember? I went back to my tent. I managed to swallow the pill without water."

"What about Mr. Jacobs? Was he around? Going to the outhouse?"

She shook her head. "No. At least I didn't see him."

"And Bruckmann?" Harry asked.

She looked at him and grimaced. "Yeah, he was out there. Smoking. Y'know, on the wall of the old homestead, like every night."

"Did you talk to him?"

"No. He's not exactly Mr. Friendly. Even he and Peter weren't talking the last few weeks. It seemed Peter was really pissed off at him about something."

"Did Peter tell you what it was?"

"No." Suddenly, she put her hands to her head. "Oh my God!

What if Gunther drove out with him that night. He's . . . he's strong enough to . . . to . . . "

"Roll a body over," Harry said, as gently as he could, "plaster it up, and lower the heavy jacket with Peter inside to the bottom of the gully."

Lynn bolted up from the chair and ran out of room, hand over her mouth.

Mazeroski sat back and shrugged. "And here I thought I might've been a bit rough on her. You're not good with women, Przewalski. Anyway, the bunch of 'em are either clean, or damn good liars. Looks like they connived to finger Bruckmann."

"Don't think so," Harry answered. "But he's the most obvious. Anyway, the killing's done. There won't be any more bodies. Marchand was the primary target. Shue and Burke were cleanup."

CHAPTER 43

BRUCKMANN FOLLOWED MAZEROSKI into the room, pulled the chair away from the table, sat down, folded his arms across his chest, and hunched his eyebrows in sullen suspicion.

"You know, I don't have to do this. I don't have to answer any of your questions."

Mazeroski eyed him like he would a Hill District punk. "Okay, Mr. Bruckmann. You can choose not to answer any questions. You can even leave. You are here voluntarily to help the police solve three murders. Two of the victims were your close associates. But, if you want to play hardball, we will arrest you on suspicion of murder, let you call a lawyer, and then start asking questions."

He paused, picked up Burke's notebook for Bruckmann to see, and put it back on the table. "What's it going to be? Talk now or talk later?"

Bruckmann eyed the ashtray, Diana's Pall Mall butts, and began to pull out his cigarettes. Mazeroski shook his head and pointed at the no smoking sign. Bruckmann had come in hostile. He wasn't going to get any breaks.

Mazeroski didn't waste any time. He pushed Burke's notebook across the table. "Okay. It's Burke's notebook. You've seen it before. We found it at the bottom of the third drawer of your office desk. You might as well have left it on top of the desk. Did you hide it there right after you killed him? Or the next day, after we found Marchand in the block?"

"Are my prints on it, Detective?"

"We're asking the questions, smart guy."

"Fuck you, Detect—"

Mazeroski leapt up, sending his chair catapulting behind him, and started around the table. "Listen, buster, you're here in this country on a student visa. U.S. Immigration is one block over. One more crack like that and you'll be back in Germany on the next Luftwaffe flight."

Bruckmann couldn't stop himself. "Surely you mean Lufthansa," he cackled.

"No, asshole, I mean *Luftwaffe*. One of the Junkers that my old man shot down. Now, let's start over again. Tell us about the notebook."

"First time I've seen it since Burke had it Monday afternoon. Look, Detective, anyone could have planted the notebook in my desk. Diana. Lynn. Simeon. Jacobs. Even one of your policemen."

Mazeroski started to get up again, but Harry held out his hand. "Wyoming, Bruckmann. I let everyone think it was an accident. But I saw you. Remember the bash on the head? The shove off the cliff? Look at me, Bruckmann. You tried to kill me, but missed. You didn't miss with Marchand, Shue, or Burke. The punishment in Pennsylvania for not missing is lethal injection. Same in Wyoming. Lucky for you, you can only be executed once. Chances are they'll fight over who gets to do it first."

Bruckmann's face curdled to chalk. He made a second pass at his cigarettes and tried to speak, then started shaking. It looked to Harry like an epilepsy of fright. He was down, but Mazeroski kicked him again.

"Okay, Bruckmann, you look like puke. There's a pail over there if you need it. I don't want you to spray that stuff over Burke's notebook." He shoved the letter from Leclerc across the table. "Or over the copy of this letter. You know, the one to Marchand detailing your traffic in stolen fossils. Yeah, your prints are all over it. No one planted that in your apartment. Your colleagues tell us you threatened to kill him. You waited up that night, whacked him, drove him to the quarries, plastered him up, and drove back, no one the wiser."

Bruckman leaned forward and clasped the table with his hands. It helped him stop shaking. "They're liars. I didn't kill anyone. Sure, Marchand gave me the letter. I explained that I was just loaning fossils to the broker. They were a demo. To show the broker the kind of specimens I could get for his private clients—legally. They were interested in fossil ivory. But he wouldn't give me an advance unless I could show him an example. I sent him some saber tooth material. It was just a temporary loan."

Harry interjected. "Try harder, Bruckmann. Marchand wouldn't fall for such lame bullshit. At best it was dirty collateral on a trade. At worst you were selling the stuff outright. What about the hit and run on me in the badlands?"

Bruckmann looked up at the ceiling tiles, the same pasty white as his face. He took his time, as if he were weighing the cost of coming clean.

"You know what? I'm sorry, Harry . . . Mr. Przewalski." His voice went from surly to sociable, almost repentant. "I didn't try to kill you. Just scare you. When you showed me the envelope from Leclerc, I panicked. I'd searched Peter's tent and didn't see it. I thought I'd gotten lucky. Maybe Peter had taken off and wouldn't come back. Maybe some jealous husband had killed him. No one would find out about the French broker. Then you showed up with the envelope. And the letter, I thought. I was planning to convince Peter to let me leave quietly. No publicity, no embarrassment about fossils disappearing from the museum. He would have agreed. But I figured you wouldn't. You would have reported me to Stewart and Mayer. And probably Diana. That bitch wouldn't give anyone a second chance. But I didn't kill anyone. I swear it."

The door opened. Nowak came in and handed Mazeroski a piece of paper. He read it, folded it, sighed, and refocused on Bruckmann.

"Okay, Bruckmann, not good enough. Shue figured out the fossil business. It's in her notebook. She called you on it when you got back from Wyoming. You went up to her place, grabbed the vase, and bashed her head in. Like you whacked Marchand. And tried to whack Przewalski. You just hit Marchand and Shue a bit harder. Either that or it's Przewalski's thick Polack skull. Then you whacked Burke. He was just down the hall from the preparation lab, where you were working last night. Plenty of time to saunter in, ask how's things, hear him explain why he's marking Marchand's plaster jacket with the red Sharpie, ping him with the rock hammer, spread a little blood over the red mark, grab the field notebook, and hightail it back to the lab. I bet—"

"No! I didn't—"

Mazeroski steamrollered over him. "I bet we won't find any blood spatter on your clothes. I bet you were wearing a lab coat. Guess what, Bruckmann? I just won both bets! You didn't have time to dump the lab coat. Roman here tells me the guys just found it in a storage closet in the preparation lab, tucked behind sacks of plaster. You were in a hurry after you killed

Burke. So you stuffed it there. It's marked 'BRUCKMANN' on the collar and it's got little red spots on it."

Bruckmann leapt up. "I'm being—" he burst out, and abruptly clamped shut. "A lawyer! I want a lawyer!"

"Get a good one. You'll need good lawyering down the road."

Mazeroski motioned to Nowak. "Roman, book Mr. Bruckmann here. Read him his rights. We got enough to hold him, enough to introduce him to American jails. Tell him we're impounding his passport."

Outside, on the Bridge of Sighs, the late afternoon air was steamy and close. Mazeroski took off his sport jacket. Sweat had already begun to stain his tan shirt below his armpits. He and Przewalski leaned against the stone railing. Muck, coins and cigarette butts littered the bottom of the shallow pond. It probably wasn't any cleaner in Venice, Harry thought.

"Christ, it's a goddamn open pit furnace out here." Mazeroski was breathing heavily, almost wheezing.

"Burke's blood on it? The lab coat?" Harry asked.

"Right now it's just blood. When the tests are done, it'll be Burke's blood."

He took out a pack of Camels and gave one to Harry. "It's the only time I smoke. When I make a case." He lit the cigarette and shook his head, almost in disgust. "I nearly lost it with Bruckmann. He's an asshole, but it's not his generation that did what they did. To my old man. To others." He flicked the ashes into the pond, took another drag of the Camel, then straightened up from his reverie. "Anyway, Przewalski, we have enough for the D.A. The lab coat makes the case. We've gotten convictions on less."

"I wondered about the lab coat," Harry said. "There were a couple lying around the Big Bone Room yesterday." He tossed the half-smoked cigarette off the bridge. "I'm going back up there to tell Mayer and Stewart that it's over. Also Diana, if she's around." She started tunneling in his head.

Mazeroski smiled at him. "Okay, Harry, this isn't my business. But that woman isn't worth losing over a goddamn case. Catch up to her. Practice a few *mea culpas* driving up Forbes. And if you run into Simeon, give him a message from me: we had Shakespeare every day in the police academy, followed by heavy doses of Latin."

CHAPTER 44

BY FRIDAY, THREE days later, little had happened. The city continued to steam. A sticky, yellow air mass liked the sky over Pittsburgh and lingered. By midday, the streets were boiling over in sweat, smog, and distemper. The National Weather Service issued an inversion alert, warning anyone with lungs to stay inside. During rush-hour traffic, air conditioners went full bore but didn't cool or condition. They coughed more smog and strangled the air. The Pirates escaped to the West Coast and dropped a series to the Giants. At least they were consistent, losing at home in the swelter of Three Rivers Stadium, losing away in the cool mist of Candlestick Park.

For President Stewart, the case was closed. He asked Harry to submit his bill, the contract fulfilled. Contrition was presidential, he added, and apologized again for blaming Harry for the murders of Shue and Burke. In an interview with the *Post-Gazette*, Stewart congratulated Mazeroski on "damn fine police work" and Bruckmann's swift arrest. He'd put the run-in with Mazeroski behind him, deposited downstream under public relations.

Attendance at Carnegie Museum boomed. Two days of death in the Big Bone Room lured more visitors than the 100 million years of death in Dinosaur Hall. A private theater firm approached the museum about staging a murder play amid the racks of bones in the crime scene in the Big Bone Room. Weekly performances, special admission charge.

Harry's fifteen minutes of fame ticked into days. To escape the media, he'd asked Stewart for an office in Carnegie Institute's Andy Warhol Museum, a recent acquisition on Pittsburgh's North Side. Stewart wasn't amused or didn't get the joke. He had no use for the Warhol, a financial albatross on the institute since it had opened. He'd told a horrified board that if it were up to him, the Carnegie would dump "Warhol and his garbage" in the Allegheny River.

During his career, Warhol's ego demanded that anything he touched go into a cardboard box for perpetuity. Chewing gum wrappers? Into a box. A half-eaten pizza? Into a box. Photos and books checked out of the New York Public Library? Into a box and never returned. Now the Carnegie Institute was stuck with 608 boxes of Warhol's detritus. Three hundred of the items were featured in an exhibition called Possession Obsession. One acerbic critic called the collection a compost heap of hubris. Another said it was a landfill aspiring to art history.

Harry's caseload was suddenly full. Lawyers called, wanting him to dig up the dirt under ugly divorce cases. Spouses called, wanting him to find extramarital lovers, real and imagined. A wealthy dowager in Fox Chapel was sure that her husband, lying under a headstone in the cemetery, had been grabbed by aliens, resurrected, and flown to Las Vegas in a spaceship. A distraught couple begged him to rescue their daughter from a Hare Krishna commune in Oregon.

On Wednesday, the day after Bruckmann was arrested, Roberta Karlsen called from Red Lodge. "Damn it, Harry, it's morbid. We were sitting here drinking bourbon and coffee while Peter was rotting in that gully at Buck Spring." She told him that the latest polls had just come out. George would be the next governor of Wyoming. His boots, Harry thought, were now covered with more cow shit than those of his opponent.

"Harry," Roberta added, "the inaugural ball is in January. It'll be at the governor's mansion in Cheyenne. Consider this an invitation for a private viewing of my portrait."

Harry laughed. "Yeah, that's how Catherine the Great trapped Voltaire in St. Petersburg. He got snowed in over the winter. What I want is time share on the portrait—half the year in your bedroom, half the year in my office." She chuckled and told him she'd think about it.

On Thursday, he'd met Cynthia Ballard for lunch at a diner downtown near the *Post-Gazette*. She was tall, trim, and neat, in a blue suit tailored to fit and flatter. Her blond shag was immaculate, coiffed around a long, thin face. She hadn't wilted in the heat. Either she didn't sweat, or she'd immersed her deportment in a tub of hold-fast hair spray.

Ballard confirmed what Harry already knew. "I found Meredith dead on the floor. The vase was beside her."

"Five days before Marchand left for Wyoming," Harry said, "he bought a ceramic vase and flowers at a florist in Squirrel Hill. It cost him $97.96, and $15.00 for the cab fare to have it delivered to Meredith's North Side address. Did she mention a gift from Marchand?"

She nodded vigorously, but her hair remained immobile. "Yes. The police asked me the same thing. Meredith told me she was flabbergasted by the gift."

"Did you notice the vase in Meredith's walk-up? Before you found it beside her body on Monday?"

Ballard thought about it. "I can't say for sure. I was at her place a few times during the summer to water her plants, but only went in once. She kept her plants outside on the stoop."

Friday afternoon, Harry didn't call ahead. He parked in the Carnegie Museum lot, strolled by the security booth, and climbed the stairs two at a time to the paleontology office suite on the second floor.

Diana was at her desk, still poring over the summer's accounts. The door behind her to the balcony overlooking Dinosaur Hall was ajar. He hadn't seen her since she'd walked out of the interrogation room Tuesday afternoon. She looked good—white shorts, tight red tank top, red lipstick, black hair parted on the side.

She iced up her face. "Who let you in?"

"The building says 'Free to the People of Pittsburgh.' I took the museum up on it."

"Very funny. Go see the new moose diorama on the second floor. It's waiting for you. I'm busy. Time was I'd make time for you—and a lot more. But that time is gone and won't come back. You can leave now."

"I didn't expect open arms."

"Congratulations! You won't be disappointed. That's the end of my sentiments. Like I said, you can leave now, Harry."

She pushed her chair back, got up, and abruptly disappeared out the door onto the balcony. Harry skirted her desk and followed. Jacobs was bent over near the barricade at the end of the balcony stacking boxes of books against the wall.

Diana spun around, seething. "I thought I told you to piss off!"

"You did. I didn't." Harry took a quick glance at the panoply of dinosaurs below. "Packing up, Jacobs? Run out of evolutionists to convert?"

Jacobs straightened up. "I'm helping Diana pack up Peter's library. She's moving into his office."

"David, that will do for now," Diana said, sternly. "It looks like Detective Przewalski and I are going to have a private conversation whether I want to or not. We can continue this in the morning."

Jacobs looked back at them warily as he walked into the office suite. Harry heard him slam the door to the stairwell. Diana crossed to her office and stood in the doorway facing Harry, legs apart, arms folded across her chest, a challenge to get past her. "Okay, say what you came to say and leave."

"There's a scene in 'Zorba the Greek.' A woman is lying on a bed in a tiny whitewashed room. She's dying. The village widows, swathed in black, mill around her, vultures pecking at the mattress. As she begins taking her last breaths, they rip the sheets from under her."

"Bravo, Harry," Diana sneered, "save the sentimental movie crap for someone else. Peter took his last breath a month ago. Gunther saw to that. We're cleaning out Peter's office. We need to decide what to do with all of his books and papers."

"I bet you won't find those Russian articles among his papers."

Diana lifted her eyebrows. "What do you mean?"

"He didn't plagiarize them."

"I know he didn't! Simeon is full of shit!"

"You did."

CHAPTER 45

DIANA'S FACE FROZE. "You're crazy, Harry."

"Not yet, but the day is long. Last Thursday we got back from Wyoming. On Friday, Meredith found the Russian journal at the Carnegie Library. She got the articles translated."

Diana shrugged. "Okay, if you say so. So what?"

"She also saw something else. You'd signed out that Russian journal a year and a half ago. No record of Marchand doing so. He never saw the Russian articles."

"You're full of crap! He asked me to check out the journal for him. I'm in the Carnegie Library weekly, catching up on the latest science."

Harry shook his head. "Nice try. Ten days ago in camp you told Simeon you'd never heard of the Russian journal or these articles."

Diana sneered, leaned against the doorjamb, but said nothing.

"You told him you'd track them down when you got back here. You played the indignant card just right. You made it personal. It was good theater. And a good plan. Blame the plagiarism on Marchand. Retract the papers you'd published with him. Apologize to the profession. You'd be seen as honorable, an innocent colleague, fooled by Marchand into co-authoring a stolen idea."

"This is bullshit. Entertaining bullshit, though. Go on, Harry. I want to see where you're going with this."

"It's not where I'm going with this. It's where you went."

Below, a busload of senior citizens came into Dinosaur Hall decked out in red visors, yellow T-shirts and white sneakers. The security guard came to life, got up, surveyed the crowd, and sat back down.

Harry turned to Diana. "We can move inside. It might be—"

"I'd rather not have you in my office," she snapped.

"Fine. Five years ago, you fell in with Marchand—in science, in bed, perhaps in love. He needed a mechanism for his radical notion about Earth's changing climate and axis of rotation. You found it for him in that obscure bunch of Russian papers published more than half a century ago. You implanted it in his mind as novel, original. Probably over wine. Or over your body. You played his conceit until he thought the idea was his. It wouldn't have been hard. In the end, you published it together."

She pushed the black swoosh of hair from her forehead, her face registering disbelief. "Harry, this is fantasy, a fable."

"I don't think so. Peter was lead author, so he took credit for the idea. You let him. You happily rode the coattails of scientific fraud. He was too arrogant to suspect he'd been duped. You were too calculating to care. You thought it would bind him to you. United in championing a revolutionary theory. Romance cemented by controversy. The cement didn't hold."

Diana raised her arms in mock gratitude. "Hey, a free psychoanalysis. You're a lousy detective, Harry. And a lousier shrink."

"Yeah, maybe so. Peter dumped you for Lynn, a newer model. You had plagiarized the Russian research for nothing. Worse,

Simeon got onto it. But he automatically fingered Marchand, not you. For once you benefited from old-school prejudice. It wouldn't occur to Simeon that you—or any woman—could be good at science. Or chicanery. Marchand became infuriated with Simeon's insinuations. He told you he'd find those Russian articles, have them translated, and skewer Simeon. You realized it was game over."

The senior citizens congregated below around the *Diplodocus* skeleton. One of them started coughing. It quickly spread into a chorus of hacking. Harry waited for the epidemic to die.

"You know where I'm heading, Diana."

She stared at him, cool, implacable, almost smug. "Go ahead, show me."

"The irony must have seemed perverse. You plagiarized the articles to keep Marchand, to anchor your intimacy. Now, unwittingly, he was going to expose your crime. You had to kill him. Then you found out Lynn was pregnant with his kid. That made it easier. Fury always does. Marchand himself probably told you. He would do that. His vanity preceded his stupidity."

Diana shook her head, her face momentarily wistful. "Why are you doing this, Harry? I thought you knew me. I thought you wanted me."

"I did. When you were smart and tough. But ruthless and killer aren't my thing."

She nodded, took a pack of Pall Malls out of the front pocket in her shorts, lit one, and tossed the match on the balcony floor. "Compared to murder, smoking in a public gallery isn't much of a crime. What's next, detective? You're forgetting Gunther. The police have him on ice for three murders, starting with Peter's."

"Both of you killed him. You got Bruckmann to help. Then you framed him for Shue and Burke."

She looked at him, incredulous. "You're mad, Harry. No one will believe this crap."

"You can hope. You blackmailed Bruckmann into murder. Marchand showed you the letter from Leclerc implicating Bruckmann in the sale of Carnegie fossils—you lied about that, too. You gave Bruckmann a choice: either he helps you get rid of Marchand, or he does hard jail time. Bruckmann told me early on that you had killed Marchand. I thought he was just mouthing off. He wasn't. He was afraid of you."

Diana ground the butt out on the floor and immediately lit another. The security guard didn't see the smoke or smell it. Neither did the senior citizens. They had tired of dinosaurs and were being shepherded out of the Jurassic into Mineral Hall.

"Go on," Diana said.

"That night, July 21, you told Bruckmann to hang around the homestead. Like he always did. You waited up with Marchand in the mess tent. He got drunk and whined on about Simeon. Then he went to his pickup to leave. You followed him. You smashed in the back of his head. Enough to knock him out. Probably while he was leaning over the tailgate. Probably with a rock hammer. The coroner will tell us. The side of his skull looked like a pulped melon."

"This is tiresome, Harry," Diana said and looked at her wristwatch. It was too nonchalant.

"Yeah, that's the problem with straight facts. Bruckmann might have helped you whack Marchand, but I doubt it. He did help you shove the body into the bed of the pickup. You and Bruckmann drove out of camp to Buck Creek and along the gully to the pile of jacketed blocks below the quarry. You grabbed the plaster, burlap strips and water, pulled Marchand out of the pickup, encased him, made it look like a jacketed sauropod femur, and put a number on him. He might still have been alive. If so, he suffocated. And that promotes

Bruckmann from accessory to first degree. The coroner will tell us that too."

Diana sank down to the floor and leaned back against the door jamb. Below her shorts, the muscles in her thighs bulged when she crossed her legs.

"Think you got it all figured out, don't you?"

"Most of it. You had four hours. You and Bruckmann left at eleven-thirty. People in their tents in camp thought it was Marchand driving out in his pickup, like he did every night. Forty-five minutes to the quarry. A couple of hours to plaster him up. Forty-five minutes back. Lynn heard the truck return, a door open and close, then open and close again. She thought Marchand had forgotten something in the front seat. But it was you and Bruckmann getting out of the truck, one after the other—a small mistake."

Diana stubbed out her cigarette and shot him a wicked smile. "You missed your calling, Harry. You should have become a suspense novelist. Active imagination. Inventive plot. Likely motives. Wrong characters, though. And a little overcooked. It would have been easier just pushing Peter off a cliff and passing it off as an accident."

"Like Bruckmann tried to do to me? Maybe one day you'll tell me if he did that solo, or on your orders. I suspect solo, because you're smarter than that. You couldn't risk not killing Marchand on the first try. He was a hefty guy. He could survive a whack on the head and a roll down a badland bluff. I did. Most of the buttes aren't steep enough for free fall. Anyway, you had limited opportunity. You were in the quarry most days, not out prospecting below the escarpment."

Diana sighed. "Might as well settle in for the long haul." She got up, went into her office, and came back with an Iron City beer and an ashtray. She shut the door behind her, slid back down to the floor, and retrieved the cigarette butts around her.

"You'll understand if I don't offer you one, Harry." She twisted the cap off the Iron City, took a long guzzle, and wiped her lips.

Harry nodded. "Nice double deception you had going. To the cops, Marchand was on the run from two murders. He was both a missing person and a prime suspect. He was supposed to stay missing in the Big Bone Room for the next fifty years. Only you and Bruckmann knew he was dead. If he was found, you made sure Bruckmann would be the fall guy. For Marchand, Shue and Burke."

She gulped another mouthful of beer, lit a cigarette, and drilled Harry with her eyes.

"Time for the facts of life, kiddo," she said, a sulfurous hiss.

CHAPTER 46

"**D**AMN RIGHT I killed Peter! I'm the one who made him! I brought him the Russian's climate stuff. His career zoomed. Speaking engagements. Symposia invitations. Even a few book offers. So, how did he thank me? He fucked me over. He dumped me for that blond bimbo. Then he threw it in my face by knocking her up. No one treats me like that. NO ONE!"

Rage had consumed her face, the skin pulsing below her temple.

"You should have let it go, Diana," Harry said calmly. "Revenge just digs more graves."

"Shut up, Harry. I don't need your fucking platitudes." She clenched her jaw till the veins in her neck stood out. "It was more than revenge. It was self-preservation. I wasn't going to let that son of a bitch destroy me over the plagiarism. The bastard deserved it. My father would be proud of me. He was the only man who was ever loyal." She flicked the ashes off her cigarette, missing the ashtray.

"You weren't going to let Meredith destroy you either," Harry added.

"Of course not. Airhead was stupid enough to be the wrong person in the wrong place. Happens all the time. Hitchcock made a career out of that. She stumbled onto me and the Russian journal. That fuckface Simeon told her where to look. Too bad. Otherwise, she'd still be alive. It's her own goddamn fault. She sat at his feet all summer, listening to that adipose Buddha pontificate. I should have pushed *him* off a cliff. That tub of guts would have squealed all the way down, like a fucking capybara. Then gone splat."

The cigarette dangled from her red lips, her eyes squinting in the smoke. She took another swig of beer, then winked at Harry. Confident. Amoral.

"Your turn, smart guy. Tell me how you figured Meredith. I like this game."

Harry tried to lean on the balcony railing, but felt it wobble and stepped back. He wanted a cigarette, but he wasn't going to ask her for one. He'd hoped to hear a trace of remorse, but he wasn't going to ask her for that either.

"Friday, second day back in Pittsburgh, your plot developed sinkholes. Shue called you—as you admitted to Mazeroski. She wanted to talk about the article in the Russian journal. What you didn't tell Mazeroski was that you paid Shue a visit Sunday night. Maybe you made an appointment. Maybe you just showed up unannounced."

Diana didn't volunteer the answer. She stubbed out her cigarette and began peeling the Iron City label off the bottle.

"You tried to convince her that you signed out the article for Marchand. Meredith didn't buy it. So you killed her with the ceramic vase. You put her copy of the Russian articles and the translation under the pile of *Post-Gazette* papers on the coffee table. It would point the police to motive. And to Marchand."

Diana held up the beer bottle in a mock toast. "So far so good, detective." She grabbed another Pall Mall, didn't light it, and offered the pack to Harry. He shook his head.

"The vase was a nice twist. Threw all of us off for awhile.

Marchand told you he had given Meredith a big pot of flowers in June. But you couldn't be sure she'd kept the pot, or whether he'd plastered it with his fingerprints at the florist's shop before it was delivered. So, you took a ceramic pot from Marchand's house on Saturday, dried grasses and all. It had his fingerprints and would implicate him. You brought it to Meredith's, ostensibly as a gift, and killed her with it. Marchand, the suspected murderer, wasn't supposed to be found. When we did, you moved quick. You quizzed Liza whether he'd asked her to send Meredith flowers before you guys left for Wyoming. You used Liza to let me and Mazeroski know that Marchand had given Meredith a pot of flowers. That would explain his fingerprints on the murder weapon."

"Gotta admit it, pretty crafty," she said.

"Yeah, crafty," Harry sighed. "Problem is, the police will find bits of matching dried grass on Marchand's rug and in your car. They'll also confirm with the florist that the vase he used for the flowers was not the ceramic pot. Not the murder weapon."

Diana finished her beer, put the bottle by the ashtray on the balcony floor, and leaned back against the door. She wasn't talking. Her face had clouded over, like a storm brewing in the badlands.

The security guard at the end of Dinosaur Hall called out "all clear." It was five o'clock. The galleries were closing. A minute later, Harry heard him flip the bank of light switches behind a panel at the end of the hall. The echo of the clicks faded with the light. The huge hall was suddenly black, except for two dim red exit signs at either end.

"We could go inside, Diana."

"No we can't," she snapped, then lit the cigarette she'd been rolling back and forth with her fingers.

Harry made her out in the glow of the Pall Mall. He was talking to a red shadow. "Then you killed Burke. You—"

"I didn't want to," she interrupted. "But I had to. Damn him, he wouldn't let the extra plaster jacket go. I told him it was a probably a stupid field mistake, to forget about it. But he wouldn't listen. He was proud he'd found it. He showed me how he'd marked it with the red Sharpie."

She started tapping the bottle of Iron City on the marble tile. "Morris hurt." She sounded rueful. "But I had no choice."

"Save the regret act for the courtroom. You were brutally efficient. Forty minutes to slip out of the International to the Big Bone Room, do in Burke, slip back, hit the ladies room, let me find you in the crowd, take the glass of wine, and toast the execution."

"No, no, no!" In a forlorn whisper, she added, "It was awful."

"Not awful enough to be careless," he said. "You put on Bruckmann's lab coat over your red dress before you went over to Burke and bashed his head in. What excuse did you give him? That you didn't want to muss up the dress with plaster dust?"

Diana didn't answer.

"After you killed Burke," Harry continued, "you quickly stashed his field notebook and the lab coat somewhere in the basement. Next day, you planted the notebook in Bruckmann's desk and the lab coat in the prep room."

"Yeah, I'm quick, all right," Diana muttered. "Anything else? This is getting old."

"Just that bit of misdirection during the International. Invite Stewart and the Princeton boys to the Big Bone Room to see the dinosaur pile. Let someone neutral find the body. Pretty artful."

Diana stood up and leaned against the wall by the door. "Y'know, Harry, turns out the biggest mistake I made was asking you to take me to that fucking art show. Anyway, this is all just talk. Talk, talk, talk. You've got nothing. The cops have nothing."

Harry debated the ethics of the next line, and lost the debate.

"Yeah, well . . . they've got Bruckmann. And he's also talking. He isn't going to take the fall without you. This afternoon he decided to follow his lawyer's advice. He copped a plea. The usual deal. He'll testify against you. He's with Mazeroski and a stenographer now. My guess is he'll claim he was only an accessory . . . under duress. He'll say you blackmailed him."

"Are you done?" she demanded, hoarse, suddenly angry. She crouched down to stub out her cigarette, scraping the ashtray on the floor. Then, without warning, she lunged at him like a coiled spring, covering the width of the balcony in less than a second. He heard the beer bottle clink on the marble tile and dove to the side. She catapulted into him head first, sideswiped his chest and shoulder, and sent him sprawling toward the edge of the balcony. Her body careened off his and crashed full force into the railing. He heard the loose iron moorings groan as they gradually gave way, slowly enough for her to know what was happening.

"HARRY-Y-Y!"

Her scream lasted twelve feet. It stopped the instant she was impaled on the sharp steel support spikes sticking up from the backbone of *Diplodocus*. The skeleton shuddered, but stayed upright.

Harry picked himself up in the dim red fog of the exit signs. His head had bounced off the marble floor. It was throbbing a dizzy bass note. His foot kicked the beer bottle and sent it spinning. He probed along the railing until he found where the wrought iron zagged off the balcony and hung suspended over *Diplodocus* and Diana's body. He backed across to her office, fumbled for the door knob, and was momentarily blinded by the flash of fluorescent light. The bass throb buzzed up an octave.

The bit about Bruckmann copping a plea had been a gambit. He could lie as well as she had.

The phone on Diana's desk was buried under the pile of the summer's field receipts for groceries, gas, plaster, motels, restaurants, beer and burlap sacks. Now someone else would do the accounts and sort Marchand's papers. Death left messy legacies, Harry thought, cleaning up the body, then cleaning up its past.

He picked up the phone, called downtown, and got Mazeroski on the line.

"There's a body here to be cleaned up. The *mea culpas* didn't do any good."

ACKNOWLEDGMENTS

I AM INDEBTED TO: The Carnegie Museum of Natural History, Pittsburgh, Pennsylvania, a grand institution where this book evolved; Martha and Jerry Masinton and the Write-On group, Lawrence, Kansas for their terrific support and razor-sharp edits; the Hendry family, Badwater, Wyoming and the Fross family, Lost Cabin, Wyoming, for their years of hospitality and friendship. And, of course, Aagje.

CPSIA information can be obtained
at www.ICGtesting.com
Printed in the USA
LVHW01s0154231018
594493LV00010B/161/P